The King's Girl

The King's Girl

SYLVIE OUELLETTE

Black Lace novels are sexual fantasies.
In real life, make sure you practise safe sex.

First published in 1996 by
Black Lace
332 Ladbroke Grove
London W10 5AH

Typeset by CentraCet Limited, Cambridge
Printed and bound by Mackays of Chatham PLC

ISBN 0 352 33095 3

Introduction

The episode of *les filles du roy* (or king's girls) was a turning point in the history of a young country now called Canada. Between 1665 and 1671, more than 950 women, ranging in age from 12 to 37, came from France as prospective brides for the settlers. The effort paid off: the population of Nouvelle France grew from 3,000 in 1663 to about 6,000 by 1672.

Most of these young women were orphans and wards of the king, but quite a few were widowed and some even came with children. Rumours about their background and ill repute abounded even then. It's not difficult to grasp their reasons for undertaking the difficult three-month crossing. France was weak from the Thirty Years' War and times were hard. King Louis XIV promised settlers cattle, money and land if they chose to go to the colony. Also, many young men sought to leave France for personal reasons, often to escape the law, creditors or a call to arms.

With *les filles du roy* came the last shipments of cattle and raw materials. The colony was now self-sufficient and grew rapidly from that point on.

History books traditionally hold the opinion that people immigrated to Canada not only to develop the land, but also to bring the Gospel to the natives. In reality, it is likely that the Crown pushed for emigration to race against the British who were also colonising the North American continent. Unmarried men and childless couples were penalised with extra taxes, whilst the Church did its best to encourage everyone to have many babies, a policy which endured well into the twentieth century.

Author Sylvie Ouellette's first ancestor to settle in Canada, Parisian René Houallet, embarked in Dieppe in 1663. He was 24 years old. In March 1666, he married a king's girl, Anne Rivet, who had arrived a few months earlier. They settled near Québec City and had three sons. After Anne's death, René Houallet married again and had seven more children. The family moved near the Rivière Ouelle, hence the change in the name over time.

The story of Laure Lapierre, our king's girl, is entirely fictitious, as are all the characters in this book.

Part One

The Old World

Chapter One

The laurel branch gently bobbed in the wind and grazed Laure's face. With a nonchalant flick of the wrist, she pushed it away and leant forward into the bushes. Above the trees, the pale, late afternoon sun barely pierced the haze of the hot, humid day. The distant rumble of thunder was growing louder and black clouds began to darken the horizon. And, in the meantime, inside Laure's hungry body, a different kind of storm was brewing.

Her emotions encompassed everything from excitement and anticipation, to silliness and even worry, for today was the day she had decided to lose her virginity. Now, all she had to do was wait for the man who would take it.

From her hiding place, she had a perfect view of the narrow creek where René would soon come to wash. Every day for the past few weeks, Laure had ritually spied on her prey, the stable hand. In fact, she had hidden behind these bushes so often, the imprint of her feet remained embedded in the ground.

All day, every day, she would wait for this very moment. And she had never been disappointed. But today she wouldn't silently slip back to her quarters, as she usually did. She would stay and seduce him.

In her mind, success was already a certainty. Judging by the compliments of all the young men who had asked for her hand, Laure knew she was blessed with what people called '*la beauté du diable*' – the devil's beauty.

Her curvaceous figure and sensual, fiery nature attracted men wherever she went, and she revelled in their silent stares. No matter how she dressed, she always felt constricted by her clothes. Her skin longed for freedom. For her, happiness was being naked or wearing the bare minimum.

No-one had ever raised an eyebrow when, as a child, she had pranced around clad only in an old shirt, chasing butterflies across the courtyard of the Château de Reyval. In recent years, however, she would be called upon to protect her modesty from prying eyes if she were to so much as remove her bodice. So Laure would tease convention, deliberately allowing her skirt to run up her calves and letting her bodice gape as her generous breasts strained at the ties. Throughout the summer, she even walked around without shoes, unable to tolerate anything between the soles of her feet and the warm, dusty earth.

Strands of untamed hair persistently stuck out from under her bonnet; that is, when she had bothered to wear one in the first place. She much preferred to let her locks cascade freely around her shoulders. Her long, dark-brown mane was just like her late mother's, and the sight of it often brought tears to her father's eyes. But, for others, it was just another reason to despise her.

Juliette, the housekeeper, never missed an occasion to scold Laure on her lax grooming. But the woman's words had no effect on the young maid, who had grown up among the staff at the château and cared little for authority. Almost everybody there had known her since childhood, and through the years Laure had learnt that she could do as she pleased. Roland Lapierre, her father, was the château's blacksmith, as had been his father before him. The staff respected him, some even feared him, and Laure, who had recently started work in the kitchens, took advantage of this as often as she could.

It had not been her choice to become a servant at the château. In fact, she had ranted vehemently in protest. But she had no alternative: her father's meagre wages no longer proved sufficient to provide for his daughter's voracious appetites. For Laure Lapierre enjoyed life and savoured everything it had to offer, down to the last morsel.

And now the old man could barely support the two of them. He had to pay rent on the little maisonette where they lived, unwilling to let his daughter share the servants' quarters. As long as he was around, Laure would have her own home. For now, at least, working in the kitchen meant she would be fed at the master's expense.

At times, her father seemed eager to marry her off. He was finding it increasingly difficult to keep an eye on her now that she had crossed the threshold of womanhood. More and more frequently, cheeky young men took liberties with his beautiful girl: he had interrupted several stolen kisses, and had seen the occasional furtive hand stroking her rounded hips.

Yet he rejected all those who asked for his daughter's hand. For although he was only a simple blacksmith, he thought no-one was good enough for his treasure, his beautiful Laure. The man who would have her had to be more than a valet or farm hand; he would have to be wealthy enough to spoil Laure in the way to which she was accustomed.

As time passed, the young woman only grew more eager to appease that yearning which had consumed her since her femininity had blossomed. Fingers brushing her cheek made her weak at the knees and bold kisses stirred even more excitement.

She knew how her body reacted under her own fingers; she had become addicted to the throbbing heat of pleasure she could bring to herself. But now she

7

wanted more than solitary caresses. She hungered for close contact, a man's arms around her; her skin burnt for the soothing touch of a warm body. She didn't want to wait any longer. The time had come, married or not, and she had chosen for herself the man who would be her first lover.

René was just a stable boy but he had the body of a god, with strong arms and square shoulders. His hair was the colour of dirty straw, his eyes the palest blue. Healthy and hard-working, he moved in a way which betrayed great sensuality. His body, strong, tall and defined, was obviously built for rugged, passionate embraces.

He and Laure were opposites, for his hair was just as wispy and fair as hers was thick and dark. His rough, tanned skin also contrasted starkly with her smooth and milk-white complexion. His lips, though full and sensuous, often tightened into the cruellest of smiles whereas Laure's mouth was a hungry furnace that could provide nothing but pleasure and joy. The way they complemented one another made them a perfect match indeed, in Laure's opinion.

René had come to work at the château just a few weeks earlier. Laure knew nothing of him, only that his body was by far the most attractive she had ever seen. They had hardly exchanged a single word. Her day-to-day work rarely took her to the stables, where he worked.

Nevertheless, she had managed to catch his eye. The rest didn't really matter as the mystery only served to excite her even more. Who else was she supposed to choose as her first lover? Certainly not one of the servants she had played with as a child. They held very little interest for her, and the feeling was generally mutual. But René was a different prospect.

She had seen him look at her longingly, whenever he came to the kitchens to fetch food. He always smiled at her and was clearly interested, yet had made no attempt to seduce her.

But Laure was completely taken with him, wanting nothing more in the world than to feel his hard, naked body pressed against her tender skin. She had thought of him so often, imagined them together, sharing a passionate embrace. In her mind, she was already his.

As usual, she watched silently as he appeared in the late afternoon sun, quickly shedding his dirty clothes before entering the stream. On his face she saw a familiar expression of bliss as he gradually sank beneath the cool water. When he emerged, the sight of water trickling down his naked body excited her as never before.

The skin of his bare chest was tanned and velvet-like, offering a sharp contrast to the pale, firm buttocks which had never seen the warming rays of the sun. Standing in water up to mid-thigh, he rubbed a heavy bar of brown soap over his chest, working up lather. The movements of his hands were blunt and powerful as they ran over his body, washing away the sweat and toil of a long day.

René was of peasant stock; his touch would be anything but gentle, as he was probably more used to stroking horses than women. Laure had seen the calluses left by pitchforks on men's palms and fingernails stained after a day spent greasing leather straps. Yet her body craved the contact of those rough hands; her skin yearned for his.

She found it hard to stifle a giggle as she watched his dangling prick moving in all directions, like a feisty fish constantly diving and emerging from the water with great splashes. It surely wouldn't remain flaccid if only she could get a hold of it and caress it. Indeed, it would come alive in her hands, like a stallion ready for mating. Her own flesh would then join with his and they would become one, like wild rivers that meet and merge under the force of their flow. She knew it would happen. Soon, very soon.

Laure still hadn't decided how to set her plan in

motion. Should she disrobe and join him in the cool water? Or surprise him as he walked back to his quarters? She waited a little while longer. The pleasure she took from simply watching the taut muscles move under his bronzed skin was almost unbearable, but just a taste of the delights she could expect once she finally got her hands on him.

After washing himself thoroughly, René splashed about in the water, occasionally looking up at the sky; menacing clouds were now drawing overhead. Soon, Laure knew, he would come out and make his way back to the stables.

Halfway between the river and the stables, along the path she had walked so often, was a clearing of soft grass. Time and again she had imagined the scene which would take place there; at that exact spot she would give herself to the man who for so long had been haunting her dreams.

Laure knew of at least three maids who had already been René's lovers, but despite her inexperience, she hoped to be like no other. She had, after all, managed to learn a great deal about lovemaking from what she had seen and heard.

She remembered Martin, the gamekeeper, with Suzanne, the kitchen helper. There had been many other couples who had had no idea she was watching. She had come across them making love in the haystacks behind the barn, in the fields, in the pantry. It was always by accident; she hadn't meant for it to happen. But each time the urge to stay and watch had been overwhelming.

She had seen it all: the men whose engorged members seemed to pierce their partners amidst cries of delight; the temptresses who enticed their man by taking his swollen penis into their mouths. The sounds of moans and gasps still echoed in her ears. And each time Laure had felt jealous. Not that she fancied any of the men, but she just knew she was missing out on something and she now wanted to discover the pleasures of the flesh. But that very first time would be the most important. She wanted her first lover to remember her; she had to impress.

René slowly waded out of the water. One step ahead of him, Laure silently slipped away to wait in the clearing.

With trembling fingers, she quickly undid the laces on the front of her chemise and drew the edges apart to expose slightly the pink skin of her cleavage. The rays of the sun hadn't taken their toll on her. This summer most of her time had been spent working in the kitchens and she hardly ever went out in the fields as she had done when she was a little girl. Her skin was still pale, soft and delicate, but burning with an ache only a man could soothe.

Her fingers nervously slipped inside the opening, gauged the weight of each breast swollen with the arousal of expectation, and caressed them as René would in just a few minutes. Would he be tempted to suck her taut nipples, or be content to just toy with them?

The thought of his hands on her body drove Laure crazy with anticipation. Already the flesh between her legs was bathed in heady musk and clenched sporadically, impatient to receive its reward.

She left the front of her chemise slightly open, just enough to tease. Not that she was bashful, but she wanted to give her chosen lover an invitation to undress her. The old, brown skirt she had decided to wear had shrunk with the years and now showed her ankles and the lower part of her calves when she walked. The frown on her father's face every time she wore it had almost made her throw it out, but now Laure was glad she had kept it. Today, the old rag was an asset.

Her bonnet conveniently left behind on her bed, Laure quickly undid the pins holding up her hair and combed it with her fingers. She stood silently in the clearing, her heart pounding, as she waited for René to come her way.

And she knew he would, and she would welcome him inside her at last.

The day was still hot and heavy as the sun started its descent. The light breeze gradually grew stronger as stormy clouds gathered in the sky. Laure didn't like thunder, but today nothing could make her seek cover, not even the fear of lightning striking her right then and there.

Her man whistled as he approached, the melody buried under the sound of the leaves rustling in the wind. Suddenly he was in front of her, naked. Droplets of water still dripped from his hair and rolled off his shoulders.

Laure's heart beat furiously. There was nothing she could do; the next move was up to him. He looked at her and smiled knowingly, pleasantly surprised, and made no effort to conceal his nudity.

At that moment the storm broke. Laure didn't move when lightning tore through the sky and the wind swept her long brown hair across her face. Thunder crashed above them and rain began to pour down. René didn't utter a word but stared at Laure, relishing her beauty.

In a matter of seconds she was drenched through. Her wet chemise now clung to her breasts, revealing her dark nipples which had stiffened under the wild caress of the wind.

She threw her head back and brought her hands to her neck, stroking her throat with her fingertips. The next bolt of lightning made her close her eyes. She could feel the water trickling down her chest; refreshing, arousing her.

René still hadn't moved. Laure looked at him through half-shut eyes and was pleased to see him feebly run his tongue across his lips. She was also delighted to see his member respond to the sight of her, its bulbous tip jutting upwards, stiff and swollen.

Dropping his bundle of dirty clothes, he took one step towards her. Laure knew at that moment she had won

12

the first battle. She looked at him and smiled in turn. As he advanced towards her, his eyes were fixed on her breasts and she felt her nipples throb and ache in response to his hungry gaze.

Roughly, without kissing her, without even looking her in the eyes, he undid her bodice and skirt. They fell immediately, dragged down by the weight of the water that soaked them.

Laure whimpered. Despite the tempest raging inside her, the coolness of the wind made her shiver. René laughed and pulled her chemise up, slowly revealing the smooth skin of her thighs, her rounded buttocks, the dark triangle of hair at the junction of her legs. The hem was wet through and left a cold, watery trace as it trailed up her body.

René clutched the dripping garment in a tight knot in one hand whilst he slipped the other between her legs. There, amidst the swollen folds of her moist vulva, beat the heart of her femininity. He pushed a long, cold finger inside her and pulled it out slowly, caressing the silken walls of her virgin tunnel, freeing the flow of dew that quickly warmed his hand.

Laure shuddered and threw her arms around his neck, nestling her head under his chin. To feel him so near was a revelation; to have him within reach, a dream come true. Against her cheek she could feel the blood pulsing in his neck. His skin, taut and smooth, felt like fine leather against her lips. His heartbeat strangely echoed the rhythm of her breathing. She tightened her embrace around his neck.

'You little witch,' René said in an amused tone. It was the first time he had really spoken to her. But she didn't want conversation.

'Don't talk,' she yelled above the thunder. 'Just take me.'

She could feel his member nudging at her, its purplish head twitching against her belly. Never before had she been so close to a naked man, although she had seen many of them. And this one was hers for the taking.

In one swift move he grabbed her hips, lifted her and impaled her on his erect penis. She felt his flesh probing into hers; she felt it pierce her. She let out a loud sigh. Now she was a woman.

He held her to him, motionless, for a few seconds. His mouth seized hers and she replied to his kiss ravenously, feeding on his lips and hungrily sucking his tongue.

As her passion mounted, she writhed against him. Her breasts were crushed, her stiff nipples grinding into his hard, muscular chest through the fabric of her chemise. Despite the pouring rain constantly showering him, he exuded a mixed aroma of soapy cleanliness and manly musk. Laure held on tight, only too pleased to give herself over to the strength of his desire.

His thighs were hard and hot against hers, as were his arms and chest. The rain seeped between their bodies but didn't seem to cool them at all. Their passion was too hot to be quelled.

For Laure, things were happening just as she had hoped. At least she had achieved her goal of making him come to her. The rest would surely follow. For the first time in her life, she could enjoy the animal heat of their passion. He was inside her; she could feel him getting harder still.

Without letting her go, he fell to his knees. As she held on to his neck, her face buried in his hair, he grabbed her buttocks and slowly lifted her along the length of his hard shaft. Its rounded head pulsed and teased at her entrance, before he let her slide back down again under her own weight. He repeated the lifting motion time and again. Each thrust was a caress, each stroke a fulfilment.

Against her bare arms she could feel his muscles play under his skin, strong and frisky like a colt. She felt him alive inside her, sliding in and out. Her pleasure mounted quickly, more intense than she had ever experienced.

14

Laure didn't mind not having had time to caress him as she had planned. He had taken control, and she was enjoying every moment of it. Gripping his shoulders, she threw her head back, letting her breasts jut out of her open chemise. The rain fell on them, hard and stinging, making her cry out. René bowed his head and took a stiff nipple into his mouth, sucking it roughly until Laure screamed, more in pleasure than in pain, now unable to control all the sounds escaping from her mouth with each breath.

His hands were still under her buttocks, his fingertips digging hard into her flesh and pushing at the entrance of the delicate, puckered rose of her behind. The sensations merged into one, powerful, overwhelming. The fire inside her grew out of control and as she climaxed her strangled groans of pleasure were lost in the uproar of the storm raging around them.

With the next bolt of lightning, he lifted her off him and laid her down on the grass. Still without a word, he ripped her chemise open in one swift motion, exposing her completely, offering her body to the storm and its elements.

She had barely recovered from the peak of her climax when he lay on top of her. His shaft, still hard as iron, was trapped between their rain-soaked bodies. He held her hands above her head and pinned them to the ground. The wet grass stuck to her skin and his grip made her feel like a prisoner. But she didn't complain; she knew she had yet to have her turn with him.

His lips nibbled at her neck, quickly making their way down to her breasts. His mouth wasn't large enough to take in her enormous, dark areolae. He almost choked on them, unable to swallow them, sucking and biting them, almost with a vengeance.

He let go of her arms and grabbed her breasts with both hands, kneading, moulding them like mounds of clay, whilst his mouth continued its assault on them. Laure went wild with the pleasure she took in his touch.

He seemed to know her body just as well as she did; he knew how to enhance that exhilarating sensation, that feeling that pleasure was near. He was dominating her, taking her with all his might.

The rain fell harder still, making their bodies slip against each other. Without any effort, he slid down her body, letting his tongue trail across her belly. Just as she had hoped, he drew back until his mouth closed over her wet, excited sex.

She offered herself to the ministrations of the rain whilst her lover buried his tongue in her thick bush, insatiably exploring her. The contrast between the fluid heat of his body between her thighs and the stimulating coolness of the rain on her breasts was intoxicating.

Her pleasure mounted again as his tongue located her bud and teased it expertly. A spasm shook her from head to toe and she dug her fingers into the earth, which was now reduced to silken mud. Suddenly she didn't feel the rain, she didn't hear the thunder, she didn't see the lightning. She could sense nothing but his wet, warm tongue licking the intricate folds of her vulva. It squirmed around, up and down, enhancing her arousal yet not bringing her to fulfilment.

His mouth covered her completely, probing and sucking, tasting and relishing. His lips drew on her bud, extracting all the pleasure from within her. She was oblivious to the world around her, and didn't even notice the rain had now stopped and the storm had passed.

Her second climax was even more violent than the first, and her screams resounded through the forest. René laughed as he let go of her and let his chin rest on her breasts.

The heat of her skin quickly evaporated the few drops of rain still dripping down her body. A ray of sun pierced the horizon and shone between the trees. Laure looked at her new lover and remembered there was still much she wanted to do.

Quickly regaining her strength, she pushed him aside

16

and rolled over on top of him, her thighs straddling his hips, her forearms on either side on his chest. Drops of water glistened on his shoulders. Laure stuck out her tongue playfully and lapped them up. Kneeling in the mud, she set out to do exactly what he had just done to her, to show him she knew how to pleasure a man.

Yet she had to struggle to stop him from moving. It was as if he didn't want to let her have her own way with him. She lay down on top of him, trying to prevent him from pushing her aside as she sealed her mouth around his nipple. But he was stronger than her and their caresses soon turned into a wrestling match, for he was half stroking her, half pushing her away.

They rose to their knees as she tried to get close again. This time she held on tight; her arms locked around his chest, her hands pressing into his back, whilst her mouth seized his nipple, sucking so hard on it that she thought he couldn't make her let go.

But he did. Though he sighed with pleasure, he would not remain passive. Encircling her waist with his leg, he tried to force her off balance and push her head aside.

Laure saw his behaviour as a challenge. She wanted to show him what a good lover she could be, yet he resisted her ministrations. Therefore she would simply have to move on to the next step.

With a grunt, he managed to get up whilst she still held on to him. In front of Laure appeared his swollen shaft, awakened further by their sensuous fight. The sight of it aroused her even more, fuelling her desire to possess him. She seized the opportunity and immediately drew him into her mouth. It was so big she almost gagged, but quickly recovered from the surprise of this new sensation. As she began sucking on it, she felt him ease up.

His hands came to rest on her head, his fingers burrowing into her mass of wet, dirty tresses. Was he giving in? She saw this as a good sign and released her

17

grip around his waist to slowly lower her hands on to his buttocks, digging her fingernails into the pale flesh.

He let out a loud moan, almost a complaint, and she felt the stiff rod pulse violently in her mouth. Laure had finally achieved what she had set out to do earlier that day, only now it seemed like a lifetime ago.

She brought her hands back around his hips and grabbed his shaft greedily. The swollen head responded by letting a few drops of salty liquid seep out of its tiny mouth. Laure's arousal intensified. How intoxicating to feed on him, how mesmerising to have him at her mercy. Once again she forgot where she was, and cared only for the marvel she held in her hands and in her mouth.

Her tongue started a strange dance along the ridge of the purple head, barely touching it and fluttering around it like a butterfly. Next, she tried to engulf all of him, pressing her forehead against his stomach, burying her nose in his forest of curls.

She let one hand slip under his heavy sac, briefly feeling the fullness of his balls before they bunched up. She felt him trembling; she heard him groan. She knew the moment was near. Soon, victory would be hers.

At that very moment, things took a different turn. Grabbing her head forcefully, he pushed her away from him. Laure was baffled. Just when she had thought she was really pleasuring him, he had not been entirely at her mercy.

Seizing her by the shoulders with a devilish laugh, he pulled her to her feet and forced her to turn around to face a large tree near where they stood. Shocked and disorientated, Laure let him push her against the thick trunk and encircled it with her arms.

The bark was cold and wet, slightly crumbly under the tender skin of her arms and chest. Behind her, René bent down and grabbed her ankles. He quickly lifted her legs up and prised them apart. Laure had to hold on to the tree even tighter, pressing her chest and face against it to avoid sliding down its length, the wet wood scraping her breasts.

Despite being in this awkward position, her arousal was just as intense. This was something she had not imagined. What would René do next? The thought filled her with excitement and apprehension.

He nudged at her behind almost immediately, holding her legs against his hips, letting his member find its way between her rounded buttocks, sliding up and down the slick valley. He probed her puckered opening for a little while before impaling her again, this time in a place even she had never explored before.

The engorged head slowly made its way inside her, using the dew from her vulva to lubricate the passage. Her delicate hole initially tightened in resistance, but was quickly vanquished by the perseverance of his virility. Eventually he took her completely, to the hilt, his thick shaft spreading her open in a sensation that bordered on pain but generated even more delight.

Still holding on to the tree, Laure felt droplets of rain falling from the leaves and trickling down her face. Against her skin the wet, old bark crumbled away to leave harder bits of wood painfully pricking her breasts. Her right cheek was pressed to the trunk and its musty scent filled her nose as she breathed harder.

Once again, she was on the verge of climax. Her pleasure knew no bounds. She had discovered a new source of joy, continually enhanced by the unusual invasion of her lover. Her encounter with René was turning out to be more than she could ever have hoped for.

The rain drops rolling down her cheeks were soon followed by tears of joy as she reached her peak. Her mouth opened to let out a cry of ecstasy, but no sound came. She held her breath whilst the wave transported her, again a result of the rapturous combination of pleasure and pain.

René screamed behind her, his voice hoarse with

exhaustion. His hands held her tight, trembling as he increased the rhythm of his thrusts. He contracted in a spasm, his straining rod finally releasing his seed inside her, surrendering to the violence of their coupling. Yet he continued his motion, the pace subsiding until he could hold her no more and he fell to his knees, letting go of her legs.

Laure let her head fall back and she tasted the saltiness of her tears on her upper lip. Still the bark bit into her tender skin, but her fulfilment was complete.

And it had all been so easy. Somehow she knew that was the key to everything she could ever want: all she had to do was ask.

Chapter Two

*L*aure's father had told her she wouldn't have to work for very long; she would soon be married to a good man who would make sure she wanted for nothing. He kept her spirits up and gave her hope for the future. When Laure was told about his sudden death, she was seized by a feeling of dismay.

More than grief, she was angry he had died. He had left her no dowry. Her mother had passed away many years before when Laure was only a little girl, so she was now completely on her own, with no-one to take care of her.

The funeral barely over, Laure was asked to go back to her tasks. As she aimlessly walked around the kitchens, she gradually realised she was doomed to a life of work and domesticity.

That morning, there was a lot of work to be done at the château in preparation for the next day's banquet. The kitchen had turned into a hive of activity. Cooks, maids and helpers ran around, screaming and laughing; everyone busy preparing dishes for more guests than had been seen in years. It was as if a fever possessed them all.

All of them except for Laure. She wanted no part of it.

She felt their heavy glances as she idly watched them, but she didn't care. There were more important things to think about. For instance, what was to become of her? An unmarried young woman could not expect too much from life once her father was gone.

René was not the type to marry; he was too busy chasing the other maids. Besides, Laure was getting bored with him, with a relationship that was purely physical. Although they spent a lot of time together, they hardly ever talked to each other, except in moans and grunts. She needed a new lover, a man who would take care of her, spoil her as her father had, so at least she wouldn't have to work.

As she pondered the possibilities, Laure went about her duties mechanically, as if she were sleepwalking. No-one paid any attention to her, no-one cared. For a brief moment, she hoped for a bit of sympathy when she heard Juliette call out her name, but when the house-keeper found her, she sent her straight upstairs to help the chambermaids prepare the rooms. Juliette had hated her for years, and the feeling was mutual. From the moment Laure's mother had died, the housekeeper had carried a silent hope that the widowed blacksmith would ask her to marry him. But as the years passed, Laure's father remained solely devoted to his daughter, and Juliette could never forgive the girl for that.

His decision to find work for Laure had not been welcomed by the staff. She had grown up spoilt and carefree, and everyone resented the way she liked to pretend they were beneath her. She had always felt their animosity, but never had it been so blatant as it was now. Laure couldn't bring herself to share the others' enthusiasm, and, compounding her misery, nobody cared that she wasn't as joyful as they were. It was almost as if they were glad she was so unhappy.

She slowly made her way to the first floor where she silently went from one room to the next, piling up the soft sheets and the thick eiderdowns over the large beds.

Her heart just wasn't in it. Moving on, she paused as she reached the top of the staircase, listening to the screams of laughter rising from the bowels of the château before closing the door behind her.

The master and his wife each had their bedchambers on the top floor of the west wing, far away from everybody else's. Laure had been there a couple of times before. These two rooms were, of course, the best ones in the house, and each had an enormous fireplace.

As she entered, she remembered the first time she had sneaked in. Back then, she was a curious, mischievous six-year-old. Those were the days when she thought nothing was forbidden. But her tender bottom had remained sore for days after her father had found out about her escapade. Since then, she had stayed as far away as she could from the top floor.

Yet the image of the room had remained with her for a long time. As a child, it seemed to her the furniture was over-sized, enormous. The four-poster bed, the dressers and everything else were made of dark, intricately carved wood. With great difficulty, Laure had managed to climb onto the bed. Her dirty, sticky hands pulled on the bed cover and the sheer strength of her tiny arms had hoisted her up.

Until then, she had never been in a real bed. All she knew was the straw mattress at the maisonette. She had let herself sink into the middle for a while, then bounced around. The linens were delicate and very soft under her rough skin. After that, it was all a blur. Somebody had come in and dragged her out, but she couldn't remember exactly who. All those details were superseded by the memory of her father's anger.

Even today, Laure didn't feel any excitement or curiosity whatsoever. And again, it was all because of her father. The sorrow of losing him compounded her fear of what lay ahead. She had no dowry, no-one to arrange a marriage for her or to rely on. She felt utterly alone.

The few servants who had come to her father's funeral

had long since gone back to work, and now they were laughing as if they had forgotten about it already. A few comforting words offered at the time were all they had for her. They had turned their backs immediately afterwards.

Laure was suddenly overwhelmed by grief. Sitting on the floor at the foot of the large bed, she hid her face in her apron and sobbed uncontrollably. She hadn't cried in years, but now loneliness, anger and pride joined forces to increase her despair.

Wallowing in her misery, she didn't hear the approaching footsteps in the corridor. She didn't see Madame Lampron, the mistress of Château de Reyval, until she was right in front of her.

A hand rested gently on the side of her head, the fingers caressing her cheek and forcing her chin up.

'What is wrong, my child?' a soft voice enquired.

Laure turned up her tear-stained face and stared at the figure standing in front of her. She immediately recognised her mistress and, ashamed and embarrassed, she jumped to her feet, flattened her damp and wrinkled apron, and bowed her head in reverence.

'I am terribly sorry, Madame,' she stammered. 'This shall not happen again.'

The other woman smiled and took Laure's hand in hers. 'What is the matter?' she repeated. 'What is the cause of your sorrow?'

Unable to control herself, Laure burst into tears again, the words strangled by sobs. Madame Lampron gestured for her to sit on the bed and sat next to her.

Laure was overwhelmed by such a display of kindness. Keeping her head down, she looked at her skirt and suddenly couldn't help thinking of how old and awful it appeared next to Madame's pale-blue brocade.

Through her sobs, she could smell the sweet scent of perfume and the powder covering Madame's flaxen hair. She felt cheap and dirty, but her mistress didn't seem at all bothered.

'You are Laure, aren't you?' she asked. 'I haven't seen you in a while. You've grown into a very beautiful woman indeed. Please do tell me what is troubling you.'

Laure took a deep breath and tried to regain her composure. Encouraged by her mistress's compassion and happy to finally find a listening ear, she explained her situation, her sorrow and her fears.

Madame Lampron listened silently and nodded with a smile.

'There is nothing to be afraid of, my sweet,' she said. Her tiny hand gently stroked Laure's back. 'My husband and I will make sure you want for nothing. In fact, I shall speak to him tonight. Come and see me tomorrow evening, in this room, after the banquet, and I will most probably have good news for you.'

'Madame is too kind,' Laure protested. 'I do not deserve such kindness.'

'Nonsense! We can help you and take good care of you, if in turn you agree to do something for us.'

Laure felt a great weight lift from her heart. She wasn't alone, after all. How nice it was of her mistress. Although she was grateful, she couldn't find words to express her thankfulness and simply smiled through her tears.

'You are very pretty when you smile,' Madame Lampron whispered. Her hand slowly went down Laure's back and encircled her waist. Laure felt uneasy with such a gesture, but Madame was so gentle and so sweet.

The woman's other arm came around the girl to close the subtle embrace. Her face drew so near Laure could feel her breath on her cheek and she blushed.

'Do not be shy,' Madame laughed softly. 'I know you are anything but bashful.'

How could she know anything about her, Laure wondered. The kitchen staff had no contact with the masters. Even Juliette, the housekeeper, took her orders from the butler. Unless the masters knew her father? That was unlikely, he was only a blacksmith.

Madame's hand slid down her hip, down her leg,

whilst her face kept getting closer. 'Indeed,' the woman continued, 'I am sure we can get along very well.'

Her soft lips swept Laure's cheek, dropping gentle kisses in a tight row down the length of her jaw, then moved up to her mouth.

Laure's heart pounded furiously. What was Madame doing? Why was she holding and stroking her like this? Why was she kissing her so? Yet even as doubts rose in her mind, she couldn't help feeling aroused. She wasn't used to such gentleness. She closed her eyes and demurely placed her arms around the fragile waist of her mistress.

Her body slowly took over from her mind. There was too much confusion. Laure didn't want to think about how awkward this situation was. Instead, she let her growing lust direct her actions.

She chose to let herself be pampered and enjoyed the smooth embrace. Once again she was happy and comfortable. It felt good and Laure couldn't help pressing her curvaceous body against that of her mistress, more slender and delicate. When a tiny tongue slipped into her mouth, she didn't refuse it but happily responded to its caress.

This was most unusual, yet very pleasant. To hold someone so slim, so petite, was almost frightening. Even more disconcerting was Madame's behaviour. Laure had never been made love to by a woman. It was very different, but gave rise to sensations just as nice as the touch of a man.

Laure let out a gentle sigh, unable to contain the excitement now mounting within her. Madame drew away from the maid's mouth and slowly traced a path of wet kisses along her neck, and all the way down until her lips met the ties of Laure's chemise.

The dainty hands moved up to undo the knot. Gently slipping her hand inside, Madame slowly cupped the large globes with spider-like fingers, feeling their weight, teasing the erect nipples with her fingertips.

Laure let out another sigh, slightly louder. So much tenderness was overwhelming and pleasurable; Madame's advances daring but welcome. She didn't resist when Madame softly pushed her back on the unmade bed.

By then she was almost paralysed by surprise, lust and curiosity. Her first time with a man had been planned, anticipated, mentally rehearsed. But what was happening now was new and spontaneous. She didn't know what to do and was excited at the thought of being taken by a woman. Happily abandoning herself, she lay back and closed her eyes.

Her breasts were carefully released from her chemise and Madame leant to kiss them with her sensuous mouth. Laure was used to having her nipples pinched and sucked greedily, whereas today they were caressed by a soft, gentle tongue, which produced the same result. Between her legs, a rush of excitement quickly gave way to an even hotter flow of dew. As was often the case, Laure now felt like a prisoner of her own clothes. She hadn't changed after the funeral and was still clad in the thick, uncomfortable dress she usually wore only at church on Sundays. This was in addition to several petticoats, which constricted her more than ever now.

Whilst her mistress so skilfully tended to her swollen breasts, Laure's mind wandered. She imagined them both naked, rolling around on the soft sheets of the large bed. If only she could get out of this dress, feel the woman's hands gently touch her throbbing skin. She moaned again.

Madame did not respond, so busy was she licking the beautiful breasts displayed before her, gently sucking the erect nipples whilst twirling her tongue around them in an attempt to arouse them still further.

She was using Laure to arouse herself as well, for it was clear that Madame was possessed with lust. Her body wriggled on top of Laure's, her legs straddling the girl, her hips rhythmically sliding up and down as she ground their pubises together through their heavy clothing.

Whilst her mouth kept busy, her hands quickly undertook the sensuous task of removing the maid's clothes. She rolled onto her back and pulled Laure on top of her. The girl's heavy breasts almost smothered her and she groaned with joy. Her hands easily managed to unfasten the skirts and pull them down, along with the petticoats.

Laure was astounded, amazed at such skilfulness, for before she could realise what was going on, all she had on was her chemise and her bodice. Her excitement grew. She would soon be naked, as long as Madame continued what she had started.

Madame pushed her aside and got up, pulling Laure to her feet. 'Let me look at you,' she said in a hoarse voice.

Laure was too embarrassed to reply. She stood silently, her cheeks red, feeling both bashful and aroused. Her breasts were jutting out, her erect nipples insolently pointing towards the woman responsible for their state.

'Look at me,' Madame commanded.

Laure looked up slowly. She had always been told to keep her eyes lowered when addressed by the masters. She didn't dare look the woman in the eye, especially under these circumstances.

But their eyes did meet. Laure barely recognised the soft-spoken woman who had come into the room just a few minutes earlier. In her place was a lustful creature, her hair undone, falling in a blonde cascade over her white, naked shoulders. The top of her dress was unfastened, her gaping chemise revealing the ivory skin of her breasts and giving Laure the briefest glimpse of a puckered, rosy nipple. The tiny shoes she had been wearing were now discarded, revealing incredibly small and elegant feet. But most impressive were Madame's eyes, which were fixed on the bashful maid, shining like a fire in the night, glowing a thousand flames, burning with desire.

And Laure realised her own desire was just as strong. She longed for the soft caresses to resume, for the mouth to tease her nipples once more, for the delicate body to reveal itself completely.

'I want to see all of you,' Madame uttered slowly. 'Undress for me.' She sat in the armchair, her back straight, her proud breasts pushing against the opening of her chemise. Her voice was low but authoritative. Laure felt happy to oblige, obeying both her superior and a new lover.

She slowly got rid of her bodice. Her chemise, worn out and transparent with age, fell freely around her body. The sun coming through the window caught her from behind and threw her shadow on the wall. Laure could see her own silhouette, the curves of her hips, the length of her legs, as if her chemise had vanished.

Madame could see it as well. She tilted her head sideways whilst her eyes travelled between the girl and her image, as if they couldn't decide which was more pleasant to behold. Her hands slowly lifted her skirts, gathering the delicate fabrics into her lap before disappearing between her sinewy, aristocratic legs.

Laure knew she should not hurry. Nonchalantly, she pulled on the laces holding her bonnet and let it fall to the floor before undoing the knot that held her hair up. Her dark mane fell about her shoulders, the long strands flowing down to brush her breasts.

She let her arms fall to her sides and grabbed her chemise at the hips. She slowly drew it up, using only her fingertips, letting the fabric bunch in her hands as it gradually revealed her legs.

Madame stirred and sighed, her eyes fixed on the maid, one hand still hidden under her skirts, whilst the other freed her breasts.

Laure's body ached for the woman sitting just inches away. But Madame was no longer paying any attention to the girl standing in front of her. One hand on her breasts, the other engulfed between her legs, she was pleasuring herself.

Her half-clothed body twitched against the richly embroidered fabric of the armchair, her legs spread wide apart. Behind her, the large portrait hanging above the mantelpiece showed a woman bearing very little resemblance to the one writhing in the armchair.

They had the same delicate features, the same tiny hands and small waist. But the woman in the portrait was calm and collected, her cool, angelic face framed in blue. Her dress trailed on the floor and revealed very little, if anything, of the body underneath. The bodice completely fastened, the arms covered to the wrists, the scarf around the neck and chest, all hid her porcelain skin; it was a body too perfect and too proper to be real.

By contrast, the woman on the chair was flushed with passion; her hair in disarray fell loosely across her naked chest and shoulders. Her face was contorted in ecstasy and her sensuous lips curled in utter delight. Her dress bunched up around her waist revealed smooth, white thighs now quivering as she approached her climax. Her breasts heaved with every shallow breath. Her body was alive, consumed with a desire no artist could ever render on a simple, cold canvas.

Laure hungered for what she could see but couldn't touch. The sight of her mistress mesmerised her and she couldn't tear her eyes away. To see Madame in such a position, in front of a simple servant – how degrading. But what a spectacle.

Almost by instinct, Laure slipped her hands under her chemise and slowly stroked the front of her thighs, bringing her hands closer to her sex with each stroke. Without even realising it, she mirrored her mistress's caresses, her eyes constantly fixed on the woman and awaiting the next cue.

The whole scene appeared unreal, bathed by the late-afternoon sun coming through the window. Madame had pulled her skirts up completely and placed her bottom at the very edge of the chair. She wasn't wearing anything underneath: no bloomers, no culottes. Who would have thought that such a fine lady would dare be so brazen?

Her legs parted even wider, exposing her delicate pink folds which she explored with her long fingers, probing deep inside the dark tunnel and stroking her stiff bud which throbbed with delight.

Laure felt her own vulva pulsating in response. Its dew flowed from her wet valley, its smell merging with that of Madame's, filling the room with a heady aroma.

Madame brought her hand to her chest, her fingers soaked and glistening. Very gently, she raised one of her breasts and stuck her tongue out to meet her nipple. All the while her eyes remained fixed on Laure and she smiled at her wickedly as she began to lick herself.

Laure ran her tongue across her dry lips. Suddenly she longed to taste that nipple too, and delve her fingers into Madame's swollen, gaping vulva. But she didn't dare move. She had been told to undress, and she should refrain from doing anything until asked. She took the hem of her chemise and slowly pulled it up above her head, before letting it fall in a bundle on the floor.

Madame smiled in appreciation. Her hands never stopped their lustful dance and her moans indicated she was close to climax. She let out a scream as the spasm of pleasure pierced her. Her legs still wide apart, her muscles tensed as her bushy mound contracted under the force of her orgasm.

She caught her breath, stood up and stepped towards Laure. Placing her hands on the maid's hips, she sighed softly, still drunk with pleasure.

'Do you want me?' she asked in a whisper. Her voice was hoarse, her breath laborious. Her entire body was trembling, still reeling from the wave that had just invaded her.

'I don't know.' Laure hesitated. But she did want her, very much. Yet she felt it wasn't her place. How could

31

she, a maid who had only known men, take this woman, a woman who was her mistress? Would she know how to excite the delicate body that so enthralled her? Would she know how to pleasure a woman?

'You do,' the woman continued slowly. 'You want to undress me, you want to kiss me, touch me, lick me, bring me to pleasure. Even more, you want me to bring you to pleasure as well. Now look at me.'

For Laure's eyes were once again fixed on the floor. Inside her, a tempest raged. She did want Madame. She wanted her with all her being. She wanted to take her, to dominate the slender body.

'Take me.' The words sounded like an order. Laure felt a surge of desire shake her. If she was ordered, she had to obey. Especially if it meant sweet pleasure.

Slowly she undid the laces on Madame's dress, pulled it down and gently folded it before putting it on the back of the chair. As she walked back across the room, she could feel her dew now bathing the valley between her legs. Her mind was racing. The woman was eager for passion to sweep them both away, yet Laure wanted this afternoon to last as long as possible.

Wearing only her chemise, Madame went to lock the door. Turning around, she pouted childishly as she slowly walked back to the bed and wantonly ran her hands over her body.

'I am very disappointed in you, Laure,' she whined. 'You are not at all what I had expected.'

Laure was intrigued. Just what did Madame mean? How could she know anything about her?

'I was told, from a very good source, you were a passionate soul. Yet it seems you are holding back.' Coming closer to the maid, she stopped just a few inches away. Her face softened and her voiced deepened. 'Why don't you just take me like René takes you?' she whispered huskily.

The mention of his name startled Laure. How did

Madame know him? And how could he have told her anything about their encounters?

Madame silently stared at her, smiling seductively. 'You are not his only lover, you know. I have been with him as well. He has told me about you, saying you were the best lover he had ever known.'

Laure felt her heart jump in her chest. In her state of arousal, images of their passionate times came back in a thousand flashes, racing through her head along with memories of the pleasures they had known together.

'Why do you think you were sent here to my room? And why do you think I showed up? It was all planned, you know. I decided I wanted to know you, to share the passion of your embrace.'

Standing mere inches from Laure, Madame paused as if to let her words stoke the fire burning within the girl's body.

Laure couldn't contain herself any longer. Once more she looked at the woman. Again she saw the lustful, inviting body; read the message in the woman's eyes. So she had been set up. Their presence in this room was not a coincidence. Madame had planned this, just like Laure had planned her first encounter with René. Only this time Laure was the victim, just as René had willingly fallen into her trap. And just like him, today she wasn't going to refuse the invitation. The last remnant of hesitation disappeared, leaving her senses raging with desire.

Leaping forward, she grabbed the opening of Madame's chemise and ripped it apart in one swift move. The delicate fabric offered no resistance. Neither did Madame. Her body trembled with a shiver of excitement and she let out a small cry. Laure stopped, breathing hard, and stood back to look at her.

Her naked body was most attractive. Unlike any woman Laure had ever seen before, Madame was truly aristocratic; from the roots of her hair to the tip of her toes. She was of average height, but slim and pale, much like a precious alabaster figurine with shapely, compelling curves.

Her silky skin, so pale, looked almost transparent. Her limbs, long and slender, offered a velvet embrace. Her breasts, rather small but well defined, were adorned by tiny nipples, rosy and stiff, seemingly in a constant state of arousal. Beneath her small and delicate waist, her hips appeared even rounder and more generous. At the base of her belly, a sparse bush the colour of straw invitingly revealed thick, engorged love-lips. This was a body made for sensuous love, a temple of quiet but profound lust.

Laure took another step forward and gently pushed the woman onto the bed, softly, almost lovingly. Just as gently, she lay beside her and took her in her arms. Only then did her mounting passion make her lose control.

Her mouth immediately found Madame's lips and sucked on them greedily whilst her hands set out to explore the body writhing beneath her. Her grasping hands seized the woman's breasts in a tight grip, covering them completely, and the puckered nipples contracted even further against the palm of her hand.

Squeezing them gently, she kneaded them with her fingertips, amazed at their warmth and softness. Madame moaned as Laure's fingers then locked on her nipples, pinching and teasing them.

The maid couldn't get enough of her mistress's sensuous mouth. She explored it with a mad fury, like a ravenous animal, parting the lips with hers and probing inside with her tongue. Madame responded eagerly, twirling around hers like a windmill in a storm, returning Laure's kisses with just as much passion. Their breathing became shorter as their excitement escalated.

Straddling her prey, Laure ground her vulva against the tender skin of the rounded belly. She couldn't remember when she had last been this aroused. For now she was possessing another body, which had never been the case with René. Today her lover truly was at her mercy.

With regret, but keen to discover the slender body, she drew away from Madame's eager mouth. She wanted to love the breasts, two mounds of hot, soft flesh which were begging to be kissed. She drew a nipple into her mouth and was happily surprised by its size and its sensitivity; by how it responded, pulsating stiffly between her lips.

Her hands continued exploring the malleable globes as her tongue began a dizzying dance around the stiff, rosy buds. Pulling back slightly, Laure teased the erect peaks with only the very tip of her tongue whilst with feather-light fingers she lightly brushed the white skin.

Their bodies melted onto one another, their embrace a soldering bond. Madame's hands, hitherto idle, also began exploring the girl's strong curves. They rolled on the bed, back and forth, just as Laure had hoped. Sandwiched between her mistress's skin and the linen, she was overwhelmed by such softness; never before had she felt so comfortably surrounded. The mattress gave and bounced under their weight, enhancing the rhythm created by their writhing bodies.

Each woman took the lead for a while, then surrendered to the desires of the other. Laure was possessive, Madame a little more sedate. Yet at times they were equals, both seeking to give and receive pleasure.

When they lay side by side, Madame turned around and crawled over the girl's body, placing her head over the maid's bush so that each could taste the other's delicious treasure.

Laure parted her mistress's legs and pressed her lips to the tantalising vulva, captivated by its musky dew and swollen folds. At the same time, she felt a delicate mouth searching her. They remained like this for an eternity: kissing, licking and sucking; being kissed, licked and sucked.

Madame gently drew the girl's bud into her mouth,

teasing its sensitive head, slowly probing its tiny length. Laure went mad with joy. The touch was so gentle, yet so intense. She reached her peak in mere seconds. Shock waves of pleasure rampaged through her, burning within her pelvis and rippling through her thighs and belly.

Despite the cries of joy that escaped her, she never stopped toying with her new-found treasure, sucking it greedily into submission. Madame climaxed soon after, her cries muffled between Laure's legs. They both released their embrace, letting the wave of pleasure slowly subside with each beat of their hearts.

But Madame did not lie still for very long. She slinkily moved about the bed on all fours, her hair falling all around her face and her hips swaying wantonly. She made Laure sit up, legs apart, then sat in front of the girl, tangling the V of their legs until their throbbing vulvas came into contact.

They caressed each other gently, using only the motion of their hips, holding each other in a close, sensuous embrace. After a while, Laure watched as her mistress leant back on her elbows and let her head fall backwards. The woman's full mouth fell open in utter delight as her flesh rubbed furiously against Laure's. A long, wailing cry betrayed her second climax.

After a while, she caught her breath and sat up. Leaning towards Laure, she held out her arms and hugged her tight.

'You are delicious, my sweet. What wonderful times we will have together. I have been waiting for you for a long time, yet you were well worth the wait. We shall never be apart again.'

Laure didn't reply. Her mind was empty, having ceased thinking to concentrate solely on the sensations her body was experiencing. Madame's embrace was soothing and comforting, not to mention arousing. They kissed and cuddled for a while, and Laure forgot everything else around her. Slowly she fell into some sort of blissful slumber, an effect of the intense sensations that had swept over her.

Then, without letting go of her, Madame reached into the drawer of the bedside table and pulled out a long, thick bundle. Undoing the silk knot, she unwrapped a velvet cover to reveal a large candle. Its wick had been cut short, its edges rounded at both ends. The grey wax had been polished to give it a soft shape.

Releasing her embrace, Madame moved back and gently inserted one end of the candle inside Laure's tunnel. Slowly, wickedly, she worked it in and out a few times in long, soft strokes.

Laure felt her arousal mounting again. The thickness of the candle was considerable, stretching her wide, the pressure enhancing her pleasure, resulting in the most exhilarating sensation.

Madame moved her hips so that she could insert the other end of the candle into herself as well. Laure understood what her mistress wanted to do and reacted readily. Resting on their elbows, their bodies began the most curious dance, each pushing and pulling in turn, moving the candle in and out of their vaginas, using its length and girth to rekindle the flame of their passion.

Laure's climax came quickly, her wet flesh surrendering to the sweet torture of the unusual instrument. Even once the exquisite sensations had passed, she continued to move to ensure her lover would also reach her peak. They both climaxed several times, captives to their own lustful hunger.

After a while, exhausted by the power of the never-ending pleasure, they had no choice but to stop. Madame slowly pulled the candle out and ran her long, polished fingernail across it, carving letters in the wax.

'This candle will have your name on it,' she uttered in a broken voice. 'You shall see it again soon, I hope.'

Still holding and stroking each other, they slowly got dressed. By the time they were finished, the sun was already setting on the horizon and filling the room with an orange glow. It was difficult to part, but Laure left happy.

'Do not forget,' Madame advised. 'Meet me here, in this room, tomorrow night. You will not regret it.' It sounded more like a promise than a request.

Chapter Three

*L*aure silently crept into Madame's room, as instructed, the evening after the banquet. The house was quiet. Six guests were staying overnight and had retired early.

She entered her mistress's room, her heart pounding with expectation, and locked the door behind her. Right away she knew she belonged there. Already the surroundings no longer seemed foreign, even in the pale light of the fire.

Madame was waiting by the fireplace, dressed only in a long white robe, her golden hair reflecting the glow of the flames. Laure didn't waste any time and seized her mistress's tiny waist in her arms, capturing her mouth and sucking it greedily. But Madame pushed her away, laughing.

'You are impatient, my dear.' Her voice echoed in the semi-darkness. 'You are not mine tonight, but I can promise your pleasure will be just as intense as yesterday. Come.'

She grabbed the maid's hand and led her into the adjoining room, the master's bedchamber.

That room was larger and lit by only three candles. Laure's eyes took a while to get used to the darkness. In the middle, near the massive bed, four men stood, naked and ready. Laure froze in surprise. She recognised Monsieur Lampron, her master, and the three gentlemen who were staying the night at the château.

The same men she had seen seated at the table earlier, eating and drinking in all civility, proper and well behaved, were now standing in front of her, unashamed by their nakedness. They looked even stranger without their wigs, but they stood proud and tall, without so much as a pair of shoes.

The only thing they all flaunted was a full erection, and Laure couldn't believe the sight of them. She looked at Madame and was somewhat relieved by the amused look in her eyes. There was a strange smell in the air, vaguely familiar yet unusual, heady and rather enticing.

'Tonight is your night,' Madame softly said. 'We are here to bring you pleasure, if in turn you agree to do the same for us.'

Laure nodded silently, intrigued and excited. Monsieur Lampron came to her and stroked her cheek with his large hand. He was a tall and heavy man, his stance straight, his head always held high. Laure had seen him before and always thought he looked majestic, especially when riding his horse. But naked, he was even more impressive.

His wigless head was shaved and showed only a thin fuzz on top. His body was very muscular, his chest broad and entirely covered by a carpet of fine curls. His flat stomach was adorned by a dark bush at its base, from which sprang an enormous member, long and thick, its purple plum glistening in the candlelight.

As her eyes travelled around the room, Laure noticed who was holding the candles and this realisation sent a bolt of excitement through her belly.

The gentlemen's wives were standing almost on their heads, propped up by piles of cushions on the floor. Legs up against the wall and wide apart, they exposed their naked flesh. But most surprising were the candles that protruded from their vaginas, securely anchored deep within them. The melting wax dripped to collect in a hot pool on the swollen skin of their vulvas. On each candle, the name of the lady had been carved. Laure immediately guessed whose noble fingernail had picked out the letters in the wax.

The trio was quite a sight and Laure suddenly realised that the aroma she had noticed floating in the air was coming from the candles, which had undoubtedly been dipped repeatedly in the ladies' most private parts before being lit.

Madame walked towards Laure and began undressing her. Her movements were quick and exact, yet so sensuous that Laure felt more excitement than shame at the notion of being undressed in front of her audience.

'Tonight we shall test your obedience,' Monsieur announced. 'We will use you and let you use us solely for pleasure. If you fail, the consequences will be terrible. However, from what my wife tells me, I have every confidence you will do well. You will follow every order we give you, without asking any questions. What you must do first is undress my wife, arouse her and set up another candle.'

Laure was happy to oblige, though she was a bit nervous at the thought of being at their mercy. She had the feeling she would remember this evening for a long, long time.

She turned to Madame and, bending down, she grabbed the bottom of the woman's robe and pulled it above her head, revealing her naked body. Madame was even more beautiful than Laure had remembered, especially in the candlelight.

The maid kissed her sweet lover gently, caressing her softly, rediscovering the tender skin she had tasted the day before. Madame stood still, as if she had been ordered not to move, and abandoned herself to the girl's ministrations.

Laure had only one thing on her mind. She dropped

to her knees and gently parted the woman's legs. Her tongue went immediately for the stiff bud, drawing it into her mouth and sucking it avidly.

Madame was already wet, her folds engorged and hot, her bud swollen and throbbing. Laure was a bit disappointed. She would have liked to be responsible for her mistress's arousal. But at least now the woman was at her mercy. Reaching up with one hand, she grabbed a nipple between her fingers, teasing it gently whilst her other hand came to join her mouth. She took to licking Madame's sweet mound earnestly, wanting to swallow all of her, all of that delicious, honey-slick flesh offered so willingly.

Already Madame was breathing hard, her body writhing with pleasure. Laure heard the men behind her breathing harder as well, obviously pleased by the spectacle in front of them. She liked the idea of being watched, of being the source of their arousal.

A hand fell on her shoulder and pulled her back.

'That's enough,' Monsieur said. 'It's time to light a candle.'

Madame walked towards a pile of cushions and picked up the candle that lay on top of it. She smiled as she handed it to Laure, who recognised the letters carved along its length. It was the very same candle they had used the previous day.

Madame bent over the pillows and threw her legs up and apart with such natural ease that Laure guessed the woman must have done this many times before. The other women looked comfortable despite their precarious positions. They paid no attention to Laure and her mistress, as if they were caught up in a world of their own.

One of them had enormous breasts and her unusual pose offered the advantage of having them fall towards her face so her mouth could reach and suck her own nipples. Another woman was pushing the candle in and out of her tunnel, moaning with delight.

Laure lit her candle on the flame of another one. She immediately noticed its scent, reminiscent of her encounter with Madame the previous day. She bent down towards the exposed flesh, licking it in earnest as if she wanted to make sure there was enough moisture, but in reality still hungry for it.

The candle glided in easily, and Laure pushed it slowly in then pulled it back out slightly, wanting her lover to enjoy the insertion. After all, she had been told to set up a candle. These gentlemen surely would not object if she managed to pleasure Madame in the process.

Soon she could feel them growing impatient behind her. She inserted the candle as far as it would go and turned to face them, bowing her head in reverence. Unashamed of her nakedness and feeling decidedly wicked, she stepped forward, knowing they were staring at her voluptuous figure.

'You shall look at us,' Monsieur ordered. 'Tonight you are not a servant; there is no difference in status in this room. You are only a slave of love, and as such your sole purpose is to pleasure and seek pleasure in return. Now get down on your knees.'

He pointed to a smaller pile of cushions at the foot of the bed, arranged so Laure could kneel and lie back comfortably.

The first of the guests, Monsieur Desgets, came to her and presented his erect phallus to her mouth. Laure didn't need to be told what to do. She took it eagerly, her arousal so intense she was ready to do anything; she was hungry for more flesh, be it male or female.

The shaft was long but thin, the purple head rather small. Electing to use only her tongue, she ran it fast and slick around the ridge, teasing his flesh and pushing the tip of her tongue into the tiny mouth. In her hand, the balls were big and full, the scrotum tight. She tickled him with her fingertips, fretting like a butterfly over his shaft and balls, at times barely touching him.

He let out a loud sigh. 'Very good,' his voice thundered as he obviously addressed whoever wanted to hear him. 'Yes indeed, she has a lot of potential. The tongue is eager, although a bit green, but certainly pleasing.' He pulled out and moved back.

'I believe I shall try it myself,' Monsieur Benoit announced, stepping forward.

Laure was greatly amused. She liked arousing them like this. But they seemed to be merely testing her, without really seeking fulfilment. Or was that to be saved for later?

The second penis thrust into her care was very different; small but thick, made to be sucked rather than licked. She set her mouth upon it zealously, accommodating it completely, and sucked so hard that he moaned in satisfaction almost immediately.

'Her mouth is a delight,' he clamoured enthusiastically. 'Only very seldom have I seen a young lady so eager to please.' He pulled out with a popping noise, leaving a disappointed Laure impatiently awaiting her next treat.

Monsieur Lampron pushed forward his third guest who was hesitant. The young man seemed in awe of the maid's skills, as if he were afraid of her.

'Be gentle with him,' Monsieur Lampron advised. 'Our friend has only joined our ranks as of tonight. Unfortunately his charming wife, although quite sensuous, is not really keen on such caresses. We think it is time for him to discover the pleasures a voracious mouth can bring.'

His phallus was quite remarkable in size, but in a limited state of arousal. Laure knew he would never forget her and resolved to give him the best treatment she could offer.

She took him in her hands and stroked the phallus to reasonable stiffness, using both her fingers and her tongue all along the length of his shaft, but without actually taking him in her mouth. He reacted quickly, his knees trembling in response to her touch. When she was satisfied he couldn't hold out much longer, she drew him in completely, gently caressing his glans with her tongue.

After just a few seconds she knew he was close to climax, but she thought it only fair to deny him this pleasure for now. She let him go with a smile. He seemed disappointed. Monsieur Lampron, on the other hand, was pleased by her initiative.

'Very good, my child,' he commented. 'I see you understand our rules. As you may appreciate, we do not seek immediate release, but rather the happiness of lasting pleasure. I shall now have the joy of surrendering myself to your skilful mouth.'

He stepped forward and offered his large member. Laure took it in her mouth and relished it like a ripe fruit bursting with juicy flavour. By now she was also serving her own needs, for she was getting tremendous pleasure out of holding him in her mouth. Long and stiff and throbbing under her tongue, he was by far the best. She circled the shaft with both hands, stroking his length whilst she sucked the bulbous head.

He moaned in appreciation. 'You are indeed very keen. My wife has made a good choice. We shall now see how accommodating you can be.'

He gestured for the others to come and join him. Laure's mouth was assaulted by the three other eager members, each begging for more. She was elated by this delicious attack, sucking and licking them all in turn. Her hands helped greet each one, endlessly stroking and rubbing the stiff shafts.

They were all around her, hard and impatient. She fondled, licked and sucked as best she could, never neglecting anyone for very long, but wishing she could do so much more.

Above her head the conversation carried on, the men commenting on her performance.

'Quite a silken tongue.'

'Do you really think so? I find it has a rather pleasant roughness to it.'

'In any case, I like the way it moves.'

'It is indeed quite skilful. And the mouth is very comfortable.'

'Yes, and eager to please, which is really what we seek, is it not?'

Laure soon became oblivious to their words, concentrating solely on the task at hand, drunk with the power. Her vulva reacted violently, aching to feel them thrust inside her wetness.

Sitting back, she shifted her weight to rest her swollen flesh directly on her right foot. Her heel pressed against her stiff bud in a pleasant way. She tried to pleasure herself, although this was difficult to accomplish without the gentlemen noticing what she was doing. Nevertheless, her body swayed to and fro, her pubis grinding onto her heel, her wet valley sliding up and down on the hard skin.

Still sucking and licking the four men, she felt her vulva burn with the fire of her mounting orgasm, and she began to sigh uncontrollably, seemingly only taking pleasure out of having so much stiff flesh to toy with. She let out a loud moan as she climaxed, pushing her vulva onto her heel with all her weight, a surrogate penetration.

'How strange,' Monsieur Desgets stated. 'It appears that the young lady can achieve the ultimate pleasure simply through the appeal of our flesh.'

'Do not let her fool you, my friend,' replied Monsieur Lampron. 'See how heavily she sits her delicious bottom on her heels. I can only conclude this little wanton has been masturbating all the while.'

'Maybe so,' Monsieur Benoit intervened, 'but is it not what we seek here tonight, to pleasure and be pleasured? I say this young wench has indeed caught on to our games very rapidly.'

'You are forgetting one thing, however,' Monsieur

Lampron continued. His voice broke to let out a groan of pleasure. For Laure, despite being the topic of conversation, had continued her ministrations. 'Our rules are very strict. Self-induced pleasure is not allowed. She must wait for one of us to bring her to climax.'

'Quite right,' Monsieur Desgets stated. 'She has strayed, and she must be punished.'

As he spoke, Laure became slightly worried. What were they going to do to her? She had always been an obedient servant but tonight she had displeased them. She knew they weren't seeking release just yet, but did this rule also apply to her? They hadn't told her so. What was going to happen to her?

Monsieur Lampron pulled away and she concentrated on the three men whose members were still entrusted to her care, seeking their forgiveness by increasing the intensity of her caresses. Two of the men were already close to climax and the treat she offered became twice as eager, her tongue a hot instrument of sweet torture. However, Monsieur Lampron again realised what she was doing and pulled his guests away from her.

'Let's not get carried away,' he ordered. 'We must not seek release at this point, it is far too soon. We have here a young person in need of correction.' He pulled a long riding crop from under the bed and held it in front of him whilst his gaze roamed indecisively from one guest to another.

Laure was still impressed by the sight of them. Four naked noblemen, their stiff rods standing to attention, unashamed of their nudity. At the sight of the crop, Messieurs Desgets and Benoit reacted like two excited children, their eyes constantly travelling between the instrument and the woman kneeling in front of them, each man eager to pounce on her.

But Monsieur Lampron had another idea. He looked at them and smiled wickedly, shaking his head. Turning to his third guest, the youngest one who had remained silent all evening, he handed the crop over to him.

'My dear friend, do us proud. You are here tonight for the first time. Although we are not testing you, you should be aware that one must conform to certain standards in order to remain part of this group. What we have here is a young lady who must be taught a lesson. It is up to you to see that she does not stray again.'

Desgets and Benoit brought forward an enormous armchair, dragging it across the wooden floor. Monsieur Lampron made Laure get up and kneel on it, facing the back to lean against it, thereby tantalisingly displaying her engorged flesh and her rounded bottom to the four men.

'I must confess I find this creature very charming,' Monsieur Benoit announced. 'I would be hard pressed to decide in which of the delicious apertures I would choose to relieve myself.'

'Fortunately, it is not up to you to decide,' Monsieur Lampron stated. 'We shall leave this decision to chance. Lebeau, my friend, you may begin.'

Young Monsieur Lebeau seemed to hesitate for a minute. Laure was horrified. Although many of her encounters with René had been rather rough, she had never been whipped with a riding crop. She hoped it would be over quickly. She would then make sure to do only as told and never break their rules again.

All of a sudden, the crop began sliding up and down the contour of her bottom, studying her curves. The leather tip scratched her bare flesh, then insinuated itself within the folds of her vulva. Laure gasped under the wicked attack. Her heart pounded furiously, yet her arousal didn't subside. If anything, it grew even stronger.

The first slap fell. Initially, Laure felt nothing. Then, her skin suddenly became tight and hot, and she held her breath. The pain, though sharp, immediately gave rise to an unusual sensation, strangely pleasant, as if her tender skin had come alive under the blow.

The second strike quickly followed. She shivered and

moaned. The pain quickly merged with unbearable pleasure. Laure whimpered as her thighs grew weak. After the third blow she realised this session was just a farce. The man holding the crop knew exactly what he was doing.

The blows kept coming, at times hard then becoming a mere brush, and interspersed with long, sensuous strokes of the crop. They rained on every inch of her buttocks.

At one point Monsieur Lebeau turned the crop around and inserted the handle inside Laure's vagina, pulling it back out slowly, letting its girth stretch her wet tunnel. Laure panted with excitement. Once again she was close to climax, and the man holding the crop knew it.

The leather tip caressed her bud for a while, teasing it endlessly, unleashing a wave of pleasure inside her. This time Laure knew they wouldn't object to her orgasm. In fact, they probably wanted her to climax right in front of them. She held out for as long as she could, but eventually a well-placed flick of the crop made her reach the point of no return. She came with a load moan, her hips pushing back and begging for more, her muscles tense under the force of her climax.

Then she fell, lifeless, against the back of the chair.

'What a wonderful performance, Lebeau,' Monsieur Desgets said. 'I can hardly believe you have never done this before. However, being a gentleman, I shall not ask for any details.'

'That was quite nice,' Monsieur Benoit admitted, 'but you didn't give us the opportunity to see whether her back passage was as accommodating as the rest of her.'

'Quite right.' Monsieur Lampron took the crop and held its handle at Laure's anus. 'We will have to proceed carefully for we wouldn't want to damage the goods.'

The leather handle nudged at her tight entrance, then invaded her slowly, stretching it considerably. Laure didn't offer any resistance. Monsieur's ministrations were just enough to tease and maintain her level of arousal. He continued to probe her back passage for a little while, before pulling the crop out and dropping it on the floor.

'I would say she is ripe,' he concluded in an authoritative tone. 'And I believe it is time for us to make the most of this evening. The time has come to choose.'

Reaching into a drawer in the table next to the bed, he pulled out four cards and set them on the table, face down. Each man in turn came to take one.

This mysterious ritual served to decide how each man would make use of Laure's charms that night. Monsieur Lebeau held out his card on which a pair of lips were drawn in red ink.

'It must be my lucky night, for I shall have her mouth,' he said happily. Monsieur Lampron gestured towards the footstool behind the armchair and helped Lebeau climb onto it to face Laure and bring his phallus level with her mouth.

'I wish I could say the same,' lamented Monsieur Desgets, 'for the card I have picked indicates I shall have her vagina.'

Laure was helped off the chair so Desgets could sit down. She was then lifted on top of him and impaled upon his length, her knees straddling his hips. He moved his head slightly to one side, so that she could still reach Lebeau's prick which now impatiently twitched just inches from her mouth.

'My dear Benoit,' Monsieur Lampron said behind her, 'since I have been awarded her tiny hands, I must therefore conclude that you shall have the pleasure of her anus.'

And so Monsieur Benoit came to straddle Desgets's lap, behind Laure, whilst Monsieur Lampron came to stand next to the chair.

Laure was assaulted from all angles, members thrust into her mouth from behind the chair, into her wet tunnel and between her buttocks. Even her hands were kept busy as she was given the task of manually relieving her master. And there began a bizarre ritual, every man driving his erect phallus in and out of Laure's various openings, each sighing with mounting pleasure. The armchair, obviously used to such abuse, squeaked in harmony with their groans.

Laure was impaled and pushed up from behind, her tender anus stretched by Monsieur Benoit's girth, his thick phallus invading her along with that of Monsieur Desgets in her softer tunnel, both men competing to occupy the adjoining entrances. In her mouth, Monsieur Lebeau once again throbbed with arousal. Tonight he would know the pleasure of coming in a woman's mouth.

Before long it was clear that these gentlemen were all ready to reach their peak, but though all were eager to release their desire, no-one wanted to be the first to climax.

Laure couldn't have been more overjoyed. Closing her eyes, she imagined a tangled mass of flesh, bodies joined in lust around her. She was the centre of attention, a source of delight for all these men. And, even more elating, she could count on pleasure sweeping her as well time and again until every man had been satisfied.

She did her best to concentrate on the members she held in her mouth and in her hands. Never would she grow tired of them. Inside her, she could feel the two other pricks possessing her, teasing her into madness.

Amidst the cries that accompanied their lustful thrusts, Laure noticed softer moans and briefly glanced at the corner of the room towards the women who had been holding the candles. Until then, she had been too preoccupied to notice what they were doing, so she was surprised to see the candles had been pulled out and properly placed in holders. They were no longer needed.

The women were on the floor, another mass of tangled flesh, stroking and kissing one another. Hands and mouths caressed whatever they could reach, each woman exploring the others' bodies with long strokes and greedy kisses. Laure watched them, fascinated and somewhat envious. There were luscious nipples begging to be sucked, pink flesh displayed and eager to be licked. Soon they began to moan louder, their cries merging with those of the men who were making use of Laure's charms.

Yet she was happy right where she was. In her hands she could feel Monsieur Lampron pulse violently, the long, stiff rod powerfully hardening. She felt her many lovers' hands on her, their fingers tangled in her hair, stroking her breasts and pinching her nipples. They were gradually losing control and giving in to their excitement.

Everyone in the room was taking care of each other, giving and seeking pleasure. The moans grew into screams as each man and woman reached the ultimate release, in turn, in harmony.

In the corner, pleasure swept the women one after the other. Laure could see their faces twist with ecstasy, their limbs contract under the force of their climax, their hips jerk as they were seized by powerful waves.

Little by little the intensity of their lovemaking subsided, and each woman lay back relaxing and smiling. Occasional kisses were exchanged, but they seemed more sedate.

Laure's own pleasure kept mounting, insidious and exhilarating. The men's hips pushed into her fast and deep, and she felt each man coming in her hands, her mouth and inside her. She climaxed in unison with each of them, highly responsive to the pleasure that shook them and reverberated through her. She could smell them, taste them. All her senses were ablaze on this, the most sensuous night of her life.

She knew everyone was pleased with her and realised she would very likely be invited to join them again. Once a poor, lonely maid, she was tonight the centre of attention and hopefully she could soon become a regular player of these games.

Indeed, this was exactly where she belonged.

Chapter Four

The following day, Laure rose late and in high spirits. Although she had returned to the grotty maisonette the previous night, she knew that it would be the last time. Tonight, and every night after, she would share her mistress's bed.

After a while, she dressed and lazily walked back to the château. She stood tall and proud, her eyes surveying the kitchens as if they belonged to her. In a way, they did. Now that the Lamprons had taken her under their wing, this was all hers.

As she swaggered around with a defiant smile, the housekeeper gave her an angry look. But Laure couldn't care less. She no longer had to take orders from a woman like Juliette. Nor from anybody else, for that matter. She would show them who was in charge.

The cook yelped out a reprimand as she grabbed a croissant in the basket bound for the dining room, but she pretended not to hear. She was above them now. She had earned the right to a better life.

Looking at the trays of food ready to be taken to the dining room, Laure concluded the Lamprons and their guests were just about to have their breakfast. Her mouth full, she didn't bother brushing the flakes of pastry off her chin and a smug smile tugged at the corner of her lips.

Nonchalantly, she walked in front of the servants headed for the dining room and, there, she flung the door open and casually walked in.

Conversation stopped as they noticed her entrance. Laure stared at them, beaming. Just as the previous day, during the banquet, they all looked so proper: the ladies heavily powdered and bejewelled, clad in layers of fine, delicate lace; the men dressed in dark velvet, their long wigs trailing on their shoulders. It was hard to imagine these were the same people who had participated in a steamy sex session the previous night.

For a short moment, Laure could almost believe she had dreamt the whole episode. But the welts on her behind were a very real – and very sore – reminder that it had indeed happened.

She heard Juliette approaching behind her and she fought a giggle rising in her throat, knowing the housekeeper would try to drag her out of the dining room. How could the woman know Laure had passed a threshold the previous evening, a threshold which now made her more than a simple maid?

She braced herself for triumph: any moment now Monsieur Lampron would invite her to join them and tell the housekeeper to leave them alone. Any moment now.

But instead they all looked at her with a haughty expression. Madame spoke first.

'What is it you want?' she asked in an authoritative tone. She addressed Juliette without even looking at Laure. 'We did say we did not want to be disturbed. What is the matter?'

'I'm sorry, Madame,' replied Juliette with a curtsy. She grabbed Laure forcefully, pulled her away and closed the door behind them.

A second later, barely muffled laughter rose in the dining room and filled Laure with indignation.

Obviously, the Lamprons and their guests had found her intrusion most amusing. How dare they?

She shook her arm violently to get away from the housekeeper. 'Let me go. What are you doing?'

'Have you forgotten your place?' said Juliette. 'Or have you just gone mad? You have no business in the master and mistress's dining room.'

'Don't I?' Laure replied defiantly. 'If I can join them in their bedchamber I can just as easily join them for breakfast.'

Juliette's hand hit her cheek and Laure almost lost her balance. 'You may go wherever they ask you to go,' the woman said in an angry whisper. 'But only if they ask. Whatever you do in their bed at night is up to them. The rest of the time, never forget that you are still a maid and you will do as I say. Now get to work.'

Laure pressed her hand on her throbbing cheek and held the housekeeper's angry gaze. What a fool Juliette was. How little she knew of what their master and mistress were up to in the privacy of their bedchamber. No doubt a woman like her would never be invited to join them. But though her cheek was still stinging, her pride had suffered more.

Perhaps it was too early. The Lamprons would wait until their guests had left before letting the rest of the staff know they had now taken her under their wing. Then, everyone would have to obey her.

Laure went about her duties only half-heartedly. Once again everyone paid little if any attention to her. Thankfully, Monsieur would let them know about the changes soon, maybe even as early as tonight.

But the announcement didn't come. As the staff began retiring for the night, Laure stayed in the kitchen. Any moment now, she would be called to the top floor. But as the evening wore on, she found herself sitting alone with only a dying candle to keep her company. The warm evening air carried with it the strokes from the village clock, half a league across the fields. Not tonight, then. Maybe tomorrow.

But the next day didn't bring the news she hoped for, nor the one after that. Laure barely did any work. She spent the days dawdling, oblivious to the tasks she had been assigned, at times even refusing to do as she was told. Everyone in turn got angry and lashed out at her, but she didn't care.

What she did mind was having to go back to the little maisonette every night. Since she had been allowed into her mistress's bed, she felt nothing but contempt for the tiny bunk in which she had been sleeping for years, with its grotty woollen blanket and pillow filled with coarse hay. Now that her father had died, she would have to move out anyway, and the sooner the better.

She longed for the soft sheets and the warm eiderdown of Madame Lampron's bed. But, most of all, she craved the contact of a sleepy body, tangled with hers in a warm embrace. It had only been one night, but that had been long enough to make her despise her old surroundings.

Why hadn't Monsieur sent for her already? He had obviously been pleased with her the other night. This, she hinted at several times in front the rest of the staff, but got no reaction, so she made sure she told everyone exactly what she had done.

'You should have seen them,' she tried telling Madeleine, the gardener's eldest daughter. 'They talked so fine, but they were all naked and interested only in one thing.' At first the girl had seemed impressed, but not enough to stop her work and give Laure her undivided attention.

No-one else would even listen to her, and they were irritated by having to do her work for her. At some point, Juliette would have to set her straight and eventually she did so right in front of everybody.

'We don't care what happened the other night,' the woman burst out angrily. 'And you should know better than to say things like this about the master and mistress.

All we care about is that there is work to be done, and you are not doing your share. Either you do as you are told, or you'll have to find work elsewhere.'

'You're just jealous, you all are,' Laure exploded. 'They will send for me. They will take me as they would their daughter and then I will make you swallow your words. Before you know it I will be the one giving orders, I will.'

Once again, a slap from Juliette shut her up.

'Enough,' the woman shouted. 'Get to work now or else.'

Laure looked at her defiantly and stormed out of the kitchen. This was too much to take. It just wasn't fair. What had she done to deserve this? The Lamprons had clearly forgotten all about her, and now the rest of the staff wanted her out.

She ran to the river; she needed to get out of that house. Why, oh why? How could they be so heartless?

Sitting on the grass, she stared blankly at the water. There was nothing for her here. There was no way she could live at the château with the memory of what had happened if she were to remain a simple maid. Why had they given her a taste of sweet life; why had they made her feel part of their group if they only intended to cast her aside afterwards? Was that to be the ultimate punishment? It was too cruel, indeed.

Laure still couldn't believe what was happening. She wasn't asking for much, just for Madame to keep her promise. After the wonderful times they had shared, it was even more difficult to go back to her old life. She wanted to be there again; in the master and mistress's bedchamber, giving and receiving pleasure.

But it now seemed the Lamprons didn't want her anymore. And what about the staff? Would she have to live with their contempt? Especially Juliette's. And all the others she had talked to about what had happened that night. They would think she was a liar. For if the Lamprons had included her in their games as she claimed, why were they ignoring her now? She couldn't comprehend it herself, so how could she expect the others to believe her? What was she to do?

The sound of hurried footsteps behind her interrupted her thoughts. She turned and saw Guillaume, the groom's son, running towards her as fast as his young legs could carry him, shouting loudly.

'Laure, Laure. You must come right away. The master wants to see you.'

Laure sprung to her feet and stared at him. Monsieur was sending for her? Finally. She hoisted her skirt and ran behind the boy who was now heading back to the château.

Her heart pounded with incredulous joy. Monsieur wanted to see her. At last. In her mind, she could already see what was going to happen: he would let the staff know Laure was now under their wing; she would be vindicated and her orders would be obeyed.

Now, she would show them. She would treat them with the disdain they deserved. They would pay for having cared so little about her.

By the time she reached the château, she was out of breath. She stopped in the kitchen and quizzically looked at everyone in turn. As usual, no-one was interested in finding out what had happened to her. Or maybe they just didn't know yet.

'There you are,' Juliette's voice rose behind her. 'We've been looking for you. Monsieur wants to see you immediately. You've kept him waiting long enough already. Now go.'

There was nothing in her voice to tell Laure what she wanted to hear. No sign of anger towards the maid, but no respect either.

She caught her breath, flattened her skirt with the palm of her hand and walked to the petit salon where Monsieur could usually be found at this time of the day. Slowly she entered the room, wanting to make as little noise as possible. Monsieur Lampron was sitting by the window. He didn't even rise as he saw her. He smiled sardonically at her, and beckoned to her to come closer.

'You little fool,' he said sarcastically. 'You think you're clever? You think you're better than the rest of the staff? Don't forget that you wouldn't even be here if it weren't for my wife.' He stood up and started to pace around a silent Laure.

A sob rose in the maid's throat. What had she done to make him so mad? He stopped right in front of her and laughed.

'You are still a simple maid. Don't forget that,' he said calmly. 'Don't you dare think everything will change for you just because you were invited to join my wife and our guests in my bedchamber. That does not, in any way, change your situation here.'

He sat back again and Laure heard him sigh. 'You will have to learn to be more obedient,' he said, almost to himself.

'You have no right to treat me like this,' Laure exploded. 'You said I was good. You said your wife had chosen well. You said I could stay. You have to keep your promise now.'

Monsieur turned livid and looked at her once again, his lips trembling in anger. 'I have promised nothing,' he snarled. 'You are not the only person here who has been allowed to play with us. And just like those others, it does not entitle you to any privileges.'

Laure held his gaze. 'Who else?' she asked. 'Who else have you used and discarded like you have used and discarded me?'

'Who we mingle with does not concern you,' he replied in the same voice. 'And we do not use anybody. We offer pleasure and we ask for the same in return. You agreed to that on the night. It is now up to you to decide what is to become of you. If you wish to be invited again, you will have to wait your turn. But if you don't follow our rules, you will be let go.'

Laure felt the hair on the back of her neck prickle. The

prospect of having to leave the château horrified her. But there was still hope for her. Just as she had been told that night she had spent in his bedchamber, she had to obey and never stray. And she knew the reward would be great.

She knelt next to his chair and grabbed his hand. 'Please do not send me away,' she said in a little voice. 'I'll be good. I'll do whatever you ask of me. You know how good I can be. Please give me another chance. Please, Monsieur?'

He remained silent and Laure sensed she had to give her all. Taking his hand, she slipped it in the opening of her chemise and guided it up and down to make him stroke her breasts. Her nipples grew hard immediately and she felt him calming down. Of course, he knew what she was capable of. He would have to be very angry to let go of her. That she could be sure of.

'Can I just have another chance?' she repeated.

Monsieur pulled his hand away and stood up. 'Very well,' he said as he opened the door. 'Come to my bedchamber tonight after dark. We will see about this.'

He left and closed the door behind him. Laure remained kneeling on the floor. She looked around, suddenly realising she didn't want to go. She was ready to do anything to make sure he would never be angry with her again.

She didn't know what to expect as she slowly opened the door to her master's bedchamber. After what had happened the other night, she knew she had to be ready for anything.

For a moment, she was tempted to turn around. Would they once again give her a taste of exquisite pleasures, only to ignore her the next morning? Was she to be one of them only under cover of darkness, yet remain a simple servant by day? She pondered the possibilities for a few seconds, then resolved if that was what they had in store for her, it was still better than nothing; better than leaving the château.

Silently, she crossed the deserted room. The door to the adjoining bedchamber was open and pitched a faint glow in the darkness. It was enough for Laure to make out the room, the very room where she had been invited not so long ago, and where she had willingly and joyfully offered her body to delicious torture in return for heady delight.

She shivered with arousal as she passed the big armchair. She paused to look at it. It was a simple item of furniture, innocuous on its own. Yet for Laure the sight of it conjured up powerful, bittersweet memories.

For a while she had been foolish enough to think she was special, the only one to give herself in that manner. There had been others, Monsieur had said. Who? How many? Was it just a game for them to pick a maid from their staff and make her theirs for the night, then send her back to the kitchens without ever inviting her back? Would it be the same tonight?

She kept on walking and stopped at the entrance to her mistress's bedchamber. Monsieur appeared in the doorway, holding up a candle in his large hand, and closed the heavy door behind him. Laure was disappointed to see he was fully dressed. He peered into her eyes.

'I am giving you a second chance, as you asked,' he said in a flat tone. 'If you obey, you will be rewarded.' He slipped his hand into the opening of the maid's chemise and roughly brushed her nipples into stiffness.

Laure gasped with anticipation. She didn't care what he asked of her; she would do it.

'You are wanton,' he said as he pulled out his hand. 'That is good. You will find that my wife, who's waiting in the next room, is also wanton tonight. What I ask of you is to pleasure her as close to her peak as possible, but never allow her to reach it. She doesn't know you are here. She thinks I have invited another player into our game. This should increase her excitement. Do not say or do anything that could make her recognise you.' He paused to catch his breath. As he spoke, his voice had gradually started to tremble, betraying his excitement.

'Do not be mistaken,' he continued, 'this will be more difficult than it seems, for you are also forbidden to seek release until I tell you otherwise. I forbid you to even undress. You may not caress yourself without my consent. And, naturally, this must last as long as possible.' His voice turned cold and sounded like a threat. 'If either you or my wife comes before I allow it, you will be deemed to have failed. But if you perform to my satisfaction, you will be on your way to better things.'

He opened the door and casually showed her in. Laure stepped forward eagerly, but at the last moment his arm blocked her way and held her back.

'One more thing,' Monsieur whispered in her ear. 'This is by no means the only test you will have to undergo. Even if you do well tonight, I shall ask even more of you.' His tone now sounded menacing. He dropped his arm and moved aside to let her in.

Laure didn't move. For a brief moment, she was tempted to turn and walk away. There would be more: more tests, more cruel games. What exactly had he planned for her? And how long would it take before she could really be one of them? Was it worth the wait, the torture?

She ventured a brief look inside her mistress's bedchamber and her uncertainty vanished. Just like the other night, she stiffened with surprise and shivered with arousal at the sight which awaited her.

Madame lay naked on her unmade bed. No pillow under her head, no blanket in sight, not even a sheet under her delicate skin. Just her nude body on a bare mattress. She was blindfolded with a black scarf, and each of her limbs were attached to a pillar of the bed.

The room was illuminated only by candles. Each threw

a different shadow, making the scene surreal: the white, naked body, like an offering on an altar, sacrificed to lust.

Her chest heaved violently; her breasts rose and fell with each shallow breath, her nipples darker than usual and erect. Between her parted legs, the moistness of her sex shimmered in the candlelight betraying her arousal. Obviously she had been told what to expect, and she was more than ready for it.

The sight of her made Laure quiver. Madame had certainly heard her come in, but Monsieur hadn't told his wife who would be joining them. Laure could feel her mistress's excitement in the air as she entered the room.

It enveloped her and only served to arouse her more. Already her flesh throbbed and she felt her dew begin to flow. She knew tonight would be good.

Without a word, she walked to the bed and knelt between her mistress's parted legs. The mattress tilted slightly. She heard the woman let out a faint cry and she had to force herself not to laugh. This was good. Cruel for Madame, but horribly amusing for Laure.

The woman had been kept waiting for a while already. She knew her anonymous torturer had arrived. Laure couldn't stop staring at her victim, oblivious to everything else around her, except maybe for the master who stood by the head of the bed.

He had not spoken since they had entered the room. He had not undressed. Obviously, he didn't intend to take part in the ritual. He was there solely as an invigilator, to see if the pupil would pass the test.

Laure waited for a moment, letting Madame calm down. She wanted to start when her mistress would least expect it. Closing her eyes, she tried to slow the pounding beat of her own heart, to ready herself for the task at hand.

Once she heard Madame's breathing return to a normal pace, she bent down and swiftly ran the tip of her tongue up the woman's slit. She barely touched her, but as she sat back on her knees she tasted the musky dew she had been yearning for. Her moan of delight echoed that of her mistress. Monsieur had been right to warn her: it would be difficult to arouse the woman to the threshold of pleasure and always maintain her self-control.

She softly lay her fingertips just above the edge of the woman's bush. The skin, hot and slightly sweaty, trembled under her touch. The woman was ebullient, like a pot of water ready to overboil. And each of Laure's caresses would inexorably bring her closer to the point of no return.

Cautiously, Laure moved her hand up. Of course, she knew exactly what to do to make her victim burst with pleasure. But she also knew how to enhance her arousal without bringing on the ultimate release: for now, she would just stay away from that gleaming valley wantonly beckoning to her.

Her hand snaked up the woman's belly and stopped right under the edge of the swollen breasts. Tantalisingly, she pulled away and returned only to flick the erect nipples with her fingertips. She paused, then pinched them hard.

Each foray yielded a loud moan, from deep within Madame's throat. Cruelty had its rewards and Laure enjoyed it thoroughly. The power which had been bestowed upon her was intoxicating. She knew exactly what was going on inside her mistress's head. Or rather, she knew how she herself would feel if she were the one to be tortured in this way.

She pulled back completely and paused. The body lying in front of her was writhing in frustration, the hips swaying and grinding against the mattress, the folds of the gaping vulva parting further.

Laure wet her middle finger, inserted it inside the woman's anus and pulled it out again. Madame whimpered and Laure knew no matter where she set her fingers, the response would be keen.

She looked up at Monsieur and saw he had remained unmoved. Of course, for a man like him, what Laure had just done was probably very mild. But there was no denying his wife found the suffering exquisite.

Laure slipped off the bed and surveyed the situation. If she were to keep Madame on the brink of reaching her peak, she had to take things slowly, possibly decrease the intensity of her caresses.

She went to kneel in the middle of the bed, right by Madame's side. Monsieur had said she wasn't allowed to touch herself, but he hadn't forbidden her to use her body to arouse his wife. Sprawling on top of her mistress, she slithered lasciviously, then looked up at Monsieur, half expecting to see a look of disapproval. But his expression was still phlegmatic.

Laure became bolder and writhed over the naked body, endlessly stroking each morsel of the tender skin with her fingers, grinding her clothed pubis over that of the other woman. She made a supreme effort to refrain from setting her lips where her hands had been. She longed to taste all of that skin, to suck on the delicious nipples and toy with them as she knew her mistress liked. But it was too early still.

The body beneath hers bucked against its restraints, the bound hands spasmodically clenching and opening wide, as if trying to grab hold of something. Laure pulled back and knelt next to the shuddering figure.

'Come back,' Madame whined.

Laure smiled to herself: she had achieved the result she wanted. She set her hands on the bare breasts and held them fast. In the middle of her palms the nipples got harder still. Laure dug in her fingertips and pressed down on the globes.

She kneaded them roughly, pinching the nipples hard and rolling them between her thumb and forefinger. The woman's hips jerked violently; her knees buckled. Her thighs pressed against each other, as hard as the restraint on the ankles would allow, then parted again. Pressed and parted. And again. Each time a distinctive, wet noise rose from her soaked vulva, a squishy sound delightfully suggestive of the amount of juice now flowing from her throbbing tunnel. Its smell invaded the air. Laure wanted to taste it again, yet she knew it was risky to even come close to the quivering flesh.

Instead she moved down and took to teasing the quaking thighs. She set down her palms firmly, one on each leg, and forced them to remain still. Yet her fingertips kept fluttering on the inner thigh and the woman moaned even louder.

The maid wickedly massaged her mistress's legs, trailing her fingers up and down in sensuous strokes, coming always closer to her wet sex but never actually touching it. She pulled back and proceeded to trail the smooth flesh with a lone finger.

She barely touched the skin, letting her fingernail trace a path and describe large circles from knee to groin, concentrating mainly on the inside of the thigh. And just when she got within reach of the pink flesh, she moved on to the other leg.

Sometimes she playfully dug her fingertips into the silken mound, bringing them down where the tiny bud protruded, although she never intended to touch it.

Madame settled down quite quickly. Her sighs betrayed her enjoyment, but she knew that Laure was only teasing. It was time to move on to something else.

Without giving any sign of warning, Laure drew one nipple into her mouth and sucked hard. Madame gasped and cried out in surprise. The maid suckled her like a hungry baby, pulling on the elongated nipple then releasing it simply to bathe it profusely with her tongue.

Getting more and more aroused herself, Laure straddled her mistress's naked body and gave her own desires a freer rein. She loved feeling the delicate skin come alive in her mouth, and she wanted more of it. Breathing fast, she covered the whole chest in warm saliva and massaged it with her fingers.

Under her parted legs she felt Madame's hips rising to meet hers. She settled back down, grinding her vulva in a sensuous rolling motion. Sensations blossomed within her. She felt her dew flow as the pressure increased. At that moment, she would have sold her soul to the devil to be allowed to undress. A moan rose in her throat but she managed to hold it back before Monsieur could hear it: she had just realised she was on the verge of disobedience.

Falling back on the bed, she quickly rolled over and stood up. She had to keep her head clear. No matter how much she longed to abandon herself to the sensuous contact of Madame's soft skin, she couldn't yield yet. She had to hold back.

She climbed back onto the bed. This time, she touched her mistress only with her tongue, using her hands to support herself as she surveyed the pale body on offer, her mouth wet with hunger for each morsel of flesh so enticingly displayed.

Like a ravenous beast, Laure nibbled roughly at Madame's nipples, engorged with expectation and puckering even further as the saliva bathing them gradually turned cool. The maid was careful to avoid any other contact with Madame's skin, allowing only her lips and tongue to touch her.

She concentrated on her nipples for a long while, bringing her prey to the peak of excitement before deciding it was time for something more intense. She returned to kneel between her parted legs and stared with satisfaction at her gaping vulva, its dew oozing profusely, the tiny shaft standing proud and swollen.

All she had to do was seize this rounded tip between her lips and suck on it. Then, it would all be over. Yet she felt Monsieur's heavy gaze on her and her thoughts turned to something even more wicked.

She let her mouth trail up and down the inside of

Madame's legs, retracing the path her fingers had followed earlier. Time and again she came close to the fragrant bush, so close she could feel its heat on her lips. But she managed to avoid temptation and obediently pulled back. Then, at last, she allowed herself this reward just once in a final caress.

She set her tongue exactly where Madame's rounded cheeks touched the mattress and pulled it up in one slick move along the swollen folds, as slowly as she could, pressing her lips hard against the labia. Madame moaned loudly and her pink flesh contracted under Laure's mouth. She pulled back all at once, leaving her mistress unsatisfied.

Laure stood again and looked at her master. He still hadn't moved. It was impossible to read approval or anger on his face. Despite her best efforts, he wasn't impressed by Laure's performance and she knew she had to think of something better.

Then, her eyes paused on a string of pearls idly left on the bedside table. A long string coiled in a heap, each tiny rounded bead reflected the light of the candle in a pink hue. The sight of them lying there triggered something deep inside Laure's imagination and she went over to get them.

As she took the necklace, she was struck by its coolness. She held it up hooked on her bent finger, not wanting to let the heat of her hand warm the beads. They had to remain cool for what she wanted to do.

Holding the necklace up above Madame's heaving chest, she lowered it gradually. Madame let out a small cry of surprise and Laure noticed her mistress's white skin break into goosebumps all over her chest and abdomen. She let the pearls do the work for her, directing them all over the reclining body from neck to knees: tickling the armpits, trickling around the breasts, up and down the abdomen, and all over the parted thighs.

Madame shivered profusely and whined endlessly. Kneeling next to her on the bed, Laure felt happy. This was interesting and new, and she was amused by her own resourcefulness. Then, another idea occurred to her.

She returned to kneel between her mistress's legs, rapidly coiled the long string of pearls around her middle finger and swiftly plunged it inside Madame's throbbing entrance. The string was too long for the length of her finger, but it didn't matter. The rest bunched in the palm of her hand and she used it to press and rub against Madame's stiff bud: cold pearls on a hot one, hard white beads on a pink, fleshy one.

Soon Laure could feel the pearls getting hot and wet with the juices exuding from her mistress's folds. She pulled her finger out a little bit at a time, then pushed in the rest of the pearls to fill the tunnel completely. Grabbing the last few beads that still protruded, she slowly twisted the necklace, sending the pearls twirling inside the other woman's vagina.

Madame parted her legs wider and gasped each time Laure gave the string of pearls another twist. Her body now writhed in unison with the movement of the beads inside her, her hips swaying sensually.

Laure could easily imagine the sensation of the knobbly bundle inside her as well, and she was proud to have thought of it. She looked up at her mistress and was pleased to see an expression of pure joy on her face, her teeth biting her bottom lip repeatedly as each cry of pleasure came out louder than the previous one.

Bending down, Laure grasped a couple of pearls and slowly drew out the whole necklace. Each pearl shone with the dew of her mistress as it came out the warm tunnel, coated with the nectar she longed to taste. Once the whole string was out and coiled in the palm of her hand, Laure brought it to her face and ran it across her cheeks and her mouth, marvelling at the sensation of the hot, fragrant pearls. She licked every last one clean before she let the necklace fall to the floor. It was time to move on.

Monsieur was now smiling. Laure was encouraged by this and quickly looked around the dark room to see what else she could use. Naturally, the sight of the candles brought back memories. She took one out of its holder and brought it closer to the bed.

Her first thought was to use the candle as her mistress had done a few days earlier. But as she moved around and felt the melting wax drop onto her hand, she had another, better idea.

Holding the candle high above the bed, she tilted it slightly to make the wax drip one exquisitely hot drop at a time, on her mistress's breasts. She held the candle steady, making it drip at a slow, maddeningly erratic pace. Each drop was received with a whimper of sheer delight, a cry that echoed in the room and unmistakably betrayed the woman's pleasure.

Gradually, the wax covered the woman's chest, one drop after another, until Laure could barely see her pale nipples through the greyish layer. As the drops continued falling, Madame's moans quietened. It was once again time to move on.

Laure placed the candle back in its holder, then grabbed a few cushions to position under the woman's hips and prop them up. The swollen flesh, now purplish after such powerful arousal, appeared clearer in the candlelight; the folds glistened with dew, the rounded bud palpitated for everyone to see.

Stealing a quick glance at her master, Laure was heartened to see that he was still smiling. As she readied herself for another attack, she noticed a bulge in his breeches. Finally, she knew she had done something he approved of.

She took the candle and brought it to the other end of the bed. Once again she felt drunk with the exhilarating power of domination, of being the master of the game. Every few seconds she would look at Monsieur. Now she knew what pleased him: he took pleasure out of pain.

70

He was the master; she had to obey. But the passive figure on the bed was hers to take and to toy with. As long as she played by the Lamprons' rules, she could do exactly as she pleased. And right now, she wanted to tease the woman who lay before her, to torture the engorged folds quivering just inches from her.

She let one fat drop fall. It missed its target, landing a bit to the right of the clitoris which retracted for a moment as the whole vulva contracted forcefully. With her finger, she wiped up the melted wax before it turned hard. This way, she could make the treatment last longer.

The wax lifted off readily, unable to stick to the soaked flesh. A long series of drops followed, each removed a few seconds later by Laure.

Her heart was beating fast. She was keenly aware of the pain she was inflicting on Madame, yet she knew the pleasure the woman was deriving from it. Like revenge, it felt sweet to the maid. Madame would suffer for her lack of consideration towards the girl she had enticed into sensuous games, only to leave her out after only a brief taste of the delights Laure had been led to expect.

At the same time, Laure could show her master and mistress how keen she was to join their circle, how much they would miss by excluding her. But, most of all, she was elated by the power she held: it was a thin line between pain and pleasure and she was the one who held the key to both.

As each drop fell, Laure felt her blood racing in her veins, irrigating that sensitive area at the junction of her legs. Excitement had built up through the evening, and the hungry beast inside her constantly craved more stimulation.

One drop finally hit its target, and the woman buckled violently despite the restraints. 'More,' she moaned. 'Please do not stop now.'

Laure stood back and looked at Monsieur Lampron quizzically. He shook his head and she understood she couldn't give her mistress the release she wanted. He came forward, took the candle from her hands and placed it back in its holder before returning to stand at the head of the bed.

Suddenly worried, Laure anxiously looked around the room. Failure was close at hand. Unless she thought of something fast, she would have to go back to fondles and kisses. It would be a regression, a blunder. She had to think of something better.

Her eyes paused on an open chest in the far corner. She hadn't noticed it before, but she could see something familiar in it: a riding crop. As she walked closer, she saw there were in fact several implements in the chest: an entanglement of leather straps, metal pieces, a number of objects she couldn't make out.

A small velvet pouch caught her attention. She opened it and found two metal clamps. Instinctively, she guessed their use. Even if she was wrong, she could still use them. She walked back to the bed and looked at her mistress's breasts. The wax was almost completely hard by now so she swiftly removed it. Underneath, Madame's skin appeared rosy and glowing.

Laure caressed the smooth globes with her fingertips, tweaking the nipples until they stood out again. She smiled to herself: Madame had no idea of what would come next. For now the woman remained passive, enjoying the softness of the maid's touch.

Without any warning, Laure swiftly opened the clamps and press them shut around her mistress's erect peaks. Madame woman gasped with surprise and a bolt of excitement pierced Laure's stomach. The woman's cry might have been in pain, but the moan which followed was one of pure delight.

Monsieur finally spoke. 'I see you are beginning to understand there is more to arousal than the mere contact of skin, kisses and embraces.'

Laure nodded with a smile. So, this was indeed what they expected of her. She went back to the chest to get the riding crop, the one Monsieur Desgets had used on her not very long ago. She remembered that evening so well: how he had carefully placed the blows on her tender behind and used it to make her achieve her climax, and the pleasure she had taken out of the pain. Tonight Laure was the one in charge. And she would be just as skilful.

She let the tip of the crop trace the contour of Madame's breasts, lifting each globe and letting it fall back again. At first, she used a smooth and gentle motion, but gradually increased the intensity. After a while, she was almost hitting them, amused at the way they quivered as she pushed them up and down and sideways.

Little by little, Madame's breathing grew heavier. And so did Monsieur's. No longer standing still, he shifted his weight from one foot to the other, trying his best to retain his composure. But obviously he was no longer insensitive to what Laure was doing to his wife.

That notion excited her even more. At last, things were happening to everyone's satisfaction. If this pleased him, Laure wasn't about to stop now. She let go of the riding crop and went to the corners of the bed to untie Madame's ankles. The wrists would remain bound for what she had in mind. Not once did she look up in search of approbation from her master. Now she knew what she was doing.

Grabbing the woman's hips, she lifted her off the bed and made her turn around. Her limp body didn't put up any resistance. Once Madame was on her tummy, Laure resumed her ministrations, this time directing the blows on the other woman's rounded, white bottom.

At first Madame didn't react. After a few blows, however, her perky bottom rose above the mattress, her knees bent and the thighs parted to offer the riding crop another, more tender, target.

But Laure refused the invitation. She knew what would happen if she were to set her instrument directly on the awaiting vulva, and then she would fail the test. So she continued to hit the rounded cheeks gently, almost nonchalantly. She took great care in keeping an erratic rhythm and varying the force of her blows. Each stroke had a powerful effect on Madame, whose voice rose above the smacking sounds.

'Now,' she whimpered. 'I surrender. I can't take anymore of this.'

Monsieur stirred and stepped forward.

'That's enough,' he said decisively. 'I think this has lasted long enough.'

Laure held her breath for a moment. Although she was disappointed the game was coming to an end, she was also relieved, for she knew she had passed the test.

Monsieur came to join her and together they untied the fragile body. Madame lifted her blindfold and let out a cry of joy.

'Laure, it was you. What a delightful surprise.' She opened her arms and welcomed the girl with a passionate kiss. 'My darling,' she said softly. 'You have made me so hungry for pleasure. Will you put an end to my suffering now?'

Her elegant hand covered her slit and she lovingly caressed it as she pressed herself against Laure. Then she raised her soaked fingers to the girl's mouth and bid her to lick them clean.

Laure closed her eyes and greedily sucked each finger in turn. The sweet dew she tasted only made her hungry for more and she groaned with desire. Slipping her own hand between her mistress's legs, she rubbed back and forth until her fingers were completely wet.

'Go, my sweet,' Madame said softly. 'Drink from me and make me come with your mouth, I beg of you.' The woman sat on the edge of the bed and placed both her feet flat on the floor. Laure knelt down and set her mouth on the offered flesh. Her mistress's thighs pressed on either side of her head and the woman moaned gleefully. Laure's tongue flicked across her moist, slick folds and as Madame became more excited she probed more eagerly.

Never had she felt such ardour and her voracity surprised her. Even more surprising, however, was Monsieur Lampron's next move: he knelt behind her and lifted her bottom up in the air.

So, he would give her release whilst she pleasured his wife. That way, everybody would be satisfied. Extending her arm between her legs, she helped him draw up her skirt. Her flesh was just as wet as her mistress's and she longed to feel him inside her.

He glided in easily but she gasped as he filled her. She had wanted this for so long. She set one thumb on her mistress's clitoris and the other on her own to rub them simultaneously. But Monsieur's hand grabbed her wrist as she began to caress herself.

'It is not time for you,' he said. 'You must wait.'

He thrust behind her and soon his grunts joined Madame's moans as the couple reached their climax. Meanwhile, Laure was still not satisfied. And she was still fully dressed.

As Madame's last sigh subsided, Monsieur helped the maid to her feet. 'Go and wait in the next room,' he ordered. 'And do not touch yourself. I will be joining you in a moment.'

Laure left obediently, but not without glancing one last time at the woman on the bed. Madame's eyes were closed and she looked as though she was sleeping. Yet the unmistakable smile on her face betrayed the pleasure which still lingered with her.

Impatiently, Laure waited by her master's large bed. In a moment he would be with her. What else would he ask of her before granting her final reward? She quivered at the thought. Anything was possible. But at least she knew he was pleased with her. She had, indeed, been good.

He entered the room and closed the door behind him. Laure's heart pounded with anticipation and she bit her lip nervously. He walked towards the far end of the room and gestured for her to join him. Sitting in the large armchair, he made her stand in front of him.

'Lift your skirt up,' he commanded. 'I want to see whether you are still wanton.'

Laure obeyed joyfully. Of course, she was hot, and now hotter still.

'Close your eyes,' he said. 'And don't you dare look at me until I tell you to.'

Stifling a nervous giggle, Laure shut her eyes tight. She was as giddy as a young girl, still unable to guess what he was going to do. She felt his hands survey the contour of her hips and her behind. His thick fingers slipped inside her for a moment then pulled out again.

There were noises. Monsieur took something from a large chest by the armchair. It was obviously something metallic and heavy by the sound of it. Laure cursed herself for not having paid more attention to what was in the chest. Now she couldn't look at it. But she would know soon enough.

A cold piece of metal glided up between her thighs and she shivered. What on earth could it be? It felt like some kind of metal strap reaching all the way up to her navel in the front and completely covering her behind.

Her legs trembled and she braced herself for a penetration. Whatever Monsieur held, it could only be an instrument of sweet torture which he would skilfully use to bring her the release she had been yearning for all evening. The notion made her breathless with excitement.

In front of her, Monsieur was breathing so hard Laure could feel his breath brush her belly. She couldn't wait. She had to look. But then she remembered his orders and she forced herself to calm down.

When she realised with horror what her master was doing, it was too late: already the metal apparatus had been fastened on each side, and the locks were shut. Disregarding what Monsieur had told her, Laure looked down, terrified: the chastity belt was in place.

Monsieur burst into loud laughter and looked at her cynically. 'Now, Laure,' he said as he made her let go of her skirt. 'We shall see how obedient you can be.' He sat back and crossed his legs.

'Starting now, you will do everything that is asked of you. Everything. Be it at work or for pleasure, and no matter who is asking. You will keep the belt on as long as I deem necessary. You must not seek to remove it, nor find a way to masturbate. But if you are asked to give pleasure, naturally you will comply. Just remember this is a test. You must be obedient or else everything you did tonight will be forgotten. And remember I have spies all over the château. They will watch your every move and report to me. You must not talk to anybody, nor ask for the belt to be removed. Now go. I shall send for you when the time comes.'

Laure stood silently for a few minutes, unsure of what she had just heard. The metal was warming from the contact with her skin and now the belt was not as uncomfortable. But it was still there. And she knew it would be hell for her.

The cruellest of all punishments. No pleasure for her tonight, although she had done everything she had been told.

She stepped back, suddenly weary. How long would this last? And who were these people who would be watching her? Obviously, there must be other servants who had shared the master and mistress's bed. She knew about René, of course, but who else?

Most of them, probably. That would explain why no-one had seemed surprised when she talked about being invited to join the master and mistress and their guests. Although everyone at the château might not have been invited to take part in these elaborate games, they all knew what went on in the west wing, behind the closed doors.

Pressing her hand to her crotch, she could feel the metal hard and unyielding against her hand. It was a punishment for a sin she had not yet committed. But, in a curious way, the idea that pleasure was now forbidden made her feel even naughtier. It was new and exciting, and she also realised that from the moment the belt had been fastened, her desire had also quickened.

Monsieur was so wicked: he knew the belt would keep her in a near-constant state of arousal, but it was impossible for the girl to relieve herself. Yet he was underestimating Laure. Given a chance, she would find a way. The challenge only served to fuel her determination and she fought to hide the smile rising to her lips. As soon as she was out of his sight, she would think of something to alleviate her predicament.

But as she turned around and slowly walked towards the door, she noticed the piece of metal between her legs didn't touch her at all. The belt was designed so as to prevent any friction on her swollen folds. There was no way she could touch her flesh, let alone stroke it. She stopped in her steps and almost burst into tears.

She was the one who had underestimated her master, for suddenly she understood pleasure would be denied as long as the belt remained in place.

As she walked back to her quarters, Laure couldn't help feeling betrayed. She hadn't received her reward. But even though she had to live with the belt for a while, at least she knew there was still hope of once again being invited back into her mistress's bed. And for that, she was willing to put up with anything.

Chapter Five

*T*he next morning Laure rose early and didn't waste any time getting to the kitchens. The idea of actually working didn't appeal to her, for somehow she suspected everyone already knew about her predicament and all eyes would be on her, but she was determined to do as her master had instructed.

There would be tests. Monsieur hadn't said exactly what or when, but Laure was both curious and excited. How difficult could it be? Moreover, she was anxious to get this behind her, to earn her reward. She would prove to everyone how good she could be. She would show them.

But from the moment she arrived at the château, nobody paid her any attention. They were quick to ask her to fetch the water, pluck the chickens and peel potatoes until her fingers turned red with blisters. And as if that wasn't enough, she was also required to help others clean the rooms, feed the animals and pick vegetables. Other than that, no-one said anything to her. After a while, Laure came to wonder if indeed anyone knew about the horrible instrument of torture she wore under her skirt.

Towards the middle of the afternoon, she was already

exhausted. Juliette took pity on her and sent her out to fetch Martin, the gamekeeper, who was supposed to be somewhere in the fields.

Laure was relieved to get away for a while; a walk in the fields would restore her. But on the other hand, she dreaded the prospect of seeing Martin. She loathed the man and usually avoided any contact with him.

The gamekeeper was about the same age as Laure's father was, yet still unmarried. He was quite good looking, but Laure had always felt there was something repellent about him. Perhaps it was the way his beady, shifty eyes always flicked away from the person he addressed. When it came to women, Martin was especially keen on eyeing them from head to toe, pausing on certain very specific places of their bodies, but never looking them straight in the eyes.

This was especially true about Laure. She had obviously caught his interest a long time ago, back when her father was still around to protect her.

There was no love lost between those two. Laure's father always distrusted and disliked Martin and his ways: how he thought the world of himself and never wore anything but crisp white shirts which he made young maids clean in exchange for certain favours.

As for Laure, she despised everything about him, especially the slim moustache that stuck to his upper lip like a limp caterpillar. She knew he wanted her but she would rather die than let him touch her. Recently Martin had become even more cheeky with her, in a lecherous, repulsive way.

She found him on horseback at the far end of the fields, almost on the edge of the forest. The men he was with stopped talking and went back to their work as they noticed her approaching. Laure felt uneasy and blushed before briefly relaying the message she had been entrusted to deliver. A second later, she turned around and headed back.

There was no way she would stay any longer than

necessary. Maybe the servants in the kitchen didn't know about those tests Monsieur had announced, but where Martin was concerned, she didn't want to take any chances.

As she made her way back towards the château, she soon heard hoof beats behind her. Then the shadow of a horse and cavalier blended with hers. Without even looking, she knew it was Martin. Bowing her head, she silently prayed he would keep his pace and pass her without a word. But that was hoping in vain.

As the horse caught up with her, Martin pulled it up to a walk and Laure had no choice but to suffer his company. Her shoulders were level with his feet and he came up so close she could even smell the leather of his boots.

Without a word, Martin suddenly brought down his crop and playfully hit her behind a couple of times. The metal resounded with a dull noise through Laure's clothes and shook her bottom. She stiffened but didn't speak.

'I see you are being tested,' Martin said sarcastically. 'I wonder what the master sees in you that would make you worth the trouble.' Using the tip of his riding crop, he pulled at the top of Laure's chemise until the laces gave under the pressure. Laure's first impulse was to move away but Monsieur had mentioned his spies would report any attempt to resist. Obviously, Martin was in on the secret and she had no choice but to obey.

With a cruel laugh, he plunged the crop in the girl's cleavage. 'Then again,' he continued with a chuckle, 'I can think of a couple of reasons.'

Laure kept walking, her head bowed. How she hated him. She hated the way he laughed, the way he used his crop to toy with her breasts. If it hadn't been for Monsieur's warning, she would have run away by now, making her way across the field where she knew the horse couldn't follow lest it trampled the crops.

Martin took his foot out of the stirrup and with the tip

81

of his boot made her chemise slide from her shoulder as she walked, exposing her right breast which joggled slightly as she kept on walking. Martin laughed again.

He pulled the crop out, bent towards her and held out the shaft in front of her to bar her way. At the same time, he pulled on the reins to stop the horse.

Laure stood motionless, wondering what idea was now germinating in his twisted mind. She hated what he was doing to her, but her heart pounded and in a curious way she was excited. The sun beat down on her chest and warmed her skin just the way she liked.

Using only the tip of the crop, Martin lightly brushed her exposed nipple to make it stiffen. Laure whimpered both in shame and as a result of this rough caress. Monsieur had warned her about this and she knew there was nothing she could do. As her heartbeat grew faster, she realised obedience was nothing more than a cruel game, and the reward would come only much later, if ever.

Martin watched her from above. The crop was like an extension of his hand, gliding on her chest and skilfully arousing her. He managed to expose her breasts completely and soon both her nipples stood proud and erect.

She felt the warming rays of the sun penetrate her bare skin and she moaned. It felt so good. Dizzy with arousal, she suddenly wished Martin would get off his horse and come to her rescue.

He wanted her. This, she knew. And the only way he could take her was by removing the belt. No doubt a man like him would find a way to break the locks. And so what if she let him have his way with her? It was still better than remaining a prisoner. She would put her feelings aside for a while and gladly give herself to him if in return he could satisfy her.

But just as she resolved to undress and beg him to help her, Martin straightened up and whipped the horse violently. Man and beast took off, leaving only a cloud of dust in their place.

* * *

Laure didn't know if she could find the strength to live through the second day. She had expected everyone to ignore her, like the previous day, but instead, everywhere she went someone sought to tease and humiliate her.

First it was Madeleine, the young kitchen maid in whom she had confided. When Laure came looking for sympathy, the gentle and innocent girl suddenly turned on her.

'I thought you said you'd be with them soon,' Madeleine said in a cold tone. 'Look at you now. You're lower than all of us. And everyone thinks you're nothing but a big mouth. Nobody trusts you, and nobody likes you. They would make you crawl in the mud just to make you pay for all the haughty airs you've put on. That's what you get when you think you're better than the others. I think you deserve to be treated like this.'

Wherever Laure went, conversations stopped the moment her presence was noticed. And right after she left, she could hear them whisper and laugh behind her back. She was glad when Juliette sent her to feed the chickens. At least she knew she'd have a moment's peace.

The birds gathered at her feet in a flurry of feathers, clucking furiously as they tried to get to the grain she tossed around. They were so funny to watch, especially the smaller ones. The more impatient hens tried to fly into her basket, but Laure raised it high above ground. She'd make them wait a while. They had no reason to be so greedy.

She was enjoying herself and felt much better. Her situation might seem desperate at times, but all she had to do was wait. Soon it would all be over. But even as her spirits improved, a voice behind her brought her sharply back to reality.

'You, come here.'

She turned around and recognised Matthieu, a groom who was about her age. They used to play together as children, but then he had gone away for a while and since his return they had not spoken at all.

Standing by the entrance to the hen house, he nonchalantly leant against the frame of the door. As she walked towards him, she noticed the cocky smile on his face and her fear subsided. Matthieu was no match for her. In a way, he was still a little boy. What harm could he do to her?

She was confident she could handle him – and whatever he asked of her – until she saw two other young men coming out of the hen house to join him.

'Come on,' Matthieu said as she approached. 'Let's see it.' One of the boys walked up to her, sniggering, and unceremoniously lifted her skirt. The others started laughing as her chastity belt was exposed. Laure felt her blood boil and remained still, cursing them between clenched teeth. Bastards.

All three of them were perhaps a bit younger than her, too young and foolish to do such a thing on their own. Obviously, they knew about her predicament. Yet somehow Laure doubted Monsieur had put them up to this. It was too crude a joke for such a refined man. Rather, she suspected the boys had heard some gossip and decided to torment her as a prank. They knew she couldn't run away from them; she had to do whatever they asked of her. That was the only way to explain how they had the nerve to do this.

She could already hear them tell the tale. This would be something to brag about for years to come, but she knew they would carefully omit to add that their cowardice would have stopped them if they hadn't already known she would have no choice but to submit to their taunts.

The boy kneeling at her feet started to tickle her thighs. 'Wooooooo,' the others yelled. 'Come on, higher, higher.'

Laure flushed with rage. How dare they? They had absolutely no consideration for her feelings. At least she felt confident that the three young men were totally inexperienced when it came to women and that they wouldn't get past the belt. For once she was glad of its presence.

Matthieu came towards her. His erection was plainly visible in his breeches. He saw Laure had noticed it and blushed a deep crimson. Yet that didn't stop him from coming towards her and kneeling next to his friend.

The boys fondled her legs hesitantly, as if they weren't quite bold enough to take her like a real man would. Their giddy laughter betrayed their youthful ignorance. They had to egg each other on to go one step further, up her thigh, then on the inside, then . . .

'Get away from her,' Juliette's voice shouted above their laughter.

They stood up sheepishly and looked at each other, then at Juliette, before taking off as fast as their young legs could carry them.

Juliette walked towards Laure and handed her a large bucket. 'We need more water,' the woman said simply. 'Bring it to me in the kitchen.'

Laure obeyed without replying, surprised to realise she might have an ally after all.

There were times during that week when Laure was tempted to go back to her master and beg him to put an end to all this. She had been lucky when Juliette bailed her out, but the housekeeper wasn't always around. And the situation became more complicated on the third day.

Laundry days were always a big affair at the Château de Reyval. There was water to boil, clothes to sort out, wash, set to dry, fold and put away. At least, Laure could keep her mind off things whilst she remained busy.

As she walked up the stairs to bring the bedsheets back to the main closet, she was suddenly aware of a presence behind her. Before she had time to turn around, a blindfold was fastened around her head and she was led into the first room on the right.

Fear seized her, but almost immediately she understood what this was all about: another test. There were two men already in the room, maybe three. She could smell them and hear them breathe, but she couldn't tell who they were. As soon as the door closed behind them, hands began to undress her.

This time Laure knew these men weren't as innocent as Matthieu and his two companions. Her heart pounded with excitement and curiosity. What were they going to do to her? What would they ask for? Better still, was there any chance they could hack the belt off if it was in their way?

Once she stood naked, someone tied her hands behind her back and made her kneel, legs apart, on the bare wooden floor. Her entire body was besieged by hands, mouths and tongues. Their wet caresses snaked all across her belly, her chest, even under her arms. Lips nibbled at her neck and sucked her earlobes whilst fingertips flickered over her nipples.

Her senses keenly acute, Laure tried to fight the bolts of pleasure now rising within her. They were skilful, whoever they were. Rough hands fondled her breasts, then a hot, wet pair of lips drew on her nipples until they became almost sore. Other hands caressed her back, her thighs and her arms.

Laure grew weak with excitement. The men took great pains to arouse her, yet she already knew this wouldn't lead to anything, at least not for her. It was another cruel test, one she wasn't sure she would pass. Her whole body shook and she struggled to muffle the moans rising in her throat.

Breathing deeply, she tried to concentrate on her surroundings, to detach her mind from her body. In doing so, she became more eager to figure out who her mysterious lovers were. She listened hard, and could hear whispers exchanged between them and another man standing at the far end of the room. Although she couldn't make out what they were saying, it was easy to guess the man was instructing the others.

Several smells floated in the air: sweat and dust revealed the men had probably spent the day in the fields. But above it all, she noticed another, aromatic, more familiar smell: her master's cologne.

He was there. This, she knew. Suddenly, she didn't care who these other men were anymore. All that mattered was that her master would see with his own eyes how obedient she could be.

Instinctively, she straightened up and forced her breathing to sound regular. He had warned her not to seek pleasure, and she couldn't betray the way she felt, not now.

Yet these men knew exactly what to do to increase her arousal. The mouth set on her nipples sucked avidly, and the hands stroking her inner thighs had found the very spot where she was most sensitive.

Behind her, an erect phallus fell into her bound hands whilst another slipped into her mouth: they wanted her to relieve them. Her fingers closed around the thick shaft and she swung her wrists in tempo with the man's thrusting hips.

Her tongue snaked skilfully around the plum now throbbing in her mouth and her lips stretched around his shaft. The third man was still busy sucking her nipples, but Laure was sure she would be required to take care of him sooner or later. He kept kissing her chest incessantly, and she could hear the wet noises of his tongue as it bathed her skin. The sound was only surpassed by the moans of pleasure from the two other men.

They used her mouth and her hands to relieve themselves, and Laure knew their pleasure depended solely on her. Once again she held the position of power, even in submission. Naturally, she would gladly give them what they wanted.

She increased the pressure on the stiff phallus in her mouth. Its tiny opening seeped and the shaft pulsed in response. The prospect of receiving him excited her but she tried not to let it show. Instead, she concentrated on pleasuring her other lover, the man she held behind her back.

She toyed with him as best she could, cradling his balls in one hand whilst rubbing his shaft hard and fast with the other. He was the first to release his seed, which spurted onto Laure's buttocks and thighs.

The member in her mouth pulsed violently just moments later and she received his semen deep in her throat. Their strangled cries rose in the room and Laure felt proud of her performance. She expected more but almost immediately, the men pulled away. For a moment she didn't know what to think. Would Monsieur come to her and finally set her free? Or was it too soon?

She wanted more: more caresses on her glowing body, more male flesh to toy with. Instead, she heard the men leave and she realised the test was over. That left her alone with Monsieur.

Laure remained kneeling on the floor. She couldn't let on she knew the master was in the room. A moment later, the squeaky floorboards told her he was creeping out. She kept quiet and pretended not to hear him. The door closed behind him only to open again almost right away.

Someone untied her hands and Laure immediately raised them to her face to get rid of the blindfold. She found Juliette standing next to her, holding her clothes. Without a word, the housekeeper handed over the clothes and left the room as if nothing had happened.

All alone, Laure didn't know whether she should laugh or cry. Monsieur had witnessed her obedience and she knew she had done well. Yet the belt remained. How much longer would she have to suffer?

Juliette was Laure's only ally, or so it seemed. She sent her on errands and made her work more than her share, but not once did she make reference to the belt.

For a while, Laure was even tempted to confide in the housekeeper, but on the fourth day she realised Juliette was merely obeying orders herself and couldn't do anything to help her. Moreover, it was she who set Laure up for the cruellest test of all.

They were alone in the larder that morning. Juliette seemed nervous and light-headed, but Laure didn't pay much attention to her until the woman ordered her to go to the far end of the south wing and wait in the small salon.

Laure hesitated before opening the door, unsure of why she had been requested to go there. But Juliette then caught up with her and told her to go in.

The door opened onto a spectacle such as Laure had never seen before. On a large table, which had been cleared for the occasion, Martin and Manon, another maid, were naked and fondling each other.

Laure's first impulse was to turn back. But Juliette pushed her forward into the room and led her to within a few feet of the couple. Martin and Manon laughed as they saw Laure come in, but nonetheless continued with what they were doing. In fact, it was as if they were expecting her. Laure understood she was meant to watch their coupling and remain idle. And this performance would not be over in a matter of minutes.

Juliette pulled up a chair and made Laure sit with her legs apart and her hands on her head. On the table, the couple seemed invigorated by the arrival of their audience. They hugged and kissed each other greedily for a while, and then their embraces became more intimate. Martin set his hand on the woman's vulva and rubbed it hard and fast. From where she sat, Laure could see the glistening dew gradually cover his fingers and its smell floated into her nostrils.

For her part, Manon took hold of Martin's engorged shaft and lasciviously squeezed it whilst her thumb slicked around its shiny head. Laure was impressed by the size of it and sorely regretted having refused him in the past. His member was magnificent: long and thick and just as self-assured as its owner.

As their moans grew louder, Martin gradually slid off the table and knelt down next to it. Grabbing Manon's legs, he pulled her towards him and directed his face towards her flesh.

Manon writhed as she slid towards him, parting her knees and grabbing her breasts. Martin's face disappeared between her thighs. Laure could hear the sound of his tongue noisily licking Manon's wet vulva and felt her own flesh twitch in response. Already Manon was moaning loudly, her breasts heaving and her nipples getting stiffer as they pointed towards the ceiling.

Laure could also hear Martin grunt as he relished the woman, his hips swaying violently and his hard phallus proud and erect. She couldn't help but admire the sight of it. Just like the man himself, it looked arrogant and assertive.

Manon's cries of pleasure made Laure hot: the man was skilful and made his partner climax repeatedly. Laure groaned with each breath, and the sounds they all made echoed in the large room lined with glass cabinets along the far wall.

Laure was both aroused and uncomfortable. Under her chemise, she felt her own breasts engorged with arousal, as if she had been the one lying on the table. Once again she felt a prisoner of her own clothes. Things wouldn't be nearly as bad if only she could get rid of her bodice and chemise, not to mention the loathesome chastity belt.

But the fire burning under her skin only grew hotter as the couple's screams reverberated around the room. Laure wanted this to stop. She had no choice but to listen, but certainly she didn't have to watch. She closed her eyes for only a few seconds before Juliette reached over and pinched her arm.

'You will watch,' the woman ordered in a cold voice. 'You cannot escape this.'

Laure immediately understood that, on this occasion, Juliette would not take pity on her. She kept watching, both mesmerised and miserable. At times she turned to Juliette in a silent plea. She didn't want to stay. As much as she might have enjoyed such a spectacle under other circumstances, today it was just too much to bear. But each time the cold and angry look of the housekeeper reminded her to remain still and watch.

Manon was panting heavily, barely recovered from her last climax, when Martin made her stand up right in front of Laure. The girl got to her feet shakily, still reeling from the after effects of such violent pleasure.

Supporting her from behind, he lifted her breasts in his cupped hands as if he wanted to offer them to Laure. Manon smiled blissfully, eyes half-shut, proud to be shown off so brazenly. She parted her legs and slipped her trembling hand along her labia to spread them open.

Inches from her face, Laure could see the pink, slick folds of Manon's flesh. She could smell it as well: a heady and enticing aroma. Instinctively, she licked her dry lips.

Both Martin and Manon sniggered, and Laure could only guess what the expression on her face revealed. True to Martin's nature, he was immensely pleased with himself, obviously taking great satisfaction in tormenting poor Laure. Perhaps it was his revenge for having lusted after her in vain for so long.

And it wasn't over yet. Already Manon was moaning as she touched herself. Martin's hand replaced hers and wickedly rubbed the tender flesh, which oozed with her love juices and covered his fingers. Together they stared at Laure, taunting her cruelly.

Unable – and now unwilling – to divert her eyes, Laure could see Manon's vulva contract under the man's hand, the tiny bud once again protruding and claiming its share of attention. The sight of Martin's fingers transfixed her as they moved back and forth along the wet slit.

More than ever, Laure knew that if only she had allowed him, he would have tortured her own flesh as skilfully. Yet despite her regrets and her desire, she hated him even more. She hated them all, everyone at the château who had joined forces to torment her.

She knew she didn't have to take this. Any moment, she could get up and leave, but then she would have failed the test Monsieur had devised for her. As hard as it was, she wouldn't let them get the better of her.

So she kept watching, concentrating on Manon's trembling knees as Martin continued rubbing the wanton slit. Manon tilted her head back against his bare chest and her mouth curled up in a delighted grin.

Laure was thirsty for the luscious wet flesh which palpitated and glistened just inches from her mouth. Her own flesh responded similarly: her petticoat was now damp and her vulva ached as her arousal grew more intense.

Manon climaxed once, and then again. Her piercing screams assailed Laure's ears and travelled down her chest and belly to reverberate in the pit of her sex. By now, Manon was like a rag doll in Martin's arms, her body occasionally shaken by faint tremors as her orgasm slowly subsided.

Against her hip, Martin's phallus seemed to be getting bigger and harder. He lifted her off the ground and guided his organ between her legs. Laure gazed at the swollen head as it appeared between Manon's squeezed thighs, rubbing against her flesh and taunting the spectator.

For Laure, anger turned to pure jealousy. She could smell his manly aroma blending with that of the woman, and by now she was hungry for them both. She clenched her fists on her head, shaking so hard with rage her breasts quivered and her nipples ached.

Manon gradually regained her senses and writhed against Martin's chest. He put her back on her feet and she knelt to take him in her mouth. As his thick shaft disappeared completely, they both groaned.

Laure sobbed. Her mouth watered; she could almost taste him. She wanted to join them; she was out of her mind with desire. Tears filled her eyes and she glanced at Juliette. The woman gave her the same, cold hard look.

The couple was just as loud as before, only this time Manon's moans were muffled by the beautiful phallus she held in her mouth. Insatiable, she cradled his balls and poked his anus repeatedly. Laure could see them from the side, not missing any of the thick shaft thrusting into Manon's mouth and the play of her fingers between his legs.

Martin stood tall and stoic, yet he sounded like he was choking, his eyes shut tight and his face contorted as if in pain. But there was no doubt that all he was experiencing was sheer pleasure.

Manon withdrew and let his member, glistening with her saliva, point directly at Laure. With a wicked smile on her face, she looked straight at the poor maid as she began masturbating him. She handled him roughly, running her clenched fist up and down the length of his penis at an amazing speed.

Laure knew she would see him come. In fact, he was so close to her she expected to be anointed by his seed. The thought made her weak with desire and she wriggled on her chair. Her whole body trembled uncontrollably. All this excitement was exhausting and she couldn't hold back anymore. She couldn't help the sigh which escaped from her throat, but only a moment later she felt the pinch of Juliette's fingers on her arm.

'Stay still,' the woman repeated. 'Don't let me catch you again.'

Martin was now huffing and puffing heavily. His knees wobbled and he fell. He pushed Manon on the floor, seized her feet and prised her legs apart. Dragging her towards him, he lifted her ankles onto his shoulders.

He grabbed her hips urgently and, pulling her buttocks onto his lap, entered her without any warning.

Manon slid towards him, lifeless, and let out a faint cry as he impaled her. By now only her shoulders were touching the ground. Martin was on his knees, holding her by the hips to bring her vagina to the level of his penis.

He thrust forcefully and rapidly, his thighs hitting her behind so hard it made her whole body shake. She regained her senses just long enough to look at Laure and smile sarcastically. Her eyes closed and once again she was as lifeless as a rag doll as Martin delved deeply inside her.

Laure fumed with rage, anger and jealousy. It should have been her on the floor, being taken by this man she loathed but who had proven to be a skilled lover. Their noisy coupling excited and taunted her, and she couldn't stop the tears from welling in her eyes.

She witnessed their orgasm and then collapsed, burying her face in her hands. This was too much. Laure realised they were probably just following Monsieur's orders, yet they seemed to take as much pleasure out of torturing her as from what they were doing. Their display was almost hateful in its cruelty, and they thrived on it. It just wasn't fair to persecute her like this.

By now Juliette no longer forced her to watch. But when Laure looked up, the housekeeper couldn't hide her smile of contentment. She, too, had taken pleasure in the girl's misery.

'Now,' she said, 'go back to the kitchen and wait on the stool by the big stove. You are, of course, forbidden to touch yourself. Everyone will be watching you. I'll be coming down shortly.'

Laure took off as fast as she could. The idea of going back to work was actually a relief. She needed to do something, anything, to take her mind off what she had just seen. So she made her way to the kitchen quite willingly, and went to sit on the stool as instructed.

But a few minutes later, she realised her torment would not be over so soon. Juliette came in and ordered her to face the wall. For once Laure wished the housekeeper would assign her some chores. Sitting idly on the stool, she could think of nothing but the scene in the salon. No matter how hard she tried, she couldn't forget the events which had taken place before her eyes. Her throbbing flesh still ached, her body was ablaze with desire, and Martin and Manon's moans of pleasure echoed in her mind. ·

She had hoped Juliette would have mercy on her and find her some work, but after a while she knew that wasn't going to be the case. In fact, she remained where she was until bedtime.

Even slumber offered no escape. All night Laure tossed and turned, her sleep constantly disturbed by images of quivering, inviting flesh displayed in front of her, but which she wasn't allowed to touch.

She rose before sunrise, feeling weak from her restless night but determined to keep her mind clear. In the kitchen, there was so much work to do she didn't even wait for her orders. She brought in three baskets full of vegetables from the garden, and had already cleaned and peeled them by the time the cook arrived. She kept constant watch for something to do, and her zeal seemed to impress and amuse everyone.

Shortly before midday, Juliette announced Monsieur wanted to see her. This time, Laure thought, it could only be good news. She had been obedient, hard working, and she had passed all the tests he had devised for her. Her feet barely touched the floor as she made her way to the day room. At last. After five horrible days, she would be free of the chastity belt.

As she reflected on the days just past, she felt proud of herself. Of course, it had been very hard, but at least she hadn't failed. How many others had been put through the same ordeal and could claim victory? Certainly not many. She was better than most – if not all –

of them. She was indeed worthy of reward. In her mind, she could already picture Monsieur offering her the key to the locks of the belt and putting an end to her misery.

He smiled at her as she entered the room, gesturing for her to approach him. As usual, he sat in the large armchair, similar to the one in his bedchamber. Laure felt elated and went to stand in front of him, giddy and excited at the prospect of finally being free.

Without a word, he undid the laces of her chemise and exposed her generous breasts. Laure smiled lasciviously, happy to offer herself to his caresses. He sucked on each nipple until they grew long and stiff, then pinched them until she moaned.

Laure cried with pleasure and relief. It felt so incredibly good, as if this were the first time a man had ever touched her. She was impatient to see what he would ask of her, but most of all she couldn't wait for him to take her, to feel his hard member inside her hidden tunnel.

He quickly undressed her and made her sit on his lap. Laure writhed in his arms, rubbing her body against his clothed chest, naked save for the belt she knew would soon be coming off. Her skin responded to the friction of his doublet, growing hotter and more sensitive.

At first, he didn't even have to move. Laure squirmed so enthusiastically he just let her use his body to caress herself. Then his mouth relished every inch of her exposed skin, licking and biting her furiously. Laure screamed with delight under the assault.

Soon he would free her flesh and take her with all his might. She couldn't wait to feel his large member impale her and thrust until she surrendered. But, for now, she was quite happy to have him sensually torment her.

Once her skin was covered with his saliva and bite marks, he made her kneel in front of him and stood up. Laure obeyed readily and watched, mesmerised, as he quickly undid the buttons of his breeches.

His member sprang out in front of her and she

pounced on it at once, voraciously taking him in her mouth and sucking avidly. The shaft responded by hardening further inside the furnace of her mouth.

Her hands clasped around it and roughly ran up and down its length. She couldn't wait for him to push her to the floor, take the belt off and have her like an animal.

In the meantime, she used all her skills to arouse him. Her tongue bathed him profusely, whilst her hands continued their exquisite torment. Already Monsieur was moaning in appreciation, his straining member throbbing against her hands. She was convinced that any minute now he would take her. She wanted that moment to be as soon as possible; she wanted to feel him inside her.

Yet today Monsieur seemed empowered with incredible self-restraint. No matter how hard she tried, Laure couldn't seem to make him lose control. For now, he was content just to let her arouse him.

His moans betrayed his excitement, but still he remained standing. She could feel him close to climax; so close she feared he wouldn't have time to enter her. Suddenly, without warning, his buttocks contracted and he emptied himself in her mouth and on her face. He had been unable to hold back.

But when she looked up at him, the smile on his face told her that had been his intention all along.

'That was nice,' he said as he fastened his breeches. 'You may go now.'

Laure was baffled. 'Go?' she whispered timidly. 'But what about me? What about the belt?'

Monsieur laughed scornfully. 'What? Did you really think I was going to let you off? My dear, it is way too early. If this is how eager you are after only a few days, I shudder to think how it will be after a few weeks.'

Laure felt her blood run cold. A few weeks? Had she not suffered enough already? She tried to think of something to say, but rage numbed her mind. Only one word resounded in her head: weeks. She didn't think she could stand even one more day.

But before she could speak, Monsieur had already left the room. As far as he was concerned, the matter was closed. Yet again, Laure was reduced to tears.

Chapter Six

*L*aure eventually decided that her only chance of escaping this horrible chastity belt was to enlist René's help. She remembered Madame saying the stable hand had been her lover. Perhaps he also knew Monsieur better than Laure did. He might not be involved in the tests Monsieur had devised for her, nor was he likely to help her remove the chastity belt, but perhaps he could suggest a way to convince Monsieur that he should free her.

In a way, Laure felt guilty that she had neglected him since she had been invited to join the Lamprons and their guests. After the night she had spent with them, the prospect of being with René just didn't hold the same excitement. Yet she knew he liked her. She had ways to get him to do what she wanted, and she was confident she would find a way to make it up to him.

Under cover of darkness, she silently made her way across the courtyard and down the short path leading to the stables. She had visited him so often in his loft above the stalls that she knew exactly how to get to him without being seen.

As she entered, the smell of hay brought back memories of happier times. This was where she played as a child on rainy days and in winter. More recently, it was the scene of wild and frenzied lovemaking with the man who lay sleeping upstairs. She paused and listened for a moment. All she could hear was the sound of faint snoring which she immediately recognised. Quietly, she closed the door behind her and lit a lamp before going up the ladder. The chastity belt impaired her movements and made it difficult for her to climb it. She couldn't hold the lamp, lift up her skirt and hold on to the sides of the ladder all at once. It was an awkward ascent, but she kept going, step by step, her heart pounding.

Would René be able to help her? Would he want to? If he refused, Laure knew she could find ways to make him change his mind.

When she reached the top of the ladder she raised the lamp to have a look at him. She saw his sleeping figure roll over under the woolly blanket, but it wasn't until he awoke and sat up that Laure saw he wasn't alone.

They silently stared at each other for a few seconds. Now she felt foolish for having come. In the glow of the lamp, she could see lacy petticoats piled on top of a woman's dress right in front of her. Obviously, René didn't have any need of her.

His companion also awoke and sat up in bed. At first Laure didn't recognise her. But there was something familiar about this woman whose flaxen hair was strewn across her face. Her perky breasts were capped with pale-pink nipples which puckered in the cool night air. Her small frame and white skin gave her body the look of a porcelain figurine.

Then, she pushed her hair away from her face and Laure let out a gasp of surprise as she recognised her mistress. Now she felt twice as foolish. Indeed, she should never have come. More than anything, she was angry at herself. Of course, René was an ally of the Lamprons, just like everybody else at the château. How could she have ever hoped he would help her?

She mumbled an apology and looked behind her. She

had to save face. She had to get down and out of there as soon as possible. But as she set her foot on a lower step, Madame called out to her in a soft, sleepy voice.

'Don't go,' she said. 'Please come and see me.'

Laure hesitated, then put the lamp down by the top of the ladder and approached the low bunk where Madame and René both sat, huddled next to one another.

Madame's open arms welcomed her and she burst into tears. The woman laughed softly and stroked the maid's long hair, kissing her forehead and wiping tears away from her face.

'Please do tell me what is wrong,' Madame said.

But Laure couldn't quell her sobs, let alone speak.

The woman held her tight against her warm, naked body. She kissed her gently on the neck, rubbed her back with long strokes and rocked her gently. At first, her movements were slow and loving. But then, as she set her hand on the maid's hip, the hard metal caught her attention and she abruptly released her embrace.

'Laure?' she asked in a worried tone. 'What is this under your dress?'

Still shaken by sobs, Laure couldn't reply and simply lifted her skirt to show her mistress the horrible instrument which had been holding her prisoner for the past few days.

Madame ran her hand along the girl's leg, stopping short of the chastity belt, as if she were afraid to touch it. She pulled back, quickly pulled down Laure's skirt and lifted the maid's face to look at her.

'What are you doing with this on?' she asked, suddenly angry. 'Who made you wear this?'

Laure managed to calm down and explained everything: how Monsieur had tricked her into wearing the belt, how she had been ridiculed, taunted, even humiliated for days on end.

Madame listened without replying. Once Laure had finished talking, she stood up and gathered her clothes in a hurry.

'My husband has gone too far,' she decreed. 'I must set him straight this time. Quick, help me get dressed. We must go and see him.'

Before Laure had time to realise what was happening, she was out of the stables and back at the château, trotting behind her mistress as she stormed to her husband's rooms. René followed behind nonchalantly, immensely amused by the turn of events.

Madame went straight to her husband's bedchamber and, without even knocking, violently flung the door open – it was amazing how strong such a frail-looking woman could become in anger. But then she stopped so abruptly that Laure almost collided with her. Obviously Madame had not expected to find her husband otherwise occupied.

Monsieur was equally surprised to see his wife. As she entered the room, followed by René, Laure bit her lip in embarrassment. The timing wasn't good.

Monsieur stood, in all his glorious nakedness, behind a young wench. She, too, was naked, doubled over and holding onto the pillar of the bed, her large breasts hanging like ripe pears above the mattress. Monsieur's enormous member stood ready and eager; he had obviously been about to enter her.

Red with anger, Madame took a deep breath and stepped forward.

'What is this?' she exploded. 'What are you doing with this girl?'

Although shocked by the party's arrival, Monsieur quickly regained his composure. 'That seems obvious, does it not?'

'Yes, I know,' his wife lashed out. 'But who is this girl? You know I am the one who chooses the girls who are to share your bed. I should have had her first.'

Laure's embarrassment at being a witness to this quarrel gave way to amusement. Obviously, Madame now had another reason to be angry at her husband, one which had nothing to do with Laure. She turned to René, who looked at her and grinned.

Madame looked tiny next to her gigantic husband, but at the moment she was clearly the one in charge. She pushed him away from the bed and gathered the girl's clothes before throwing them at her and ordering her out of the room.

The girl didn't even take the time to get dressed. She held the bundle of clothes against her chest and ran from the room without looking at either of the Lamprons. As she walked past Laure, however, she looked up, her face red with shame.

Only then did Laure recognise her friend Madeleine. She moved aside to let her out, but she was so profoundly angry she felt more like hitting her.

Madeleine – the sweet and gentle girl who didn't even believe what Laure had told her about the Lamprons. All this time, her stunned reaction and bewilderment had been just an act. Or maybe Madeleine genuinely didn't know anything. For judging from Madame's reaction, Madeleine was probably Monsieur's latest conquest.

This notion only made Laure angrier. How could Monsieur put her through the ordeal of the chastity belt and prefer to take a girl like Madeleine instead? How dare he give Madeleine the attention she herself so yearned for and knew she deserved? It wasn't fair. Luckily, Madame would soon set him straight.

The woman ordered René to come in and close the door. By now her husband had lost his erection and Laure looked with amusement at the once-proud phallus which now hung limply.

Madame paced around the room, screaming at her husband. 'We agreed never to have secrets from one another. We also agreed that I would pick all the girls whom we would invite to join us. Yet you did not ask me about Madeleine. You never consulted me. That was a mistake.'

Approaching Laure, she grabbed the maid's skirt and lifted it. 'And you didn't ask me about this,' she yelled as she pointed to the chastity belt. 'You have no right to test anybody without my expressed consent. You know that very well.'

She walked up to him and lifted her face towards his bowed head. The big bear seemed cowed by the feistiness his little mouse of a wife displayed. All of a sudden, Laure suspected Madame was in fact the real master of the game.

'You will be punished for all this,' the woman said crisply. 'You are quick to punish those who stray, so now let us see if you appreciate a taste of your own medicine.'

Standing back, she looked at his pathetic face and pondered the situation for a moment. Then she paced around him slowly, her eyes lighting up as she became more and more excited: she had a plan.

She came back to Laure and took her in her arms whilst staring at her husband. 'You will pay in kind,' she announced. 'It is time for Laure to be rewarded, and for you to be punished, and I think we can do both at the same time.'

She looked at René, gestured for him to join his master, then turned to her husband again. 'You will watch,' she said to Monsieur. 'And just as you instructed Laure when you devised this horrible test, you will be forbidden to touch yourself until I tell you otherwise.'

Still holding Laure in her arms, she turned to her and closed her eyes. Tightening her embrace, she rested her cheek on Laure's. 'Now, my darling,' she whispered softly. 'I believe it is time to put an end to your ordeal.'

She walked over to Monsieur's bedside table to retrieve keys from the drawer, then came back to Laure and undressed her. Once the maid stood naked, Madame knelt in front of her and for a minute she just looked at the belt which glinted in the candlelight.

She ran her hands lightly over Laure's smooth thighs

and the part of her buttocks not covered by the back panel of the belt. For a moment, Laure worried that Madame might in fact find this sight quite captivating and decide not to free her just yet. She held her breath as her mistress's fingers tried to glide under the metal panels. Then, without further hesitation, Madame undid the locks and the belt clattered to the floor.

At first, Laure didn't feel anything. Then cool air brushed her moist skin and her knees parted involuntarily. She looked at the belt, now lying harmlessly at her feet, and knew she was finally free.

She wanted to cry, laugh and yell all at once. She felt vindicated. Madame's hands then stroked the skin that had been shielded for so long, her touch now almost foreign to Laure. Her fingers gently dug into the warm buttocks and her mouth came to kiss the hot flesh.

Monsieur watched the scene blankly. He didn't appear to care much for what his wife had just done, but Laure knew no matter how he felt, his pride would never allow him to let it show. Anyway, soon he would suffer as much as she had. Her mistress would find a way to make her husband respond.

Madame stood and quickly shed her clothes as she crossed the room. Laure shivered when she saw her stop by the large chest. That's where the belt came from. What else was in there? More torture for her?

Without hesitation, Madame took out a large whip and paused to contemplate it. A wicked smile slowly played across her face. Despite her delicate features and her angelic looks, her mind was conditioned to think of how to get the most out of mingling pain and pleasure in a variety of different ways.

She coiled the long and supple lash around her body, twisted it like a snake around her naked waist and slid it upwards to caress the underswell of her breasts. The handle drooped limply over her forearm and she let it swing as she walked to her husband. Nonchalantly, she used it to smack his bottom a couple of times.

Monsieur didn't move. His face remained impassive and he stared straight ahead. Madame seized his flaccid prick and fondled it until it regained its erection.

Laure's feeling of relief quickly gave way to sheer excitement and her heart beat faster at the prospect of witnessing a whipping session. Yet she was also uneasy. It seemed the couple had completely forgotten they had spectators and Laure didn't dare move for fear of disturbing them. Then, she felt René's hands reach for her from behind.

There was no reason for her to worry about anything. She was meant to be there. Knowing how keen Madame was to turn the tables on her errant husband, the maid knew this would be a once-in-a-lifetime demonstration. Already dew was collecting between her legs both as a result of the scene in front of her and René's expert caresses on her swollen breasts.

Somehow she doubted it could ever be more intense than this. But when Madame walked up to her and handed her the whip, Laure knew she had been mistaken.

'You know the rules,' Madame said. 'You will punish him. Do whatever you like, but remember he is not allowed to climax.'

Laure turned around to look at René who smiled and encouraged her with a silent nod. Then she looked at the Lamprons. Monsieur still stared in front of him, docile and resigned. Vengeance would be sweet.

Madame climbed onto the large bed and reclined against the pillows to watch the scene. Hesitantly, Laure walked up to her master, letting the whip trail behind her. Where to begin? As she approached, she sensed he was stoic but probably wouldn't remain insensitive for very long. Already, she detected a faint quiver in his legs. Perhaps anticipation was the best aphrodisiac.

Her instincts took over. She didn't know what she was going to do, but first she wanted to make him harder than he had ever been. Seizing his prick forcefully, she ran her hand up and down the thick shaft until she felt him harden. She let go, stepped back, and contemplated the scene. Now, it was time to get to the matter at hand.

The whip was heavy and difficult to handle. Laure raised her arm and brought it down as fast as she could. The lash whistled faintly through the air and landed on Monsieur's bottom with a dry smacking sound.

He started under the blow. The lash fell limply to the floor and Laure suddenly worried she wouldn't be strong enough to give him a proper punishment. But then, across his tight buttocks, a pink line appeared. She looked at Madame and smiled triumphantly. It had only just begun.

Taking strength in this satisfaction, she raised her arm again and again, repeatedly aiming for the man's bottom which was soon crossed with raised welts. Better still, each blow only served to increase his erection which, before long, stood proud and stiff.

Laure could hardly control herself, feeling elated despite the pain now shooting through her shoulder. She didn't know how long she could keep this up but it was so good, so intoxicating to walk around naked, finally free of the horrible belt which had been tormenting her for so long. It was even better to vent her frustration at the man who had devised such a cruel, undeserved punishment.

She was immensely aroused at the sight of her master's prick now begging to be fondled to release, but Laure wouldn't dream of touching him at this point. She would do anything in her power to stop him from getting his reward tonight. It would be the best revenge.

On the bed, Madame sprawled naked. Her hands idly caressed her pale skin and she writhed as she watched Laure exerting herself. After a while, she extended her open arms towards the maid.

'Let René take care of him now,' she suggested. 'Come and join me, my darling.'

Laure dropped the whip and ran to her mistress. She

107

was hot and tired from whipping the master so forcefully; she needed to rest a while.

Madame made her lie next to her so they could both watch what was to happen next. René had already taken off his clothes. He was as hard and ready as his master. Laure bit her lip and pressed her body against her mistress's. The stable hand was strong – who knew what kind of treatment he would inflict on Monsieur? But to her surprise, instead of picking up the whip, René looked at Madame with a knowing smile.

'Yes,' Madame said. 'You know what to do.'

She pulled Laure closer still and caressed her smooth curves. Their legs entwined and the woman's dainty hand gently brushed the maid's inner thigh.

Laure moaned with satisfaction. It felt good to be held close, to feel the contact of soft, delicate skin again. Madame's passionate kisses on her neck soon turned into long, lascivious licks.

Yet neither woman wanted to abandon herself completely, for they were enthralled by the sight of Monsieur kneeling on the floor, his hands now tied behind his back.

René went foraging in the chest and brought back a sort of cod piece sewn onto a harness with which he tightly muzzled Monsieur's stiff prick. A wooden phallus attached to one of the straps was then promptly inserted in the man's behind. René finished buckling the straps, which left the master plugged and unable to take anything off or fondle himself.

On the bed, Madame made Laure sit in front of her, facing her husband. She spread the girl's labia to show Monsieur the pink, wet flesh now eager to be teased.

Laure smiled wickedly as she saw him lick his lips. He would be taunted just as he had taunted her, perhaps even more. He trembled feebly, aware that he wouldn't be allowed to join them. Now, it was clearly a game of role reversal: today the master would obey the stable hand and watch the women pleasuring each other on the bed. His arousal would be kept constant, but he would be denied the ultimate release. His eyes betrayed his anger and regret as Madame's fingers repeatedly ran up and down Laure's slick flesh.

Laure leant back against the woman's bare chest and let passion consume her. Her orgasm was long and smouldering, neither as violent nor as powerful as she would have liked, but it was all hers. Monsieur couldn't stop her from getting the release which was rightfully hers. Yes, it was only fair. But could it make up for all she had endured the past few days? It was up to her to make sure it did.

Seeing René's magnificent penis standing to attention, she freed herself from her mistress's embrace and walked towards the men. It was time once again to take an active role in Monsieur's punishment.

She knelt in front of the two men, just inches from the master. But he wasn't the one she wanted. Tonight, she had absolutely no fancy for aristocratic flesh. Instead, she seized René's prick and took it into her mouth, thinking somehow he tasted better than her master. In any case, he had always been more grateful, not to mention eager to return the favour. He deserved her hot treats more than Monsieur.

Above her head, she could hear the men's breathing grow shallow. Perhaps Monsieur could imagine he was the one being fellated at that moment, but he would soon have to face the harsh reality: the maid wouldn't touch him tonight.

Madame came to join Laure and together they took care of René's hard member. They each took turns sucking the swollen plum whilst the other gently licked the long shaft.

Laure soon grew oblivious to Monsieur's reaction, but Madame never completely abandoned herself to worshipping the marvel she held in her mouth. It was important that her husband should keep watching.

René thrust forcefully into his mistress's mouth whilst

Laure stood and stroked his muscular body, pressing her bare chest against his back. Madame withdrew and fondled him to orgasm with both hands. Laure knelt in front of him and his seed spurted into her mouth.

The stable hand roared as he climaxed. Next to him, Monsieur stood stoic, knowing he wouldn't receive the same treatment that night.

The women went back to the bed. Madame was still unsated and threw herself at Laure's quivering flesh. Rolling around on the bed, they writhed and rubbed against each other. Their hands ravaged the other's flesh, and pleasure rampaged through their bodies again and again. Each time Laure looked up, she was pleased to see Monsieur's face now livid with envy.

Finally, Madame made Laure sit on the edge of the bed with her legs wide apart. Under René's guidance, Monsieur obediently went down on all fours, close enough to see and smell the displayed slit, but still too far away to be able to touch, let alone taste it.

Laure was happy to let Madame pleasure her. The maid climaxed one more time, right in front of her master's eyes. By then she was exhausted, yet her happiness was complete. Monsieur had paid for all the torment he had caused her. Better still, he had been made to suffer in the same way he had devised for her. Now they were even.

Chapter Seven

*L*aure woke up feeling thirsty. Her throat was raw and she coughed repeatedly. Next to her in the bed, Madame's idle body was also shaken by occasional fits of coughing.

Laure decided to get up and lazily pulled back the curtains around the bed. At that moment she knew something was wrong, terribly wrong.

A flickering, yellow glow shone through the window. It could have been sunrise, save for the way the light wavered. And from where she was, Laure could only see it through a haze, a mist. Horror seized her as she realised the room was filled with smoke.

Now fully awake, she understood what caused the acrid taste in her mouth and why she couldn't quell her coughing fits. The glow in the window could only mean one thing: fire. She shook her mistress in an attempt to wake her, unable to talk as her throat grew hoarse and thick.

Madame responded faintly, and Laure had to drag her to her feet and help her slip on a robe. Together they crawled to Monsieur's room, closing the door behind them. Still on all fours, Laure crept towards the bed, only to find it cold and empty. She pulled herself to her feet, grabbed the jug of water on the bedside table and quickly swallowed a large mouthful before taking the jug to Madame and helping her drink from it.

The woman was weak. Her frail body trembled against Laure's. Her coughing eased up somewhat but Laure knew that wasn't good enough. She had to act fast. They had to get out, but going back to Madame's room was too dangerous. Smoke was already seeping under the door adjoining the rooms.

Still holding the candle, Laure made her way out to the corridor, half dragging and half carrying her mistress. The floor was warm under their feet, but as they progressed towards the back stairs she was relieved to notice that the smoke had only just started to invade the west wing of the château.

By the time they got to the ground floor, they could both breathe more easily. Laure held her mistress's hand and guided her through the dark corridors, past the laundry rooms and servants' quarters until they arrived in the hall. There, she pushed the door open and the cool night air welcomed them. They walked across the fore-court, oblivious to the sharp gravel under their feet and warm debris raining down on them from above. Laure kept dragging her mistress until all she could feel was wet and cold grass under her feet. Then they collapsed, breathing deeply to cleanse their lungs of the smoke.

Sitting up, Laure looked at the blaze, aghast. Already the east wing was a black shell, orange flames voraciously licking at the charred beams. All around them, screaming men ran with buckets of water in an attempt to contain the fire.

Next to her, Madame sat up as well and cried out for her husband. She sprang to her feet and took off towards the raging inferno. 'My husband, my husband. Where is my husband?'

People took little notice of her cries. Laure ran after her and held her back. Amidst the crowd, she was relieved to see Juliette. The housekeeper saw them too and came up to them. 'Monsieur is out,' she said. 'I saw him earlier. I don't think there is anybody left in the house.'

She led them away to allow the men to work. The three women huddled together and watched, powerless, as the roof above the great hall collapsed and sent thousands of sparks flying through the black sky.

Juliette was the first to point out the sun had now risen. Madame stood with a doleful expression on her face, her arms clutched tightly around Laure's waist.

Monsieur had been to see them several times throughout the night. Each time his face had become dirtier, blackened with soot and ashes. Sweat trickled down his temples as he exhausted himself trying to retrieve as much as possible from the burning building.

A servant had brought them chairs, but Madame had refused to sit down. In all, not much had been salvaged. Even the big armchair from Monsieur's room was beyond repair. Its legs were charred and the fabric along the armrests was completely burnt. Laure looked at it one more time and closed her eyes. She knew things would never be the same again.

'You may stay here a while,' Mother Superior said. 'But I strongly urge you to make other arrangements as quickly as possible. I cannot leave you without shelter, but your presence here is most inappropriate.'

Laure was baffled. How could Mother Superior be so cruel to the Lamprons? This was a charitable order of nuns who zealously helped the poor and the sick, so why couldn't they welcome the people from the château?

Monsieur replied courteously but didn't look surprised. He thanked the Mother Superior and gently led his wife out of the parlour. His hands were still black and dirty, but he had washed his face. Laure helped him put Madame to bed, for she was now as weak as a child with no will of her own.

'Stay with her,' Monsieur ordered in a broken voice. 'I have business to attend to.'

Through snippets of conversation with his wife, Laure had managed to ascertain that Monsieur hadn't been able to retrieve his money and precious deeds from his room. She had also heard some of the servants talking about where they could find work. It had appalled her to see how quickly people were planning their lives even before the ashes from the blaze were cold. Laure hadn't had time to think about what would become of her.

For the past few days, she had been sharing her mistress's bed. Madame was still angry at her husband, although his demeanour towards Laure had been very different since the night he had been punished. He was docile and gracious, eager to join his wife and her protégée in bed. But Madame didn't want him. She was eager to make Laure forget the horrible ordeal of her husband's tests.

Laure hadn't even returned to the kitchens. Instead, the servants had been waiting on her, just as she had hoped. Madame had promised this would be permanent; Laure would never have to work again. Obviously, neither Madame nor her husband could keep that promise anymore. They didn't know themselves how they would recover from the loss of their property.

Laure wiped a fat tear rolling down her mistress's cheek. Madame hadn't uttered a word since they had escaped from the fire that morning, and until now her face had remained frozen in an expression of dejection.

'What are we to do?' she finally asked in a broken voice as she lifted her tear-stained face. 'My husband fears we may not have anything left.'

Laure took the frail body in her arms and gently rocked her like a child. 'We are safe,' she said, trying to reassure her. 'We will find a way. And we will stay together.'

Her last sentence was more a question than a statement. She was in no position to demand anything from

114

the Lamprons at this point. Bewildered and confused, she looked around the room and took in her strange surroundings. The bare walls were whitewashed; there were no curtains around the tiny window. The only decoration was a wooden crucifix around which hung a rosary. The two narrow beds consisted of simple metallic frames topped with thin mattresses. The bedsheets were rough and there were no eiderdowns, just thin, grey woollen blankets. Only one pillow on each bed, and a rather flat one at that. Between the beds, a small chest of drawers and a praying stool. What a change from the lavish quarters Madame was used to.

The hand on her arm went limp and Laure realised Madame had finally fallen asleep. She got up as quietly as she could, not wanting to disturb her mistress. She needed to see the other servants to find out what was going to happen to them.

As she walked down the long corridor, she couldn't help venturing a look into each of the tiny rooms she passed. If Madame's room was simple, these were sinister! They were all identical and contained a single bed made of a wooden box upon which lay a bare straw mattress. A thin blanket was neatly folded at the foot of the bed and some didn't even have a pillow.

In the corridor, the marble floor was so clean and shiny Laure could see her reflection as she quickly made her way back to Mother Superior's parlour. As she approached, the sound of raised voices caught her attention and she stopped short of entering the room. She crept up to the door and pressed her ear against it.

'I cannot believe you are the same woman I once knew,' she heard a man say. 'Dear Eloise, you used to have such an engaging personality.'

Laure recognised her master's voice. But who was he talking to? As she pushed against the door, she realised it wasn't properly shut and she managed to open it enough to see who else was in the room.

Just like before, Monsieur was talking with Mother

Superior. Only now, their conversation was much less formal, as were Monsieur's manners. Coming close to the nun, he encircled her waist and fondled her breasts through her habit. Mother Superior shuddered but didn't push him away.

He grabbed her hand and pressed it against his crotch. Mother Superior looked down, her cheeks red with embarrassment, but still she made no effort to free herself.

'You remember,' he said, 'all those years ago. How you used to scream when I caressed you so exquisitely you could barely stand it; how your beautiful body came alive under my hands. I remember the taste of your quim. My word, I wouldn't mind having you right now.'

As he spoke he lifted her habit and ran both his dirty hands up her pristine legs. Under the many layers of linen, the nun's thighs appeared, white and smooth, in sharp contrast to her black habit. Laure watched with wicked curiosity as Mother Superior allowed Monsieur to kneel in front of her and kiss her trembling legs. She let out a small cry as his tongue lost itself in her curly bush and he relished her hungrily.

From where she stood Laure could hear the wet noises of his mouth on the nun's flesh and she felt her own suddenly moisten with arousal. Framed in the tight coronet, the nun's face reflected the pleasure raging within her. Laure heard a sharp intake of breath followed by a moan, and a second later Mother Superior pushed Monsieur away.

'You are the devil, Emile Lampron,' she cried out in disgust. She pushed her habit down and braced herself against the edge of the large desk, regaining her senses. 'You had your way with me when I was young and foolish, but I know better now. You and your depraved ways are not welcome here. You will leave by the end of the week, and take all your people with you. I will not have you corrupt this holy house. Your mere presence

116

here is an insult to everything this order stands for. Now go. I do not want you setting foot in my parlour again!'

Monsieur slowly stood and laughed dismissively. 'You may feel this way now,' he said. 'But just give me a few days and you will change your mind. I know where your weakness lies, and you know you stand to gain a lot by befriending me. I will be back.'

Laure barely had time to move away from the door and hide behind a pillar before he left the room. Obviously, Monsieur and Mother Superior had known each other in the past, and she suspected this information could have very interesting advantages.

That first night she slept on the other bed in Madame's room. Monsieur had said he would be away for a few days and had instructed Laure to stay with his wife.

Yet Madame wanted to be left alone in her bed. Laure couldn't help feeling sad, remembering how uncomfortable her mistress's bed was, and how she could have cuddled up and held her through the night.

But Madame hadn't been herself all day. After a private talk with her husband, she had been saying things that Laure couldn't quite grasp but didn't like the sound of nonetheless. Madame had talked about paying the price for their excesses, about how her life would now be lonely, and other things Laure simply didn't understand.

The other servants hadn't been much help. Those without family had already gathered their meagre possessions together and left to find work elsewhere. They didn't want to wait around, only to be told there was no work for them in the area. Others had found shelter with friends or relatives.

Only Laure was left with no way out. She had to rely on her master and mistress to see what was to become of her. And she wasn't even sure they knew themselves.

When Monsieur unexpectedly returned the next day, he went straight to Mother Superior's parlour, although she had forbidden him to. Just like before, Laure silently stood right outside to eavesdrop. She missed the beginning of the conversation, but what she heard was enough to understand what it was all about.

'This is blackmail,' Mother Superior hissed. 'You have no right demanding anything from me.'

'My dear,' Monsieur replied, 'I've said it before and I'll say it again: it would be in your best interest to do as I say. Surely you wouldn't want anyone to know we were once such good friends. And, should you agree to my conditions, we could be friends again.'

Laure could hear the nun pacing behind her desk. 'Can you imagine,' Monsieur continued, 'what the bishop would say if he heard you once gave birth to a child, my child.'

'You have no right.' Mother Superior repeated.

'I have every right,' Monsieur burst out. 'I know where to find him and I can prove he is ours. All I ask is that you let us stay for as long as we need, and that you help provide that small sum of money I will require.'

Laure moved away from the door. She had heard enough. At least she knew that as long as she was here with the Lamprons, she didn't have to worry. But soon Monsieur would want to leave. There was no way he and Madame would stay here any longer than necessary. What would happen then?

From the first day, Laure had had very little contact with her master and mistress. Both Monsieur and Madame had other things on their minds, secrets which they wouldn't share with Laure, and the atmosphere between them all had been tense.

She didn't mind not knowing about their private affairs, but she missed the cuddles and caresses. She had often tried to climb into bed with Madame, but each time she had been denied the warmth and softness of her dainty body.

The troubling question of her immediate future greatly

vexed Laure those few days, and she was to discover the truth when a letter Monsieur had been anxious to receive finally arrived. Madame was the one who broke the news to Laure. She entered the room wearing a light coat and her gloves. Her hair was powdered and neatly tied in an elaborate chignon.

There could only be one explanation for the way she was dressed: the Lamprons were leaving. And since Laure hadn't been informed of this departure, it could only mean one thing.

'My darling,' Madame said with a blank expression. 'Despite our misfortune, we are blessed with a good family. My husband's brother has agreed to let us live with him in Paris.' She paused and stepped away.

Laure held her breath. Judging from her mistress's tone, it wasn't good news for her.

'We cannot take you with us,' Madame rapidly blurted out. 'There is very little room, and no work for you. My husband is expecting news from one of the king's envoy. We will try to make sure you want for nothing.'

She turned to face Laure. The maid wanted her mistress to come forward and take her in her arms one last time. But instead Madame stepped back. Her eyes were fixed on the floor, her face pale and lifeless.

Slowly, without even daring to look up, she turned and left the room. She paused one last time, her hand on the door handle and let out a faint whisper: 'Goodbye.'

When Monsieur appeared in the door frame, he only had the courage to glance at Laure for a few seconds before looking away. 'You will stay here at the convent,' he said sternly. 'Mother Superior will explain her terms to you.' His arm around his wife's shoulders, he ushered her from the room and closed the door behind them. Laure stared at the door, desperately hoping it would open again and they would come back for her. But soon silence told her she was waiting in vain.

* * *

119

'It would be in your best interest to marry the first young man we find for you,' Mother Superior advised. 'You are in no position to be choosy. Being orphaned, you would be nothing if Monsieur Lampron hadn't arranged for you to become ward of the king. And since you made it clear you did not wish to take the habit ...' Mother Superior paused, looked contemptuously at Laure and sighed. 'Considering the place you come from, I doubt you would make a good nun, anyway,' she mumbled as if talking to herself.

'But you also made it clear you didn't wish to find work elsewhere,' the woman continued. 'Therefore, we shall endeavour to find you a suitable husband. In the meantime, you will be expected to live as we do, to practise charity and humility. Take this time to reflect on how you came to live here. Remember, everything happens for a reason. Do not blame fate for what has happened to you and the Lamprons. God has His ways of making people pay for their sins, one way or another. Now go. Sister Pauline will give you chores for this morning. Then you can attend Mass with the other girls.'

Chapter Eight

When Laure awoke, she found the girls who shared her cell were already gone. The five narrow beds were empty, the blankets neatly folded. She imagined they were probably attending early Mass. So much the better. She didn't want to see any of them. Over the past couple of days, she had established all she had in common with them was that they were orphans and staying at the convent until they found a suitable husband.

But, unlike Laure, the girls didn't seem to resent this Spartan lifestyle. They had been here far too long. This had been obvious when Laure told them of the libidinous activities she had engaged in whilst living at the château. Their shrieks of horror when she described pleasuring four men at once said it all.

For her part, Laure was ready to sell her soul to the devil for the pleasure of feeling the warmth of a lover, a naked body writhing against hers; if only for one night. But instead she was alone, lying in her hateful little bed.

From the moment the Lamprons had left, she had been instructed to keep her hair out of sight, and forced to wear layer upon layer of petticoats on top of thick bloomers which completely hid her thighs. Her whole body was trapped, out of reach, out of touch. All her senses were numb. And, deep within her, the fire of desire burnt brighter than ever.

Her sleep had been constantly disturbed by images of naked bodies lasciviously dancing in front of her. Men and women had taunted her, caressed her voluptuously, only to run away when Laure had tried to touch them.

Just now she had dreamt she was wearing a chastity belt. Only this one had covered her from neck to ankles and left only her hands, feet and face free. She had struggled to take it off, pulling at the metal edges. After a while, she had overcome the horrible device and managed to free her legs and hips. Hands fondled her thighs and she parted them wantonly, eager to make her anonymous lovers see how she yearned to abandon herself.

The sound of her own sighs had woken her up. Now she knew what she had been fighting with in her sleep had been her own clothes. Her chemise was rucked up around her waist and her bloomers lay, ripped, on the floor. The hands which had been stroking her inner thighs were her own.

Laure laughed and cried at the same time, relieved to see the chastity belt existed only in her imagination, yet disappointed to find herself alone again. Mindlessly stroking her slit, she was mildly surprised by how wet she was. The dream had obviously had a powerful effect on her.

With her foot, she kicked the blanket onto the floor. Since she was alone, she saw no reason not to make the most of it. Her pelvis lifted off the bed repeatedly and thumped down as it rebounded against the motion of her hand. Her other hand snaked under her chemise and she groaned as she felt her nipple grow harder under her expert fingers.

Her flesh quivered and she rubbed herself hard and fast, increasing the momentum of her hand and hips.

122

Already she felt her vagina clench as her orgasm approached.

She bit her lip to muffle her cry of joy. So far away from everybody else, no-one would hear her, but she didn't want to attract attention should someone be passing in the corridor. The fire of climax built up within her. She was almost there. Her hand slid faster over her flesh, massaging it powerfully. The muscles in her thighs contracted and a sob rose in her throat. Only a few more seconds . . .

Suddenly, Mother Superior's hand slapped hers and pulled it away from her crotch. 'You little wanton,' she croaked. 'How dare you abandon yourself to such lewd pursuits when you should be praying in the chapel?'

Before Laure realised what was happening, the woman had grabbed her arm and pulled her to her feet.

'How dare you?' the nun screamed as she shook her violently. She raised her arm and hit Laure across the face several times. 'You will pay for this. You will answer to God. You will do penance and pray for Him to give you the strength to overcome this lust.'

Without letting go of Laure's arm, she dragged her out of the room and down the corridor. Laure stumbled as she struggled to keep up with the woman. Mother Superior walked in long, rapid strides, and she kept on hitting Laure with her free hand.

'I should have known.' Her angry voice echoed in the dim, empty corridor. 'I should have made you expiate your sins when you first arrived here. You are weak, woman. And God disapproves of such sinful weakness.'

As Mother Superior shoved her roughly into the room, Laure slipped and fell on to the polished marble floor, winding herself slightly. She heard the door slam shut, and, looking up, saw the nun advancing on her with a small whip in her hand. Laure shivered, as much in anticipation of pleasure as pain. Seeing the girl's apparent fear, the nun paused, lowering her whip.

'You understand and accept why I must do this?' said Mother Superior.

Laure nodded meekly. She could have protested, yet she consented to her punishment, failing to retaliate even when the nun reached forward to raise her chemise and expose her thighs. The first lash fell just above Laure's knee and the girl flinched, despite herself.

'You will stay still,' thundered Mother Superior, as she dragged Laure across the room by her chemise, then forced her to kneel over the praying stool, bent forward at the waist. 'You will suffer in silence and contemplation.'

Laure didn't dare to move a muscle. Mother Superior was incensed, her eyes bulging and her face red. Her anger made her strong. That strength, combined with the wrath she displayed, could only be appeased by obedience.

Laure braced herself and stared at the painting of Christ hanging on the wall in front of her. Behind her, she could hear Mother Superior breathing hard. She didn't dare defy the woman. Even turning around could fuel her wrath. It was best to let her calm down first.

A trembling hand lifted her chemise. The first blows fell, but they were not as hard as Laure would have expected. Besides, she had experienced worse.

For a brief spell, Laure couldn't help but think the nun would perhaps take perverse pleasure in lashing her. She knew how she had felt the night of Monsieur's punishment, and that made her wonder whether there might have been such wicked encounters between the nun and the master of the Château de Reyval.

Laure's suspicions grew stronger when she thought of how quickly Mother Superior had decided to punish her and taken out the whip. Although she couldn't see the nun, she could very well picture the expression on her face each time she brought the lash down. There was no doubt in Laure's mind that the relationship between the woman and Monsieur Lampron had been quite tumultuous. In fact, lashing Laure could perhaps serve as a vengeance for Monsieur's blackmail.

The girl's doubts were confirmed shortly thereafter. As the whip fell repeatedly across the back of her thighs and buttocks, she could hear the nun sigh in exaltation. Her throbbing skin easily tolerated the pain until the force of the blows lessened. Mother Superior was already growing tired.

When the nun knelt next to her, Laure decided to turn the tables on her. She spread her legs slightly to expose her pink flesh. She could feel it still wet and suspected Mother Superior might not be able to resist the sight of her glistening folds.

She tried to stifle her excitement, but fighting it was pointless. Indeed, her time at the château had taught her well how to extract the most pleasure out of pain. Today the only difference lay in the intentions of the nun, who had no idea that punishing Laure in such a way would have the opposite effect.

The whip fell to the floor and Mother Superior continued hitting the exposed bottom with her bare hand. Little by little, the slaps turned lazy and soon Laure was puzzled as to whether they were meant to hurt or caress her.

Turning her head slightly, she saw the enraptured look on Mother Superior's face. Her eyes were closed, her lips slightly parted and trembling. Laure couldn't help but smile. Here was her chance. She pushed her bottom higher and parted her legs further. When the nun's hand landed on her slit, she heard the woman give a strangled groan. The hand landed again and then lingered, and Laure brought her legs together to trap it. Immediately she felt the crooked fingers fondling her wet folds, and she heard the nun breathe even harder. By now Mother Superior was hunched over the girl's hips, her chin just inches above the throbbing skin.

Monsieur had spoken the truth: Mother Superior had hidden desires she would never want anyone to discover. Had she taken the habit as a penance for her own wantonness? From what Laure had seen, very few people at the convent, if any, knew of their superior's true, lusty nature.

The beauty of it was that Laure had done very little to incite this sort of behaviour from the nun. She truly believed Mother Superior initially intended to punish her, but then had fallen prey to her own instinct.

The woman's fingers moved expertly up and down her slit, and Laure knew she would climax soon. Yet her arousal gave way to surprise when she felt Mother Superior crawling behind her and licking her quivering slit.

Still kneeling over the praying stool, Laure spread her legs and looked behind her. The nun never even looked up: she immediately went down and fastened her dry mouth on the girl's moist flesh.

This was more than Laure could ever have hoped for. The woman was bent over between her parted legs, hungrily licking her to climax. Laure squirmed and raised her bottom, moving it lasciviously to grind her flesh against Mother Superior's mouth.

The nun grabbed Laure's legs and pulled her back, making her turn around to lie on the floor with her legs parted. Never once looking at the girl, she quickly dived towards the displayed flesh. Now Laure could see nothing but a black, veiled figure writhing between her parted legs. She squirmed and raised her legs to bring her knees back towards her chest. A second later, Mother Superior reached up and brought her legs over her shoulders.

Against her thighs, Laure could feel the rough cloth of the habit and the points of the cornet digging into her as the nun's head moved over her flesh. Confident that Mother Superior was totally enthralled, she lifted her chemise higher still. She would have liked to be naked, to let the cool marble floor quell the fire burning on the surface of her skin.

When the nun's hands, wet with the girl's juices, came to join hers, Laure knew her own prayers had been answered. She moaned as together they worried her nipples and squeezed the pale globes voluptuously.

Laure's arousal had been restrained for so long she climaxed several times under the woman's expert tongue. The nun's fingers dug deeper into her flesh, revealing the intensity of her own arousal.

Suddenly, Mother Superior looked up, gave a frightened cry and jumped to her feet. Laure heard her breathing hard as she quickly flattened the wrinkles of her habit, straightened her cornet and swiftly picked up the whip to stash it in the bottom drawer of her desk.

'Go back to your room,' Mother Superior rasped in a shaky voice. 'Don't you dare breathe a word of this to anyone. Ever.'

Laure left the room feeling little concern for the threats. In fact, she danced across the marble floor in her bare feet. Her flesh still sporadically clenched as her climax slowly subsided. What more could she have asked for?

To her, there was no sin committed that day. The only sin was that a woman who knew how to give such pleasure had condemned herself to a life in which she wasn't allowed to give her passion free rein.

Chapter Nine

*I*t was no surprise when Sister Germaine advised Laure she wouldn't sleep in the same room as the other girls. Instead, she was to share a cell with three nuns.

Her new roommates were on a constant vigil, praying day and night and hardly ever sleeping. They even took their meals in the cell. At least one of them was awake at any given time so that, under the pretext of fervent contemplation, they could keep an eye on Laure.

If this was the Mother Superior's idea of a penance for Laure, it was more effective than any form of corporal punishment. Her new bed was a plank of wood covered with loose straw and for the first three days her meals consisted of bread and water.

The nuns prayed constantly but never spoke. Although Laure wasn't required to join them in prayer, she could nevertheless feel their eyes on her whenever she lay down to sleep. No privacy, not even the cover of a blanket. Yet, for her cell mates, this was the life they had chosen.

Sitting with her back against the cold stone wall, Laure looked at each of them in turn. Three heads tilted to the side and staring at the crucifix on the wall, all identically framed by the black cornet; eyes filled with adoration and shining in the light of a single candle.

Thankfully, they hadn't asked her why or how she had sinned. If only someone had asked, Laure would have been more than happy to tell them what kind of woman Mother Superior really was.

But she didn't dare reveal the secret. With the exception of Mother Superior, whom Laure hadn't seen since that cosy afternoon, everyone at the convent had been extremely kind to her. Usually, she would have thrived on that kind of attention.

Yet the bleak atmosphere soon weighed upon her. This Spartan life had its limits. She needed to get out. She needed to get out before she became too much like them.

Salvation came in the shape of a man named Father Olivier. Laure and the other girls knew nothing of his visit. They didn't know what to expect when they were asked to report promptly to Mother Superior's parlour.

The other girls took the time to comb their hair and change their aprons. As for Laure, well, she just couldn't be bothered to straighten herself up, knowing it was pointless to try attracting anybody's attention by looking prim and proper.

So when she came to stand next to her fellow convent girls in the parlour, she immediately sensed the image she projected was starkly different than the charming tableau Mother Superior had hoped to present to their visitor.

Yet it was Laure, with a loose strand of hair falling across her face, her bonnet all askew and her shoes muddy who immediately caught the priest's attention.

About the same age as Monsieur, Father Olivier was a skinny, rather quaint man. He would have been better looking if only his hair had not been so short and slicked back, and if he had a bit more colour in his face. In any case, he didn't look like a priest.

'As you may already know,' he began, his eyes travelling from one girl to the next, 'our good King Louis has claimed possession of the land across the Atlantic Ocean. We now have a thriving colony, and many people have left France to establish new territories.' He stopped and pretended to stare at his shoes.

Her head bowed but her eyes constantly watching him, Laure noticed he was in fact examining her.

'I know from Mother Superior that you young ladies have no family, and that you are eager to be married and bear children. Naturally, the last few years have been difficult for everyone across this beautiful country and in this area there are very few suitable young men looking for a bride.'

Mother Superior rose and came to stand next to him. 'My dear girls,' she said. 'It is the wish of the king to send you abroad so that you may become brides to the settlers in New France. Should you accept, his majesty will of course increase your dowry substantially. At this time, there are many men and not enough women in the new country. Your king needs your help.'

Laure stiffened. Although what she had just heard seemed innocent enough, she sensed something wasn't quite right. Mother Superior's tone of voice was too sweet; she was usually much more stern. It was almost as if she was trying to convince them that they should go. Laure kept her head bowed and closed her eyes.

Indeed, she had heard of the new country. More precisely, she had heard it was a godforsaken place, teeming with savages who had already killed some of the settlers, and where winters were long and hard.

She wondered how much of this Mother Superior – or even Father Olivier – knew. But she remembered what she had heard from Raymond, who had worked as a valet at the Château de Reyval. He was supposed to have gone to the new colony to join his brother, who was already there. But within a year he had cancelled his plan. His brother had written to warn him life in the

130

colony was rough and he shouldn't attempt the trip unless he had nothing to look forward to at home.

This, along with Mother Superior and Father Olivier's unctious tone of voice, led Laure to think she shouldn't commit herself just yet. She needed to know more. She needed to know precisely what she stood to gain if she decided to go.

But as the priest kept talking, two of Laure's fellow convent girls, Thérèse and Jacqueline, were already giddy with excitement. They were not especially pretty, and since they hadn't met a single suitor in the past few months, they knew they probably stood a better chance of getting married if they agreed to leave.

Things were different for Laure: she didn't want to get married. All she wanted was freedom to come and go as she pleased; without having to work, of course. Becoming a settler's wife implied not only a husband to answer to, but a lot of hard work. Yet life at the convent was just as hard on her. She had never been so restrained, and she knew she couldn't take the lack of freedom for much longer.

When Father Olivier announced he would be around after Mass to answer any questions they might have, Laure decided to come back and find out more.

The look in his eyes said it all. Father Olivier may have been a man of the cloth, but he was still a man. And the way he greeted Laure as she entered the parlour didn't leave any room for confusion.

'I am glad you asked to see me,' he said as he ushered her in. His hand on her back slid down across her buttocks and his fingers dug in slightly through Laure's dress. 'I can tell you have several questions for me,' he continued as he sat her next to him on a wooden bench. 'But first, I must tell you something I neglected to tell the others.'

He huddled close to her and set his hand on her lap. His nose practically touched her cheek as he leant to whisper in her ear. 'You see, my child, not every girl who wishes will be allowed to go. I am on a great quest to find the best young women who will serve God and their country. Should you wish to be chosen – and I know you do – you have to prove you are worthy.'

His arm snaked around Laure's waist and pulled her close, so close his fingertips now reached around to her breast. Laure couldn't help but be amused. Of course, she had a feeling he would try something like this. It was precisely what she had been hoping for.

She smiled demurely and pretended to pull away. 'But, father . . .'

'Shhhh.' He put his finger on her lips. 'You must obey. Obedience and servitude are the paths that lead to God. Now close your eyes.'

Laure enjoyed playing along. If the man wanted to believe he was seducing a young and coy virgin, that was the illusion she would give him – as long as she got what she wanted out of him.

She sighed faintly as his hand slid up her leg under her dress. At the same time, he pulled her closer and kissed her neck. His fingers quickly found their way under her bloomers. At first she didn't know if she should help him. But when he pulled his hand away and grabbed hers, she decided to make the most of this encounter.

He placed her hand on his member, pulsing beneath his thick cassock. Laure feigned surprise, but in reality she had no qualms about playing the role of a demure yet eager pupil.

She rubbed him through the heavy, rough cloth, purposefully making her caresses clumsy and none too gentle. This was a wicked man, a man who had taken a vow of chastity and was now trying to seduce what he obviously thought was an innocent girl. This servant-of-God-turned-sinner needed to be punished.

She dug her nails into his member and squeezed until

he gasped in pain. Yet the way it stiffened and twitched left no doubt as to the effect she had on him.

He pushed her backwards on the bench and made her lie with one leg on the floor and the other on the seat. 'Be good,' he whispered as he lay on top of her. 'Be good and God will reward you.'

Laure whined with excitement. The priest's mouth brushed against her ear as he whispered to calm her down. 'Don't be afraid,' he said. 'This is God's will. You are His servant and you owe Him obedience.' His mouth nibbled at her neck and bathed her skin in warm saliva. As he writhed on top of her, she could feel his member, hard as iron, even through several layers of clothing. From the pressure and hardness against her crotch, Laure determined with satisfaction it was quite sizeable.

Father Olivier grunted like an animal, excited by the idea of forbidden pleasure. The man had a passion for women which his position prevented him from enjoying.

Laure couldn't remember the last time a man had been so enthralled by her he couldn't restrain himself. Knowing she was the object of such desire excited her even more. She moaned as he lifted his hips and his hands frantically searched amongst the layers of petticoats for a way to her flesh.

He finally reached the waistband of her bloomers, ripped them in a frenzied twist of the wrist and tore them off her. Now she was amused by his behaviour. He couldn't wait, could he?

As he drew up his cassock and was about to enter her, however, she pushed him off and he fell to the floor. The time had come to turn the tables on him. With a devilish laugh, she ran to Mother Superior's desk to retrieve the small whip she knew was in the bottom drawer.

When she turned around, Father Olivier was sitting on the floor, legs bent and apart, his garment rolled up to his waist and his stiff member pointing up for anyone to see. His bewildered look was unmistakable.

133

'You naughty priest,' she croaked sarcastically as she walked towards him. 'Look at you.'

His face crimson, Father Olivier fumbled with his cassock, trying to cover his throbbing penis, but Laure stopped him with a well-placed blow of the lash to his wrist.

'Leave it,' she ordered. 'God is watching. We do want him to see how you worship your master, don't we?'

She drew up her dress until her curly bush appeared in plain view then came closer, lasciviously swinging her hips. Standing in front of him, legs apart, she rotated her pelvis to repeatedly bring her pussy within inches of his face. Father Olivier gasped and tried to grab hold of his member. Once again, Laure was quick enough to stop him.

'Not yet,' she ordered as she hit his hand. 'We have a few things to discuss.'

She sat on the floor, facing him, and threw her leg over his. His eyes caught sight of her glistening vulva, just as she had expected. She rubbed her slit nonchalantly, spreading her labia to tease him.

'Now,' she said with a sweet voice. 'I need you to help me get out of here.'

His face lit up. 'You accept?' he said in a syrupy tone. 'You want to leave for the new country?'

'I want to get out of here,' she countered. 'I don't care much for that colony of yours, but . . .' She bent towards him and roughly fondled his prick.

The priest grabbed her hand and forced her to tighten her hold on his member.

'I see,' he said in a whisper. 'Be good, and perhaps I can help you.'

Laure managed to pull away and stood up, laughing. 'This is all you want, you lecherous old fool.' Walking around him, she playfully hit his thighs with the lash, making him squirm and crawl backwards. 'What's in it for me?' she asked defiantly.

'Well, recruiting young women is a rather difficult

task,' he said. 'We could tell Mother Superior I shall be taking you with me to help out. Once we are done, I can take you on as my servant.'

This last word made Laure's blood boil.

'Servant!' She hit him harder, watching his member rear, and a drop seeped from its lone eye in response. Laure didn't much care for it at this point. She wanted to secure her passage out of the convent, but being a servant was totally out of the question.

As she was about to hit him again, Father Olivier managed to catch the lash and pulled her towards him. Thrown off balance, Laure fell to her knees, her body landing on top of his.

'I see you are not made for obedience,' he whispered. Laure felt his warm breath brush her face, and his bare leg rub against hers. Her heart pounded fast.

'Be good,' he repeated. 'I can probably arrange for you to get what you want.'

He pulled her towards him and kissed her on the mouth. Laure felt a rush of moist heat flow within her. She caught her breath just as his hand trailed up her leg and pulled away.

'Not so fast,' she said. 'I want some assurances.'

'Like what?'

'I want you to promise me you will get me out of this convent, but at the same time I do not want to spend the rest of my life in servitude.'

'Don't you?' He got close again and this time pressed his hand directly on her wet slit.

'Being with me has advantages ...' Once again his kiss almost made her lose control. She set both hands on his shoulders and pushed him away. But he was stronger. His arm around her waist held her tight and she surrendered to his embrace.

'We will tell Mother Superior you have agreed to go to the colony,' he whispered in her ear. He stopped talking for a moment to nibble at her neck and Laure instinctively parted her legs to give him closer access.

'At the last minute, just before you get on the boat, I will send for you. You will come with me to Paris, as my maid.' Laure stiffened in his arms but he calmed her with yet another kiss. He pulled back slightly and looked into her eyes.

'Only you and I will know you are in fact my mistress. Does that sound better to you?'

'Will I have to take a husband?' Laure asked hesitantly.

'Only if you want to. But even then, we will remain close, won't we?'

Laure smiled. The prospect of being a priest's mistress sounded very appealing. As for being his maid, it was but a small inconvenience.

'I will agree,' she said, 'but only once you show me what I gain from being your mistress.'

She barely had time to finish her sentence. Already his hands were climbing up her belly, under her dress, in search of her breasts. She caught her breath as he found them.

The priest might have made a vow of chastity, but he surely was no stranger to the pleasures of the flesh. His fingers tweaked her nipples until they were hard and swollen, his touch rough but eager. His mouth devoured hers endlessly, and Laure responded to his kisses just as passionately.

After a while he pulled away and made her sit up. His thick phallus appeared in front of her face and she engulfed it readily. It seemed years since she had taken a man in her mouth. Finally, here was a man who wanted her, wanted her so much he was willing to risk eternal damnation for the pleasure of her body.

She moaned as she felt him pulse in her mouth. He tasted new and she wanted more of him, sucking him so hard she almost choked. As he began thrusting she eased her embrace and looked up at him.

'Me first,' she said.

The priest smiled contemptuously and made her lie

back before kneeling to kiss her belly. His hand foraged through her slick flesh, making her writhe uncontrollably.

She lifted her legs and pulled them back towards her chest. The priest continued to lick her smooth skin and slid his mouth inexorably towards her fragrant bush. His fingers followed his tongue and soon entered her. Meanwhile, his thumb rubbed against her bud, up and down and in small circles. Her flesh contracted around his fingers and he looked up at her.

'Do you want me to make you come now, child?'

'Yes, yes.'

'Then you have to ask politely.'

'Please make me come.'

'And you have to call me father.'

'Make me come, please, father.'

'That's better.'

His fingers, slippery with her dew, rubbed her harder, faster. Laure whimpered with pleasure. It was only a matter of seconds now, yet it seemed so long.

'You are a sinner, aren't you, child?'

'Yes, father!'

'Your flesh is wanton. We will have to tame it.'

Laure couldn't reply. Pleasure rampaged through her and her hips jerked violently. The hand on her flesh nonetheless continued its assault. She climaxed again and again, calling out each time, and his mouth came up to stifle her cries. As he continued fondling her, she sucked greedily on his fingers, hungry for more.

Father Olivier crawled on top of her and straddled her chest. His member found its way inside her burning mouth and she welcomed him with a loud moan.

'You naughty little girl,' he croaked. 'Here is your penance.'

He thrust into her mouth a few times before pulling back and lying on his side. Laure turned around to take hold of him again from another angle, positioning her hips in front of his face. His mouth readily set on her slit and she gasped with delight.

He sucked avidly, thoroughly relishing her wetness. His tongue slid deep inside her and probed around her slick folds to taste more of her. His moans of appreciation rose and joined hers in a medley of wet noises and throaty grunts.

Grasping his member tightly, she ran her tongue along its length, caressing him from the base of the swollen shaft to the very tip of his slitted plum. She inserted her tongue in the tiny mouth and pushed in to extract drop after drop of salty tears.

His hips bucked against her face and she knew he was on the verge of climax. Releasing the pressure on his member, she took hold of the whip that still lay on the floor and pushed at his arsehole with the handle.

His knees trembled as she worked it in and out several times. His mouth moved away from her bush and she heard a strangled sob. In front of her eyes, the erect phallus throbbed violently and she saw his sac tighten and retract.

Knowing he was almost at the point of no return, she pulled out the handle and quickly seized the base of his shaft in a tight circle, holding him tight until his erection subsided slightly. He protested loudly at her initiative, but Laure shut him up with a quick slap on his bottom.

Without letting go of his prick, she turned around to face him.

'Now, father,' she wheedled in a childish tone as her hand quickly coaxed him back to stiffness.

He turned to mount her and this time she didn't try to stop him, digging her nails into his buttocks and pulling him deep within her. His girth filled her tunnel and stretched her pleasantly. He thrust powerfully, at a pace more devilish than godly.

His clothed chest was heavy on hers and it occurred to Laure they hadn't even undressed. This made it seem forbidden and even more exciting, as if they were shielding their coupling from God's eyes. His thick cassock now smelled of his sweat and his arousal, and Laure knew the scent of their pleasure would also remain on the fabric.

They writhed against the marble floor, their bodies united in a deliciously shameful embrace. His pubic bone rubbed against her swollen clitoris and she climaxed again. He twitched several times inside her and reached his ultimate release with a cry. Laure was elated as his warm seed flowed freely. Thankfully, the man knew how to give as well as take pleasure. Better still, he was her way out of the convent.

Part Two

The New World

Chapter Ten

*L*ife at the convent might have been hell, but the three-month crossing to New France was even worse.

From the moment Laure had found herself standing on the dock at La Rochelle, she knew something was wrong. Father Olivier was supposed to have shown up already, as they had planned, to engage her services as his servant. But he was nowhere in sight.

Instead, dozens of priests and nuns gathered around her as they prepared to board the *Marie-Louison*. Large crates were being loaded onto the ship as passengers exchanged tearful goodbyes with relatives.

Sister Mélanie, Laure's chaperone for the trip, wouldn't let her out of her sight.

'I am very excited about this,' she said as she slipped her arm under Laure's. 'Let's stay together. I want to make sure you don't leave without me.'

Leaving was the furthest thing from Laure's mind at that moment. Father Olivier should have shown up by now. What was she to do if he didn't?

She couldn't help shivering in the early morning light, trembling from head to toe.

'What is the matter?' Sister Mélanie asked.

'Nothing. I thought I saw Father Olivier earlier. Did you see him at all?'

Sister Mélanie gave her a quizzical look. 'Father Olivier? I saw him at the convent two days ago and he said he was on his way back to Paris. You must be mistaken.'

Laure grew colder still. He had gone back to Paris? That wasn't the plan. Or had he simply been lying to the nuns yet planned to show up as promised? By the time the boat was loaded, Laure realised perhaps she had been the one he had lied to.

She looked around desperately, the last of her hopes vanishing as Sister urged her to embark.

'We must go now,' she said in an exasperated voice. 'We cannot miss the tide.'

Still watching for Father Olivier, Laure sheepishly followed her chaperone. Even once she got on the boat, she continued to search the crowd of on-lookers waving to them from the dock. Father Olivier hadn't come.

As the sails were hoisted and the ropes untied, she knew she had been abandoned. Anger set in and remained through the better part of the voyage. His betrayal was hard to accept. She should never have trusted him.

Yet again she found herself alone, unsure of what lay ahead. There was no way to know what to expect when she arrived in the colony. All she could hope for was that it would be better than life at the convent.

Once on board, she suffered from the moment the ship left La Rochelle. Passengers, cattle and cargo filled the ship and left her little, if any, space to move. She resolved to spend most of her time up on deck to escape the stifling atmosphere below. There were times when she thought they would never make it across the ocean. Successive storms threatened to destroy the ship. Heavy rain and wind often forced her to stay below deck, feeling desperately ill as the boat rocked furiously.

Three babies were born during the crossing. Two passengers died. After a while, many lost hope of ever seeing land again. The voyage took longer than had been expected, and everyone worried there wouldn't be enough food to last until they arrived in the town of Québec.

Laure was especially nervous about that. Her dowry from the king consisted of two cows, a pig and six chickens. She owned more than she ever had done before. But as rations grew thin, there was talk of taking it all away from her to feed the passengers.

Thankfully, the ship entered the mouth of the St Lawrence river before it was too late and row boats were dispatched to several settlements along the shore to bring back food. Laure wanted to get off the boat and stay there, but all her requests were met with concern. She had signed a contract stipulating she would be going to Québec City. Should she wish to leave now, she would lose all her possessions. Moreover, leaving without a chaperone was naturally out of the question.

As the boat continued its journey upstream, Laure's spirits gradually returned. When she learned they would be docking in less than two days, for the first time in a long while she felt excited. On the very last night, she couldn't sleep. She had made it so far, she was ready to make the most of whatever she found when she disembarked. Her true self and insatiable lust for life was slowly returning.

More than anything, she hungered for the contact of another human body. For the past three mouths she had been denied the physical contact she had learned to crave so much, unable even to enjoy her own body. The entire trip had been supervised by members of the various religious communities who had organised it. Even husbands and wives were denied privacy. This was no time to fornicate, they had been advised before departing. Prayer would ensure the bodies and souls remained pure during the crossing.

At first, it hadn't been too difficult. But now she had become so wanton she would willingly do anything to feel a man's naked chest against her stiff nipples, fingers probing at her moist flesh. It was especially hard on that last night, with Sister Mélanie lying next to her in the short bunk, her slender body moving languidly in sleep.

Laure had seen her chaperone almost naked, on those rare occasions when the women had been allowed some privacy to wash, and she had been disturbingly aroused by the sight of the woman's thin figure.

Without her habit, Sister Mélanie was a strange creature. Her cropped hair and small breasts gave her a rather masculine allure, as did her thin, boyish frame. But the curve of her hips and the swell of her bottom were unmistakably female.

Laure had often let her imagination run wild, remembering the times she had been with Madame Lampron and superimposing the image of the nun over that of the woman who had taught her how to love another woman's body.

She missed life at the Château de Reyval. She missed her old self, her own wantonness and hunger for pleasure which had lain dormant since she had boarded the *Marie-Louison*. Right then, she would have settled for anyone, even her chaperone.

Sister Mélanie was odd, in her own way. She appeared to be strong and severe, but Laure suspected this persona was perhaps all a front. Indeed, the nun was probably sweet and gentle but had to keep a stiff upper lip, remain impassive and show no emotions, like all the nuns of her order.

This only made her more mysterious and attractive in Laure's eyes. During the crossing, they had often shared a bed: two bodies lying side by side in slumber, but never seeking each other's touch, each other's warmth.

Tonight Laure's pangs of desire were eating away at her. However, in the open room into which all the bunks were crammed, and where some people even slept on the bare floor, would Laure dare extend her arm and encircle the tiny body lying peacefully next to her?

If she were to act, she had to be careful. Even though it was the middle of the night, some of the lamps were still lit, casting a strange glow around the room. Most passengers were sound asleep, but their snoring kept others awake.

Under the rough blanket, Laure's hand slowly snaked towards the nun who lay with her back towards her bedmate. It stopped to rest on the rounded hip, gently pressing to feel its heat through the coarse cloth of the grey, shapeless robe she wore under her habit, which doubled as a night-shirt. Sister Mélanie didn't move, her regular breathing indicating she was deeply asleep.

Slowly working her hand upwards, Laure felt the inward curve of the nun's waist and cautiously moved on in search of a pert breast. She found her prey and gently cupped it. The nipple stiffened readily and Laure was delighted by such an immediate response. Sister Mélanie slowly turned onto her back, still asleep and totally unaware her charge intended to explore her chaste body so daringly.

Laure continued her search, lowering her hand to the hem of the nun's robe. Her fingers slid under the fabric, gently caressing soft skin as they glided back up the slim leg.

She paused mid-thigh, resting the palm of her hand on the inside, where the flesh was smooth and warm. With her other hand, she drew her own chemise up above her waist, her fingers quickly aiming for that space between her legs where the dark curls were growing wetter with each excited beat of her heart.

In slumber, Sister Mélanie parted her legs slightly, as if to invite Laure's hand to explore further. The maid continued her caresses up and down the nun's thigh, whilst her other hand promptly started its sensuous dance on her own moist folds.

She could hear noises coming from above, a surge of activity on deck. The shouting and the pounding of the boards covered the sigh which rose from her throat as a bolt of pleasure pierced her throbbing bud. She turned her face towards her companion and found Sister

Mélanie was awake, watching her through half-open eyes.

She slowly brought her hand up, all the way up, until her fingertips brushed the nun's pulsating vulva. The wet folds were eager for Laure's touch, the swollen kernel of joy stiff with anticipation. At the same time, Sister Mélanie's hand ran up Laure's thigh as well, in an attempt to reciprocate and to discover her charge's own centre of pleasure. The women lay side by side for a moment, silently fondling each other whilst the noises above them grew more insistent.

Soon their mouths found each other's. Laure, becoming bolder as the commotion up on deck created a greater diversion, quickly took hold of Sister Mélanie's thin lips, gently capturing her mouth in a warm kiss.

The nun lay idle, except for the fingers which demurely tried to find their way between the girl's legs. Suddenly, she pulled back.

'We should not . . .' she protested weakly in a whisper.

Laure moved closer and cuddled up against her in an effort to quieten her.

'Don't talk,' she advised. 'Let us enjoy in silence; we have very little time.'

Once again her lips pressed against the woman's mouth. It was clear the nun had never been touched before, but was willing to be seduced by her lovely charge.

They lay still as some of the men got up and walked across the room, dodging sleeping bodies. Curious to know what was happening on deck, they took the lamps out with them, leaving the room in darkness.

Laure immediately made the most of this unanticipated privacy and quickly pulled up both their chemises. She rolled over on top of Sister Mélanie and let their breasts brush against each other's. Laure's large, smooth globes entirely covered those, small and pert, of the nun.

Their hands blindly explored each other's sensuous

curves and warm flesh, before rediscovering the moist folds. Laure became the teacher, her expert touch soon echoed by the nun's tiny hands as their mouths remained glued together in a passionate kiss.

Their wantonness was unleashed: Laure's urges had been repressed for so long; the nun's sensuality finally allowed to reveal itself.

The commotion outside the room increased as more passengers awoke and made their way onto the deck one after the other. No-one noticed what was going on in the small bunk near the far wall, where the nun and her charge lay.

A few minutes later, a message was relayed all across the ship: they had arrived in Québec.

Clamours of joy erupted all over the ship, drowning out Sister Mélanie's sighs. Totally oblivious to what was happening, Laure was more excited by the thought of taking the virgin lying next to her. Two of her fingers penetrated the nun fully, engulfed by the warm flesh that throbbed in excitement. The bud was stiff and protruded invitingly, aroused out of its imposed slumber.

By now the nun was learning quickly, her hands finding their way over the maid's body, demurely flickering over the wet love-lips, discovering another woman's flesh. Laure sighed as well. At last, after such a long deprivation, she was enjoying the close contact of warm flesh.

Sister Mélanie was hot, her skin burning under the force of passion surpressed for so long. Laure tasted the softness of the woman's neck before her mouth settled on those small breasts. Her nipples were irresistible and the nun moaned with each lick of Laure's tongue.

The woman was now passive, eager to be taken down the road of pleasure. Laure was happy to oblige. There was hardly anybody left in the large room. Most of the passengers were on deck, waiting for the cattle to be unloaded before they would be allowed to leave the ship.

But Laure and her chaperone were oblivious to the world around them and their moans and sighs grew louder with every embrace. Laure could hardly stand the violence of the passion mounting within her, pushing to be released. Her mouth still glued to the nun's breasts, she rolled onto her side and slipped her hands between her own legs.

Her stiff bud was begging for a caress, a caress strong enough to make it burst in pleasure. She rubbed it forcefully with her fingertips, her hand too small to cover the whole of the wet, swollen vulva. Sister Mélanie's hand joined hers amidst the slick folds, resulting in an exquisite torture which soon translated into a wave of ecstasy contracting her whole body, lifting her hips off the bed as her back arched in a spasm of fulfilment.

She let go of her own vulva and once again reached out to explore the nun's. But Sister Mélanie did not cease her caresses. The soft touch of her novice fingers was enough to bring Laure to her peak again, sending her hips up and down in a second, pulsating climax.

Laure reciprocated, determined to give the nun a taste of what she had undoubtedly never felt before. Kneeling down between the woman's parted legs, Laure bent to kiss her flesh, her tongue expertly teasing the tiny, swollen shaft whilst her fingers kept penetrating the virgin tunnel.

Sister Mélanie lay back, abandoning herself to the maid, grabbing and kneading her own breasts in an effort to enhance her pleasure. She finally came with a sob from the heart of her desire, repressed since she had taken her vows.

Silently, they lay side by side for what seemed an eternity. Laure was feeling sleepy now, happily fulfilled by the sweetness of the pleasure, still reeling from its fire. Her limbs were heavy with exhaustion, and she couldn't move even though she had wanted to be off this ship for many weeks. But she felt warm and secure in the arms of her lover, even after such a brief encounter.

The ship was being unloaded and shook under the heavy movements of the cattle. Sister Mélanie slowly got up and dressed without uttering a word, trying to keep her balance despite the swaying of the boat. Not once did she look at Laure, as if she was ashamed of what had just happened.

Laure didn't have any such regret. All that really mattered was that she had taken and received pleasure, something she could not live without. With luck, she never would again.

Sister Mélanie made her way out of the room. Laure turned over and went to sleep. She would let the others disembark first. Now that they had arrived, she was in no hurry to leave the ship. She was enjoying the beginning of her new life. For it had just started off on a good note.

She was aware of the hand on her, but she was sleeping so soundly she didn't react immediately. The fingers were soft but strong, slowly tracing the contours of her bottom. The blanket had been tossed aside and Laure lay naked on her stomach, eyes closed, legs slightly parted.

The hand continued its exploration, fingers gliding into the cleft of her behind, sliding down the valley that was still wet, until they brushed against her sleepy bud. Only then did Laure open her eyes. Her dark mane had fallen over her face, forming a curtain through which she could see without being seen.

The orange glow of a lamp provided enough light to see the hand holding it, a hand probably similar to the one softly caressing her at that very moment. Laure shivered in excitement at the thought. The man holding the lamp had long, pale fingers, crooked around the handle. She could also see that the first two fingers twisted in a funny way.

Now fully awake, she noticed a peculiar bump on the

side of the man's wrist, just above the cuff of his white shirt, as if the bone had been broken and had not set correctly. The stranger's arm looked strong but that was all she could see, for the rest of his body was under cover of darkness.

She was being caressed by a stranger, a man she couldn't see. The notion aroused her. She could hear him breathing and felt the warmth of his breath on her naked back. She forced herself to remain still, although the finger torturing her wet slit was doing its best to make her respond. She pushed her hips sideways lasciviously, as if asleep and pretending to unwittingly escape from the invasion.

He moved closer to the bed and she could almost make out his face in the shadows. Now she could see his eyes, two black pearls which shone as they quickly travelled over her body, not noticing she was awake and watching through the curtain of her hair. He held the lamp steady whilst his other hand intimately explored the sleeping beauty.

Laure couldn't help a faint sigh. There was a fingertip on her swollen bud, tormenting her. The finger slid up and down at a slow, maddening pace, swaying sideways and toying with the tiny shaft which seemed to have a life of its own. The pressure was at times strong, but often subsided to a mere brushing, and she felt her pleasure mounting quickly.

Once again she looked at him. This time she could see a square jaw, a slightly open mouth encased by sensuous lips, and his dark eyes shining with desire. She would have liked to turn over and offer herself completely, yet she sensed he preferred her like this; a naked, sleeping figure half hidden under the dark carpet of her hair, a mere slave to his expert fingers.

This man knew how to bring a woman to her peak by giving her, slow-building sensual exhilaration. Laure wanted him, whoever he was. She wanted him first to pleasure her, then to join her in bed. For now, he was doing as she had hoped, and she went on pretending to sleep. She didn't want to move, afraid of breaking the spell. But she couldn't help jerking her hips as the wave of arousal inside her grew stronger. She knew her ultimate release was near.

She came violently, the muscles in her legs tensing under the strength of her climax. She closed her eyes and felt his hand move away as he stepped back. In just a few seconds, she would turn over and invite him to join her. Right now she was still transported by the subsiding waves making her vulva clench sporadically, sending shivers through her whole body.

She took a deep breath, preparing herself to face the stranger. She opened her eyes and threw her head back, tossing her hair away from her face. But all she could see was darkness. The man had gone.

Quickly turning her head the other way she saw the glow of the lamp disappearing up the ladder leading to the deck.

Chapter Eleven

*L*aure almost lost her balance as she took her first few steps on the shore. It felt awkward to walk on dry land again and not have to counteract the swaying motion she had grown accustomed to during the long crossing. She breathed in deeply, almost surprised not to smell the salty sea water.

Instead, she noticed the scent of pine needles, freshly sawn wood and wet grass. She felt happy, hungry, restless. She longed to run in the forest, lie in fresh hay and dig her fingers deep into the soft earth.

The strange faces at the dock were a welcome sight to her. Onlookers watched from a distance as the dockers unloaded the many cases of goods from the ship. Laure was quick to notice Father Olivier had not lied when he had said there were too many men and not enough women in this town.

Judging by the way the dockers looked at her and the other girls who had just disembarked, Laure knew she was also a welcome sight to them. She basked in their attention for a moment, all smiles and beaming as she casually walked among them, mesmerised by the half-naked bodies glistening with sweat in the early morning light.

During the trip, everyone on board had been very

proper indeed, even the sailors. Despite the harsh conditions, there were no ankles, no forearms, and certainly no bare chests on display. But now she was back in the real world. Priests and nuns blended with the townspeople and now became a minority. Sister Mélanie seemed to have disappeared, and for a moment Laure felt free, happy to be alive. Men brushed passed her and never missed an opportunity to flash her a smile or a wink. In every man she greeted she looked for a sign, knowing the stranger from the boat could not be far away. She would find him, and recognise him, if only her eyes could meet his.

But as the loaded carts slowly made their way to their various destinations, so did the passengers and soon Laure was left alone once again with a group of nuns and priests.

'There you are,' Sister Mélanie's voice came from behind her. 'We must go now. Come.'

Laure was ushered into a coach where the other girls were already seated. She cast one last glance back before climbing on board and noticed two men looking at her with keen interest. She heard them whisper, but couldn't make out what they were saying. Two words reached her ears and echoed through her head: king's girls. The town knew they had arrived.

Laure was pleased to have made such an impact. But she was more anxious to find her mysterious lover from the boat. As the horse slowly pulled the heavy load up the steep hill to the higher part of town, Laure kept a vigil by the window. He had to be somewhere nearby; and he had to know who she was. If he had any common sense, he would have figured out that a young woman travelling alone and escorted by nuns could only be a king's girl. But would he make the effort to find her?

She studied every face she saw. By now the sun had risen and the town was bustling. The scene was surreal: men – soldiers, clerks, farmers and workers – as far as the eye could see. The crowd parted to make way for the coach and hats were deferentially lifted in greeting. Laure felt like a princess.

Within one day she was desperate to get out. She was sharing a room with seven other young women: a dormitory on the top floor of the convent where beds were arranged in neat rows, each with a large chest at its foot.

Laure had been separated from the other girls who had come over on the *Marie-Louison*. They were sleeping in another room, which didn't really matter to her anyway. Despite having spent more than three months with them, she hadn't made any friends.

The girls who shared her dorm had been there for a while and friendships had already been formed. Laure felt like an outsider, but she had no intention of making any effort to mingle, figuring she was better off on her own.

The girls were all friendly and cheerful, except for Marguerite, a tall redhead who took satisfaction in bossing everyone around. The first evening, as Laure examined her trousseau, Marguerite walked towards her, flanked by two of the other girls. She looked at Laure disdainfully, then turned to talk to one of her companions who also looked at Laure and giggled.

'So,' Marguerite asked. 'What do you think men will see in you? What do you have to offer as a wife?'

'I don't know,' Laure replied cautiously. 'I just think there are too few of us, and we are all bound to find husbands soon enough.'

'She is right,' a girl called Angelique said from the far end of the room. 'We are the ones with plenty of choice. And I, for one, am in no hurry.'

'Me neither,' another girl said. 'As long as he has a big farm and plenty of animals.'

Marguerite burst into laughter. 'A big farm! My dear, what he owns does not necessarily make a man a good husband.'

'Quite right,' her companion said sarcastically. 'We also want our husbands to be pious and good, don't we?' The trio laughed loudly as Louise slowly walked over. Laure noticed that she looked older than the others, and was not at all pretty.

'You seem so contemptuous of the young men who have called on us recently,' Louise said to Marguerite. 'What exactly was wrong with them that you refused their marriage proposals? If I were lucky enough to have received a proposal, I would have been married a long time ago. All your suitors are nice, hard-working men. Once they marry they will have their own land. What more do you want?'

Marguerite turned to Laure. 'Let's see what our new friend has to say,' she said. 'If you could have any man at all, what would you look for? Someone with his own farm? A few horses? Vast amount of land?' She paused, looking at Laure.

Laure held her gaze. Marguerite reminded her a bit of herself, in a way. The laces of her bodice were only loosely tied, and under her bonnet her hair appeared to be undone. Just from the way she walked, it was clear Marguerite, like Laure, knew enough about men not to settle for any husband unless he was a good lover.

Marguerite's question remained to be answered. Laure looked at her and smiled. 'A good body, of course,' was her reply.

'Naturally,' Louise said. 'I also want a man who is healthy. But that is not a priority, is it?'

Laure and Marguerite looked at each other. They didn't need to speak anymore to know they shared a common passion, a yearning for flesh that couldn't be appeased by just anyone.

The long coach ride was uncomfortable. Laure tried to rest her head on the thick pile of clothing on the seat next to her. But the bumpy road made it impossible for her to get any sleep.

They had left before dawn and had stopped only once to give the horses a rest. The coach was loaded with food and clothes the nuns were taking to a remote village. The trip there and back would take the whole day, and Laure had been asked to come with them. This way, she could better see the land to which she now belonged, and hopefully get acquainted with what was expected of her as a settler's wife.

They arrived at midday. The late-August sun was hot and beat down on her head. Even though Laure wore only a thin, grey dress, the layers of petticoats underneath were irritating. Unbeknownst to the nuns, the thick bloomers they had provided for her had remained in her room, tucked away under the pillow. Laure would rather risk a scolding than wear yet another layer of clothing.

The forest suddenly opened onto vast fields, and Laure straightened up. For a moment, she could have believed herself back in France. The crops were plentiful and harvest was in full swing. Wheat bristled in the soft breeze. Further afield, she could just see the heads of the men at work.

As soon as the coach came into view, several young men dropped their tools and began running after it, not slowing down until it reached the tiny village. Laure leaned out of the open window, mesmerised by the sight of all the men chasing them, not slowing their pace until the coach stopped.

'They have been expecting us,' Sister Agathe explained. 'Sometimes it takes months before we can bring them the supplies they have been waiting for.'

The village itself consisted of a few cabins arranged in a square around the church. A man with his wig askew opened the door of the coach and greeted the nuns. 'Welcome, sisters, welcome.'

The man was obviously important in the village, but his state of dress left much to be desired. Though his shirt was made of expensive fabric, it was torn and dirty, and worth no more than a rag. His breeches were in better shape, but his feet were bare.

In fact, most of the people who had gathered around the coach were dressed simply in work clothes. Some of the nuns averted their eyes as bare-chested young men began unloading the boxes perched on the roof of the coach. Great clouds of dust rose around their stamping feet and cries of joy surrounded the nuns and their charge. Laure was distracted and confused but she hadn't missed any of the shy smiles cast in her direction, even though right now everyone seemed much more interested in the goods the nuns had brought with them.

Behind her, Sister Jeannette took Laure by the arm and led her away. 'Come, child. We will attend Mass and this afternoon we will go to the farms to distribute the rest of the supplies.'

Laure turned towards her and immediately stepped back, gasping with horror. Right behind the nun stood a man who could have come right out of her worst nightmare. He was a sinister creature, with skin the colour of bronze and straight, jet-black hair tied in braids. But most frightening was the paint on his face, a series of bright red stripes drawn diagonally from his nose to his ears. A strip of leather around his head was tied at the back and sported a bundle of dark feathers. His piercing eyes were dark and inscrutable. He showed no expression and simply stared at Laure. Sister Jeannette gave her a puzzled look, turned around and started shaking with laughter, along with all the villagers when they realised what Laure had been so frightened about.

'Have no fear, my child. This is Falcon Eye, a member of the Huron tribe. He lives here with the farmers. He does not speak our language very well, but he is a good Christian.'

As they made their way to the church, Laure looked over her shoulder. Indeed, Falcon Eye was helping the men unload the coach and, from a distance, he didn't look at all frightening. His clothes were made solely of deer skin, as were the weird slippers on his feet. So, was he one of those savages she had heard so much about? Still uneasy, Laure didn't waste any time following the nuns, eager to put some distance between herself and this unusual man.

The coolness inside the church was soothing. In the sacristy, Laure was given a towel and fresh water to wash her face and hands. She felt better, though tired. During Mass she dozed off, kneeling with her forehead propped against her clasped hands. The nuns didn't dare interrupt what they assumed was fervent prayer. The bells woke her and she walked out refreshed and rested.

The first farm they visited was located further up the dirt road. The house itself was enormous, as were the barn and the stables. The coach hadn't even stopped before the farmer, his wife, and their twelve children rushed out to gather round it.

Noticing Laure's astonished expression, Sister Jeannette smiled at her. 'They are also good Christians,' she said. 'As you can see, families here are very large.'

Behind the children, several young men also came running out. No doubt a farm this large needed the help of many extra hands.

The young men seemed happy to see the nuns, but even happier to see Laure. One of them, Louis, caught her eye right away. Maybe it was his beard, so pale it looked almost white. His curly hair was tied at the back of his neck and, though not as pale as his beard, made his tanned skin look even darker. Indeed, he was by far the best-looking lad, and he held Laure's gaze for a moment.

Through his sweat-soaked shirt, she could see the sinew of his muscles, and she realised how hungry she was: hungry for young, male flesh. When he casually offered to show her around, she didn't wait for Sister Jeannette's approval. After all, she had been sent here to find a husband.

He proudly gave her a tour of the barn and the henhouse as if they belonged to him, talking incessantly.

'You know, Mademoiselle Laure, I work very hard,' he explained. 'I need a lot of money if I am to buy my own farm next year. But if I were to marry, the governor would then give me the land for free.'

But Laure wasn't really listening. As they walked from one building to the next, she constantly looked around to see whether they were alone. Unfortunately, there was always a child in sight, and she quickly grew impatient.

When Louis mentioned that prior to her arrival he was working behind the barn to sort out the corn crop, Laure suddenly displayed a keen interest and asked him to take her there.

Just as she had thought, they were alone there, away from prying eyes. Yet that wasn't enough to give Louis any ideas. Maybe all this talk about being a good Christian had blinded him to other delights the world – and Laure – had to offer. He continued his lecture on crop harvest, taking an ear of corn and peeling back the green skin to show Laure the golden kernels arranged, row upon row, in a thick cylinder.

She closed her hand around it and was amazed by its warmth. Each rounded bud shone in the sunlight, soft and firm. From the corner of her eye, she watched Louis's reaction as she tightened her grip around the shaft and slowly ran it up and down its length.

At first, he didn't seem to make much of it, but the look she gave him was enough to make him understand what she wanted. He blushed a bright crimson and stepped back. Never ceasing her suggestive caress on the ear of corn, Laure brushed up against him. Louis seemed surprised, but didn't try to move away.

His manly scent made her even hotter and she pressed her hips against his thighs. Hesitantly, he laid his hands on her shoulders and blushed further.

'Mademoiselle Laure? What are you doing?'

In reply, she dropped the ear of corn and quickly undid his breeches. She felt him tremble, but again he didn't stop her. Slipping her hand in his trousers, she grabbed hold of his turgid phallus and expertly coaxed it to stiffness.

It felt good to have him come alive in the palm of her hand. Only then did she remember how long it had been since she had been so close to a man.

She fondled him with both hands, looking down at this marvel now awakening and twitching. Louis moaned uncomfortably and Laure was amused at his reaction.

'What is the matter?' she asked. 'Have you not been with a woman before?'

'Oh, yes, Mademoiselle,' he stammered. 'Only . . .'

'Only what?'

'Well, it was a long time ago, and she wasn't a nice girl such as yourself. Now, I do think we ought to be married if . . .'

She silenced him with a kiss. Her sex was already wet with desire and she knew she had very little time. Licking the sweat off his neck, she grew even more excited and could feel him warm up to her as well.

She undid the buttons at the front of her dress, and then the laces of her chemise. Louis was still unsure, but once she took his hands and set them on her engorged breasts, he suddenly lost all his inhibitions.

He laid her down on the pile of corn and lowered himself between her parted legs. In a fraction of a second, he glided within her and Laure gasped with joy. Sensations almost forgotten resurfaced and she moaned against his chest.

Birds chirped in the distance and the hot summer sun reminded her of those careless days at the château. Maybe her presence here was meant to be. She was, after all, just as untamed as this land, wild and free for the taking.

She let pleasure transport her as Louis's thick shaft thrust back and forth inside her. They climaxed together, almost immediately. Louis then rolled onto his back and closed his eyes and Laure looked in despair at his phallus, now rapidly shrinking, and cried out. 'What? Is that it?'

He gave her a puzzled look. 'Well, for now . . .'

Laure lasciviously climbed on top of him and rhythmically pressed her crotch against his. She wanted more. Rubbing her chest on his face, she writhed endlessly, wanting to feel more of him and hoping to reawaken his manhood.

It had very little effect. Despite his youth and desire, Louis was probably too exhausted from working in the fields to be able to satisfy her. In the meantime, her own flesh yearned for more stimulation. She slid off him to lie on her side, took his hand and put it on her wet slit.

He stroked her rather clumsily, just enough to maintain her excitement. Laure bit her lip, realising that if she was to have more, she would have to take matters into her own hands.

The ear of corn she had dropped on the ground lay just inches from her head. It caught her eye and its phallic shape gave her the most wicked idea. Looking at Louis defiantly, she grabbed the corn and inserted it in her vagina.

He watched in dismay as she began to masturbate. As she approached her climax he took hold of the ear of corn and pushed her back. She lay with her arms open wide and her knees up against her chest as her lover manoeuvred the improvised phallus inside her tunnel. With his other hand, he rubbed her swollen bud hard and fast. Indeed, he had potential, Laure thought. She climaxed again, moaning as pleasure swept through her.

When she glanced down at him, she saw his member still dormant. Suddenly angry, she pushed him away, drew down her skirts and fastened her bodice. Though her whole body still shuddered as her orgasm slowly subsided, she knew this one time with Louis would be their last. She wanted nothing more to do with him.

As she walked back towards the farmhouse, she saw

no sign of disapproval from her chaperones. Obviously, they had no inkling of what she had been up to. Stifling a groan of satisfaction, Laure realised it would be rather easy to escape their watch and meet men behind their backs. She resolved to keep an eye out for any opportunity, and any able – and willing – body.

Louis had barely shown up behind her when Sister Jeannette announced it was time to leave. Just before she climbed into the coach, she felt his hand on her shoulder and she turned around, irritated.

'Mademoiselle Laure,' he said uncertainly. 'Will you marry me?'

Laure gave him a blank look and climbed on board. 'I'm sorry, Louis. I don't think I like you all that much.'

His sad eyes followed her as the driver whipped the horses on. Laure looked away. 'It was very wise,' one of the nuns said. 'You shouldn't accept the first proposal you get. There will be other young men, not to worry.' Laure didn't reply, but deep within her she hoped the nun was right.

The ride back to Québec City was more comfortable, as the coach was now empty except for the passengers. Yet, for Laure, it seemed to take longer. They stopped at the village to get some food and then the sun began its descent in the West.

Laura let her head bob against the back of her seat. It had been a long day, she was very tired and she drifted off to sleep.

Suddenly, a loud cracking sound followed by a violent jolt woke her with a start. The driver cursed loudly, then immediately apologised to the nuns. Laure had to maintain her balance and brace herself against sliding off the wooden bench. She didn't have to get out to know a wheel had broken.

Outside, the sun hung low and painted the sky with streaks of orange and yellow. The driver insisted they stay inside whilst he surveyed the damage.

'Bad news, sisters,' he said through the window. 'This

is a nasty break and I don't know how long it will take to fix it. Do you think anyone at the convent will send for you?'

'Not for a while,' Sister Jeannette replied. 'They are expecting us back quite late.'

The man took his cap off and scratched his head quizzically. 'Well, I'll try my best.'

He barely had time to finish his sentence before a man came out of the woods and approached the coach.

'Can I help?'

Sister Jeannette looked out, her face lighting up. She thanked the stranger and ordered the nuns and Laure to get out.

'Are you sure about him?' Sister Laurette asked in a whisper. 'Do you know who this young man is?'

'Yes,' Sister Jeannette replied. 'But we need help right now. Come.'

The driver helped them get out whilst the stranger knelt down next to the broken wheel. Normally, Laure wouldn't have even looked at him, but what she had overheard stirred her curiosity. She moved away from the coach, keeping her eyes on the stranger. She was surprised to see how young he looked; his deep and mellow voice sounded like that of a more mature man.

The two men worked hard, and Laure had plenty of time to examine the stranger. There was something very attractive about him. His untamed hair was dark and loosely tied with a black ribbon at the back of his neck. He wore peculiar boots, made of deerskin and adorned with colourful beads. Under his rolled up sleeves, his arms were tanned and muscular; his skin covered in fine black hair. In the fading sunlight, he looked even darker: hair, eyes and complexion.

His strong jaw and aquiline nose made him definitely handsome. She especially liked his smooth hollow cheeks and jutting cheekbones. They gave him character.

In fact, the more she looked at him, the more Laure found herself attracted to him. Keeping her ears open to

165

catch snippets of the nuns' conversations, she managed to learn the man was a fur trapper, one of those people who had turned their back on civilised life to mingle with the natives and learn their ways.

This, in fact, was the opposite of what the king wanted. Everyone in the colony was to strive to teach and educate the natives, not the other way around. Worse still, the man hardly ever came to church anymore. But these were minor flaws as far as Laure was concerned. She moved closer, trying to catch his attention, but unfortunately, he was totally immersed in his work.

It was getting dark and cold, but Laure didn't mind. She just couldn't take her eyes off him, and was delighted when she heard the driver ask him to fetch the oil lamp. At last, she would see him better. As she tried to make out his face in the flickering light, she knew there was something familiar about him, but she couldn't tell exactly what.

It wasn't until he held up the lamp and her eyes fell on his hand that a bolt of excitement pierced her. She recognised that hand: the long fingers, the way the first two twisted around the handle, and the peculiar bump on his wrist. He was the stranger from the boat.

'Is this going to take much longer?' she heard herself asking in a shaky voice. She didn't really want an answer, but hoped the man would look at her.

He did. But the look he gave her was disinterested and far from friendly.

'It won't be long now, mademoiselle.'

And he was right. Moments later, the wheel was repaired and the nuns climbed back on board. The stranger gathered up the small bundle of tools he carried with him as he prepared to leave, while Laure desperately tried to think of something to make him recognise her. Of course, he had never seen her face. On the boat, she had been lying on her stomach with her hair around her face.

Then she had an idea. It was unimaginative, but worth a try. Subtly, she undid the ribbon of her bonnet and quietly pulled down the pin that held her hair up underneath. She walked up to the stranger who was standing by the coach, helping the nuns get in.

At the last minute, she pretended to trip and threw herself forward. As she landed, face first in the dirt, she shook her head in an attempt to make her hair fall in disarray around her face.

The nuns shrieked. As the stranger came down on one knee to help her up, Laure let out a faint moan. He grabbed her by the arm, pulled her to her feet and brushed her hair away from her face with his dirty hand.

Their eyes locked and they held each other's gaze. She saw the sparkle in his eyes and knew for certain he had now recognised her. His hold on her arm tightened slightly and she moaned again.

'Have we met?' he asked in an amused tone.

'I wouldn't think so,' Laure replied. 'I just arrived on the boat yesterday morning.'

'I see.'

He helped her brush the dirt of her skirt and, without releasing his hold on her, ushered her into the coach.

'Are you all on your way to the convent?' he asked deferentially.

'Naturally,' Sister Jeannette replied. 'That's where we live. Where else would we be going at this hour?'

He closed the door and leant through the window. 'I wish you all a safe trip then,' he said.

'Thank you very much for your help,' one of the nuns said. 'And we hope to see you at Mass on Sunday, François.'

He smiled and looked at each of them in turn, letting his eyes linger on Laure perhaps a little longer. 'I will definitely be there if I am in town.'

He stood back, waved at the driver and watched motionless as the coach took off. From where she was sitting, Laure could see his silhouette gradually disappearing in the dark. François. At least now she knew his name. And he had recognised her.

He would come for her soon. She just knew it.

Chapter Twelve

*L*aure shivered in the cool night air. It was her third night spent by the open window, hoping to see a dark figure prowling around the building, looking for her. François would come for her, she was certain of that. But when?

Each night she waited patiently as the other girls lay sleeping. Nobody could see her in the dark. Although she was frozen to the bone, she didn't dare shut the window. What if he came? Would she be able to pull up the large pane of glass quickly and swiftly enough to call out to him? She didn't even want to take that chance.

As dawn rose beyond the trees, she finally decided return to her bed. She only had a few hours before attending morning Mass. Of course, there were plenty of opportunities to doze off whilst pretending to pray.

On the fourth night, noises stirred her. She straightened up, her heart beating fast, and anxiously searched the dark night. At first she couldn't tell where the sounds were coming from, but she was sure she could hear whispers and giggles.

Then, she saw them: three silhouettes, clad in black cloaks, running across the lawn and disappearing into the trees. Laure thought she recognised the tallest woman as Marguerite, but she couldn't really be sure. Her curiosity soon got the better of her and she left her vigil by the window.

As silently as she could, she walked around the dormitory. When she reached Marguerite's bed, she saw a sleeping body neatly tucked under the blanket. So it couldn't be her. Or could it?

Moving closer, she failed to hear any sounds coming from the bed. She pulled down the blanket, and her suspicions were confirmed: the sleeping body was in fact a bundle of rags arranged to look as if a person was lying in bed.

She then checked Marie's and Antoinette's beds. As she had thought, the trio was out for the night. So it was them she had seen running away. They would have to come back eventually, Laure assumed, so she stayed by the window, waiting for them.

This proved to be much more exciting than waiting for François. She knew they would have to return before dawn, and she was impatient to find out where they had gone.

It was hours before they came back. Although Laure was quite sure she hadn't fallen asleep, she didn't see them returning across the courtyard, and it was the sound of squeaking floorboards that caught her attention.

They had sneaked back in and were getting into bed by the time Laure caught up with them.

'Where have you been?' she whispered.

Startled, the girls looked at one another. Obviously, they hadn't heard her approach and were surprised to have been discovered.

'This doesn't concern you,' Marguerite replied coldly as she took the rags out from under her blanket.

Laure came closer. She noticed the smell of alcohol floating around the girls and guessed they had been drinking. But as she walked up to Marguerite, she noticed another scent, one far more enticing: the scent of a man.

Her flesh started to moisten as she realised what the girls had been up to. For there was no mistake to be made: she knew that aroma well, the perfume of a man's honey as it flows from his rod and splatters across a lover's belly.

She felt hot and hungry. Just knowing her companions had found a way to get out at night and meet with men was enough to arouse her. She wanted so much to join them. But still Marguerite paid no attention to her.

'Take me with you next time . . .' she ventured.

'What?' Marguerite asked, annoyed. 'Take you where? How would you know where we have been?' She turned and tucked the rags into an open chest.

Laure was incensed. She had to convince Marguerite to take her with them, but first she would have to let them know she had figured out where they had gone.

Lifting Marguerite's dress, Laure quickly slipped her fingers between the girl's legs and touched her sex. Marguerite gave a little cry but didn't try to pull away.

And just as Laure had thought, Marguerite's pussy lips were wet, swollen and slick as she lightly brushed them. Marguerite finally reacted. She grabbed Laure's hand and pushed it away, then turned around to face her.

'Well,' she said with a knowing smile. 'Maybe you would enjoy coming with us.'

Laure pressed her body against hers. 'Take me with you next time,' she said again as she ran her hand across Marguerite's chest. 'And I will do anything you want. Anything.'

'We'll see,' Marguerite announced. 'Now go to sleep. And be quiet: I don't want anyone else to find out we were out.'

The girls walked so fast Laure had a hard time keeping up with them. But she was too wise to complain. For the past three days now she had been waiting impatiently for them to tell her when they planned their next outing. Since the night she had found them out, her level of excitement had been constant.

She had also given up on her idea that François would come for her. Right now she wanted a man, any man, and the prospect of feeling male flesh pressing against her once again made her pussy quiver with expectation.

They headed for the soldiers' barracks. From what Marguerite had explained, Laure knew that twice a week the young men had an evening off, when they drank and sang until the early hours of the morning.

About three months ago, Marguerite, Antoinette and Marie had started visiting them. Of course, the evenings then took on an entirely different atmosphere. The girls always left as soon as they were certain the nuns were asleep. That was Marie's job. And they had to be careful to return before anyone awoke. To date, everything had always gone according to plan.

The barracks were quite a long way from the convent, and as they walked through the woods, Laure breathed in the musty scent of the cool air. Tonight she was at one with nature.

Since arriving at the colony, life had been easier and the rules a bit more lax, but Laure didn't enjoy as much freedom as she needed. As at the convent in France, she had to wear layer upon layer of clothes, at times so thick she couldn't feel her own body through them. Naturally, she had tried as often as possible to discard the bloomers. That was her little secret. She liked the way her thighs rubbed together, freely, as she walked. The nuns had no way of knowing, and the notion made Laure feel even more wicked.

It made up for her time on the boat, where Laure was scolded time and again when she dared to forget a single layer of clothing. Of course, the many ladders made it easier for everyone to see what she wore under her dress and she couldn't escape her chaperone's prying eyes.

But here, in the colony, the dress code was relaxed due to the intense heat of the midday sun. That was no excuse not to wear a minimum of layers, but at least Laure didn't feel so constricted anymore.

Tonight, God willing, she would be able to undress and luxuriate in her own nakedness. She longed to feel the contact of another body against hers: a man, any man, with hard muscles and smooth skin.

Her heart pounded fast as they approached the barracks. They couldn't afford to be seen here either. Marguerite went first, venturing behind the row of small wooden buildings, along the edge of the forest, and ducking as she passed the windows. The others followed, one at a time, and they finally met up by the side of a longer cabin filled with the sound of loud voices and laughter. Marie stood guard as the girls went in, one after the other.

Laure followed Marguerite and Antoinette inside. The trek had made her nervous, but her fears vanished the moment she entered the room and saw all those gorgeous young men who were, naturally, delighted to see the girls.

Marguerite and Antoinette went from one young man to the next, greeting them with warm kisses. Laure stood back and looked around. The room was bare, except for a few tables and chairs; the floor covered with chunks of caked mud. Bottles and hats had been casually dumped on tables, tunics thrown over the backs of chairs. Then Laure suddenly noticed a lone riding crop discarded on a table, and for a moment, bitter memories dampened her excitement, but soon the voices around her brought her back to reality.

'And who have you brought with you?' one lad asked as he looked Laure over.

'This is a new girl, Laure. She was quite eager to come with us. Weren't you, Laure?'

Laure smiled and followed the other girls, hugging the men and pressing her body against theirs. There were six of them, all wearing the same bright-red army breeches and white shirts. Some still had their tunics on, but a few had already unfastened their shirts. All of them leered appreciatively at Laure. Of course, as the new girl, she expected to be the focus of attention tonight.

She could see her companions already quite busy kissing and pawing some of the soldiers, but true to her old self, Laure had something quite different in mind. She didn't want to be like the others. She would show them how special she was.

The man who had spoken was still looking at her, clearly interested, so she went to him. He kissed her on the neck, roughly, then pushed her back.

'You smell nice, sweety,' he said. 'Now show us some skin.'

The other soldiers gathered around eagerly. Delighted by such a keen invitation, Laure casually let her cloak fall to the ground, set her foot on a chair and slowly raised her skirt. Inch by inch, her pale skin was exposed, the men cheering her on as she progressed. Suddenly, one of them leant forward and caressed her leg.

This was what Laure had been hoping for. Without wasting any time, she grabbed the riding crop off the table and slapped his hand. He stood back in surprise and the others burst into laughter.

'You cannot touch until I give you permission,' Laure said defiantly.

The poor lad looked around, not quite knowing what to say. Laure brought the tip of the riding crop to his chest and used it to undo the laces of his shirt. Not a word was spoken. The only audible sound was that of heavy breathing.

The man let Laure unfasten his shirt without protest. She walked around him, caressing the back of his legs and his bottom with the crop. The breeches were tight and showed every contour of his muscles. In front, his hard phallus pushed against the fabric and visibly twitched.

'Undress, young man,' Laure ordered. 'Let's see what you have to offer.'

Hesitating, he looked at his fellow soldiers.

'You heard the lady, Gilles,' Marguerite shouted. 'Do as you are told.'

He undressed silently, without looking at her. Marguerite came to stand by Laure's side and kissed her on the cheek. 'I am impressed,' she said before stepping back.

Laure smiled and looked around. The men all had visible erections by now. And they were all looking at her in awe, almost as if they were afraid of her.

'Kneel on the chair,' Laure ordered Gilles once he stood completely naked. 'Face the back and lean over.'

He obeyed, showing off his muscular buttocks, his cock bobbing in the air. Standing behind him, Laure ran the tip of the riding crop up along the inside of his legs. He quivered and his knees trembled as she got closer to his dangling balls.

That's where she hit him first, with a light flick of her wrist. He gasped and bucked, then reared backwards as if he wanted her to do it again.

She didn't. Slowly walking around him, she caressed him with the crop, toying with his nipples which puckered under the rough touch of the leather tip, tickling and gently whipping his flanks, flickering his prick which grew harder still.

She heard him moan as she teased with him. With a faint gesture of her head, she invited Marguerite to come forward.

'Sit on the floor with your back to the chair,' she ordered. 'Then lean your head back beneath him. I want you to lick him until he's ready to come, but don't allow him to spill a drop until I say otherwise.'

Marguerite promptly obeyed. Tilting her head back on the seat, her mouth was mere inches from his pulsing member. Her tongue nudged it playfully at first, at times barely touching him.

Laure went around the room and examined all the men in turn. 'Who are you?' she asked one as she fondled him through his breeches.

'My name is Laurent, mademoiselle.'

'You have a very big cock, Laurent. Tell me: how long would a woman have to suck you to make you come?'

He swallowed hard before replying. 'I don't know. Perhaps not very long at all.'

'Not good enough,' Laure decreed. 'I want a man who can last a long, long time.'

She stepped back and looked at the group.

'Which one of you gentlemen can hold back the longest?' she asked.

The men looked at each other and shook their heads quizzically. No reply came, so Laure turned to Antoinette and Marie. 'Would you ladies be able to tell me?'

Antoinette laughed and pointed to the man farthest from them. 'That one, Hubert, I would say.'

'Good,' Laure said as she resumed her inspection. She noticed one of the men keenly watching Gilles's bottom, now held high as Marguerite licked his prick. She followed his gaze and walked towards him.

'What are you watching with such interest?' she asked. 'And what is your name?'

'My name is Pierre, mademoiselle. And what I am watching is him.'

From where he was standing, he had a perfect view of Gilles's parted arse-cheeks and could plainly see his puckered ring contracting sporadically.

'Do you like what you see?' Laure asked in a low voice.

He licked his lips and took a deep breath before replying. 'Yes.'

Looking around at the other men, Laure caught exchanged glances. 'I should have known there would be at least one amongst you,' she said. 'Does his arse make you hard?'

'Yes.'

She fondled him through his breeches, then undid the buttons to release his dick from its constraint. He was of considerable size, and very hard. She stroked him up and down a few times but he never even looked at her.

'Go ahead,' she hissed. 'Let us watch what you'll do to him.'

His dick standing proud from the opening of his breeches, Pierre advanced slowly, as if mesmerised, towards Gilles.

'Take your time,' Laure said. 'Make him quiver.' She turned to Marie and Antoinette. 'It is hot in here,' she said. 'You girls should undress. Undress each other, that is.'

The girls joyfully obeyed, slowly shedding their dresses and petticoats, at times stopping to fondle each other and exchange hot, passionate kisses. The men watched intently, enthralled by the unusual show. Laure suspected the girls' regular visits were much more boring, the men simply taking them one after the other.

But tonight she was in charge. Although they were soldiers and she a simple maid, her skills were clearly superior. Being good soldiers, they knew obedience would have its rewards.

'Now,' she said as she turned to the naked girls. 'Let's see.' She ran her hand along Marie's slit, back and forth, and was pleased to find it wet with arousal, then did the same to Antoinette.

'You have to make a choice tonight, my darlings. One of you will get a soft tongue to tickle her clit until she begs for mercy. The other will get the big dick hiding in Laurent's breeches. Which will it be?'

The girls looked at each other with knowing smiles. Marie walked towards Laurent and began undressing him without hesitation. 'I want him,' she said in a decisive tone.

Laurent stood motionless as she undressed him before

she went to lie on a table. Meanwhile, Antoinette had also made her choice. She went to a tall, dark man and grabbed the laces of his shirt. She led him across the room and made him kneel in front of her whilst she sat on a chair, her legs parted.

There were only two men left. Laure knew she wouldn't have to choose between them: she would have them both, together. But first, there were more pressing matters at hand.

Pierre was still busy with Gilles, and he sounded as though he was about to come. Taking the crop once again, Laure decided to help him with a few sharp blows to his behind. 'Faster,' she yelled. 'Harder! Don't hold back.'

Pierre gave an ultimate push and his buttocks visibly contracted under his breeches. He roared as he released his seed, thrust weakly a few times and pulled out, looking totally exhausted.

'Very good,' Laure said, beaming. 'As your reward, you get to pleasure this poor Marguerite who has been so good and obedient tonight.'

Still sitting on the floor, leaning back onto the chair, Marguerite parted her legs and raised her knees towards her chest. As Laure expected, there were no bloomers in sight.

Her exposed pussy was fat and red, glistening brightly and twitching as she spread her knees wider still. Pierre seemed to hesitate for a moment. Laure waved the crop in his direction.

'I will say "please" but only this once,' she advised. 'Now show us what your tongue can do.'

Pierre went down on all fours and lowered his face to Marguerite's flesh. The girl's thighs came down on his shoulders and held him there.

'Good girl,' Laure said to herself before turning to face the two gentlemen with whom she had yet to have her way.

They stood in front of her, boyishly fidgeting, constantly giggling and exchanging glances. Laure took three chairs and arranged them in a circle, then made them sit down. She remained standing and set one foot on the last chair. She lifted her dress onto her lap then parted her pussy lips with her fingers to show the men her pink flesh.

'Please introduce yourselves,' she said casually.

'I am Yvon,' said the taller soldier. 'And this is Claude.'

'Pleased to meet you. Would you like to lick me?'

Without even replying, Yvon went down on his knees and stuck out his tongue, unwilling to waste anymore time. A blow of the crop on his shoulder stopped him cold.

'I only asked if you would like to,' she thundered. 'I didn't ask you to do it. Sit down.'

He crawled back to his chair.

'You have been a naughty boy,' Laure announced. 'You will be punished for that.' She turned to Claude. 'What about you? Would you like to see me come?'

Claude looked at his mate before replying with a faint, 'Yes, mademoiselle.'

Laure quickly ran her fingers up and down her slit. She had been so excited by all the activity she knew her first climax was just a few strokes away.

Pleasure rampaged through her almost immediately. Her thumb flickered forcefully over her swollen bud and she gasped as a violent bolt pierced her. She heard a man groan and when she opened her eyes, she immediately noticed the large, wet patch now adorning Claude's breeches. Just watching her climax had been too much for the poor lad.

Laure laughed scornfully. 'You silly, silly man! You can't even hold back for me! You're not worthy!'

She raised the crop, prepared to strike him. A powerful hand seized her wrist and stopped her arm in mid-air. She had been so caught up in what was happening, she hadn't seen the officer come in.

He took the crop from her hand and gestured for her to sit down. Laure was suddenly worried and looked around. Nobody else seemed to pay any attention to the man, so she concluded perhaps she wasn't in trouble after all.

She glanced at him with devilish eyes, yet bowed her head coyly. His arrival changed everything. The officer was by far the most attractive man in the room. Letting her eyes wander, she ventured a quick look at his breeches, but was disappointed when she saw no sign of arousal. He was obviously stronger than her, both in body and in spirit. And that only made her want him more. She would have him. On her terms.

She raised her skirts completely, sat her naked bottom on the wooden chair and parted her legs, hoping the sight of her still throbbing pussy would have some effect on him. He turned the tables on her by placing his foot on her chair, and setting the tip of his leather boot less than an inch from her flesh.

They held each other's gaze for a moment, totally unaware of anything else going on in the room. Laure didn't care for the other soldiers, nor for her companions anymore. On the whole, they had proven to be rather weak and easily manipulated. The new arrival, however . . .

'I am Laure,' she said politely as she undid the buttons of her bodice. 'And who might you be?'

'Just call me lieutenant,' he replied.

'Well, lieutenant, I must say your arrival is most opportune.'

'Is it?' he interrupted as he leant towards her. 'How so?'

'You see, I am quite disappointed to find that none of the young men here would be able to satisfy a woman such as myself.'

'And?'

'And now that you have shown up, I think my luck has changed.'

179

'Pray, do explain. What exactly does a man have to do to satisfy you?'

Laure leant forward as well, hugged his boot and rubbed her chest against the soft, pliable leather until her nipples grew hard under the friction. 'I want pleasure,' she whispered huskily. She sighed and, jerking her hips, she pushed herself forward until her swollen bud pressed against the tip of his boot.

He let her writhe on his foot without saying a word. Her juices flowed freely and soon the boot looked even shinier than before. Looking at him through half shut eyes, Laure was momentarily incensed by his lack of response, but she stopped caring soon enough. As her hips ground against the lieutenant's foot, she could feel ripples of pleasure gathering again. Soon, she knew, her climax would overtake her. That was all that mattered.

Writhing endlessly, she rode the whole of his boot from toe to ankle, swaying back and forth, rotating her hips languidly. Yet, whenever she looked up at the lieutenant his eyes showed no sign of excitement. At times he seemed amused, but no more.

Her flesh contracted violently and she gasped as pleasure pierced her. She jolted up and down on the man's boot, throwing her head back and forth before finally collapsing against his leg. Her hips twitched involuntarily as the sensations gradually subsided, and then she slumped forward, exhausted.

'Have you had enough yet?' the lieutenant said with a laugh.

Laure looked up at him. All around her, she could hear a medley of moans and squeals, and as she cast a quick look behind him, she saw that the couples had reformed without her directions. They were no longer paying any attention to her, but it didn't matter anymore: Laure had now set her sights in another direction.

She licked her lips and pouted. 'Enough? I've only just started.'

The lieutenant pulled his leg away and wiped the tip

of his boot against the back of his other leg. Laure's eyes fixed on his crotch once again, but saw no sign that he was aroused. He caught her glance and bent forward.

'What are you looking at?' he asked in a menacing tone. 'Do you have any little plans for me?'

Laure licked her lips again. 'I'm hungry,' she said huskily as she sensuously rubbed her slit with her fingertips. She tilted her head back and closed her eyes. Her flesh clenched against her fingers and she gasped. 'I want male flesh,' she continued as she stared at the lieutenant through halfshut eyes. 'I want *you*. Now.'

The lieutenant moved back and began to pace around her. 'And what makes you think *I* should want you?'

Laure stood up and stopped him by placing both hands on his chest. 'Oh,' she said, 'I think that you simply should know what you would be missing out otherwise . . . '

His hands cupped her shoulders and he held her at arm's length. Their eyes locked for a moment. His apparent lack of enthusiasm only served to fuel Laure's desire for him. But she knew better; she was confident she could win him over in the end. She had briefly felt his chest through his uniform, and now she longed to feel his bare skin. She was hungry for a man, a real man, not some inexperienced soldier.

The lieutenant's restraint told her that she had met her match. She sensed he wanted her, otherwise he would have left. Already, she could feel his nipples hardening under the thick fabric, and then, there was the smile she had noticed on his face as he had let her abuse his boot.

He made her sit down and then he casually grabbed a chair and sat astride, resting his arms on the back of it. Flippantly, he grabbed a bottle of whisky off the table next to him, took a swig from it then handed it to Laure. His silent eyes dared her to do the same.

Laure hesitated for a moment. Her experience with alcohol was quite limited, and she knew she needed to keep her mind sharp to win this battle. For she was set on seducing him. Her mind raced and she started to doubt whether he did want her. Why was he daring her to take the whisky? Obviously, he didn't have to get her drunk to have his way with her!

Or was that his way of testing her: to see how much she could take and prove he was able to resist her? She took a sip and let the liquid caress the inside of her mouth before she swallowed. It tasted of peat and warmed her insides as it went down her throat. The burning sensation radiated through her body and made her nipples erect.

She breathed deeply, her chest heaving and her nipples proudly pointing towards the lieutenant through her chemise. Parting her legs again, she slowly stroked the insides of her thighs. There was no way he could remain insensitive to such an inviting display for much longer.

For a fraction of a second, he showed signs she was getting to him. He shifted in his chair and she saw his throat contract as if he was having difficulty swallowing. She handed the bottle back to him.

Raising her foot onto the chair, she off took her shoe and fondled herself with her bare heel. The skin felt deliciously rough on her swollen folds and she smiled wickedly. The lieutenant returned her smile.

'You are quite a wanton little girl, aren't you?' he finally said.

'So I've been told,' Laure replied with a triumphant smile. For as the lieutenant swallowed yet another gulp of whisky, she finally saw something twitch in his breeches. He looked around the room, as if worried someone might have noticed, then turned to Laure again.

Sensing she had to make the most of his predicament, she released her breasts from her bodice, pushed them together and up towards her mouth. 'I am so hot,' she breathed before sticking her tongue out to lick her nipples. 'Let's go outside.'

Still holding the bottle, the lieutenant stood up with a

182

smile. Laure re-fastened her bodice and stepped out of the barracks cautiously. She made her way around to the back of the building, then into the forest. He followed, but not closely enough for her liking.

The ground was wet and cool under her bare feet. Twigs and dead leaves tickled her soles and she laughed. The air didn't seem as cold as earlier, but she felt much more comfortable than inside the barracks. She turned around, leant against a tree and watched her lover approach. The moonlight filtering through the trees was enough for her to see that his member had grown bigger in proportion and now tensed his breeches.

'Kiss me,' she whispered as she took the laces of his shirt. Holding on to the trunk for support, he leant forward but didn't touch her. His mouth covered hers in a passionate kiss, and she slipped her hands inside his tunic and pulled him towards her. He pulled back.

'Not so fast,' he said. 'You still haven't told me why I should give in to your charms.'

She took his hand and brought it to her mouth. She licked his forefinger then slipped it inside her chemise to circle her erect nipple. He took another sip of whisky, kissed her and filled her mouth with the hot liquid.

'That's not enough,' he said as he stepped back. 'I need more proof that you are as special as you claim to be.'

'Why are you making this so difficult?' Laure said. 'You know I want you.'

'Yes, but why should I give in on this occasion?'

'Because I know things you can't even begin to imagine. And also because I might get angry if you keep refusing me.'

'And then? What happens if you get angry?'

'Let me suck you and then I'll tell you.'

'You may, but I have to warn you that your jaw will be sore long before I even begin to lose control.'

'We'll see about that.'

She dropped to her knees and undid his breeches. His

dick sprang out, hot and stiff. She drew him into her mouth and sucked him hard. When her hot tongue had very little effect on him, she pulled back, took a mouthful of whisky and engulfed him again.

His hips bucked under the burning assault of the alcohol. Yet Laure's lips tightened around his shaft and he was unable to pull out. She heard him breathe deeply and figured he was probably trying to fight the over-whelming sensations she had triggered in him. In return she sucked him harder, grabbing his sac with one hand and fondling it.

She was dizzy from the alcohol, but drunk on her desire for him. She licked and sucked his hard rod endlessly, letting her tongue trail along its length for a while before taking him back in her mouth.

Although his erection was now straining at its limit, the lieutenant remained stoic. She felt no pulse in his rod, and he made no thrusting motions as other men usually did.

'I did warn you,' he said after a while. 'It takes much more than this to make me come.'

As he spoke, Laure only became more determined to make him lose control. As she put her hand on the ground for support, she felt something which gave her an idea. She pulled his breeches down completely then grabbed the large twig that she had found. Sucking still harder to make sure he couldn't pull out, she lashed him across the buttocks.

He bucked under the assault, growled like a madman and seized her jaw in his hand. He forced her mouth open and pushed her away.

Laure fell on her backside, and before she realised what was happening, he had grabbed her arms and pulled her to her feet.

'Nobody hits me,' he said angrily, his face so close to hers she could smell the alcohol on his breath. 'You want to play rough, do you? Well, I say let's play, then.'

He dragged her deeper into the woods, stopping

occasionally to examine the big trees until he found one with a low, sturdy branch. He undid his thin belt, then raised Laure's arms above her head and tied her wrists to the branch.

Her feet barely touched the ground. He stood back, looking smug.

'You're not so bold now, are you, mademoiselle?'

Laure had no reply. His behaviour was frightening, yet tremendously arousing. He came up to her, undid her bodice and exposed her breasts to the cold night air.

Reeling from the effect of the whisky, Laure didn't feel any pain in her wrists but her entire body was twice as sensitive as usual. She moaned and let her head fall forward.

The lieutenant came close, held her against him and cupped her chin in his hand.

'What now, Laure? Do you still want me?'

'Yes,' she sobbed.

He raised her skirt and uncovered her flesh. 'Then take me,' he said.

She could feel his dick now throbbing against her bare tummy. He stood motionless, and she knew she would have to make the effort. Circling his waist with her legs, she grabbed the belt to lift herself higher, then rotated her hips until she felt the head of his dick nudging at her entrance. The alcohol and her arousal increased her strength. Once aligned, she lowered herself until he pierced her.

'Very good,' he said sarcastically. 'Now let's see if . . . '

He didn't have time to finish his sentence. Laure clenched her vagina and her control surprised him. Her hips now swayed upon his rod and he sighed with satisfaction.

'You are quite something,' he conceded.

He placed his hands on her buttocks and lifted her to release the strain on her arms. His mouth then settled on her breasts and devoured them hungrily. All the pent-up desire he had suppressed emerged with amazing voracity.

His mouth seized her nipple and sucked so hard Laure could feel the pull all the way down to her groin. He hauled her closer, penetrating her fully and pressing the root of his member against her swollen bud.

She cried out with delight as her weight crushed her flesh against his. He lifted her again and held her right against the tip of his dick. He then thrust again, not deeply but so rapidly that she climaxed instantaneously.

Slipping his arms under her knees, he made her swing back and forth onto him, in longer, deeper strokes. Laure brought her knees to her chest and rested her ankles on his shoulders. He thrust for a short while in this position before pulling out and raising her hips towards his face, his hands holding her buttocks.

Laure was stretched horizontally in mid-air, her thighs resting on his shoulders and her wrists tied to the branch. His mouth was as rapacious on her flesh as it had been on her breasts. His tongue foraged with devilish intensity, gliding deep inside her tunnel and twirling expertly.

His upper lip trembled against her bud and she climaxed again. He sucked and licked more avidly, now losing control. As pleasure swept through her, her whole body tensed violently then went limp.

He sucked at her clitoris until she felt as if all life had been drained out of her. When he sensed she was no longer responding, he grabbed her legs and lowered them to his hips.

He impaled her exhausted body slowly, inch by inch, and began to thrust – leisurely at first, to rekindle her arousal. When she finally recovered her strength, he gradually increased his speed and intensity.

Soon she could feel the branch swaying as the power of his thrusts carried in a wave through her body, along the branch and up the trunk. Leaves rustled wildly above her head and the branch creaked a few times.

But Laure was totally oblivious to everything but her

own body. Pleasure swept through her again and again, and she screamed loudly. The lieutenant kept up his pace until her flesh burnt. Yet she didn't want him to stop.

The muscles in her legs contracted forcefully as she pointed her toes. Her vulva clenched around her lover's prick and she heard him breathe harder. She ached all over, but pain gave way to pleasure so intense stars danced behind her closer eyelids.

She finally felt him climax within her. His hands clasped the back of her knees and held her so tight she felt his tremors as well. She encircled his waist again and used the heels of her feet to push him further within her. His seed gushed forth and then oozed back out along her slit and down the valley of her buttocks.

He held her against him with one arm whilst he untied her wrists. She threw her arms around his neck and he held her close for a moment before falling to his knees. The evening mist still pearled on the fallen leaves and cooled her hot skin.

Lying next to her, he picked up the discarded bottle of whisky and took another swig. She took the bottle from his hands and helped herself to a mouthful. Her head was still spinning, but she didn't care if she was drunk. She felt good.

'It is getting late,' he said as he stood up and buttoned his breeches. He bent down, took her hand and gently kissed it. 'It was a pleasure meeting you, mademoiselle. Pity I will be heading back to France on the next boat. My wife is impatiently awaiting my return. I hope you find yourself a good husband.'

He turned around and disappeared into the trees, leaving Laure sitting on the ground, feeling somewhat nauseous. A short while later, Marguerite showed up.

'There you are,' she said as she helped Laure back on her feet. 'We have to leave, it will be dawn soon.'

Laure could barely stand. Her legs were weak and she was still reeling from the intense pleasure that had recently overcome her. But this soon subsided to make way for something much worse: a horrible feeling that she had drunk too much.

She couldn't keep up with the girls as they hurried back to the convent. Laure staggered behind and soon lost them completely. Marguerite had warned her that whenever they went out it was every girl for herself. If Laure ever lagged behind they wouldn't wait for her.

Right now she didn't care. She wanted to die. Her stomach was churning and horrible cramps ravaged her insides. Then she stopped completely, and fell onto her back, and now she lay staring at the stars as they spun all around her. She shivered and ached, but she didn't have the strength to get up again.

She passed out to be awakened by a whisper in her ear.

'What are you doing here?' a man asked. She knew the voice, but it was still too dark to see who it belonged to. She felt him lift her and carry her in his arms.

'Dear God, you stink of whisky. I wonder what the nuns would say if they could see you.'

Laure nestled her head in the groove of the stranger's neck and threw her arms around his neck. She felt good in his embrace; safe.

As they came out of the woods, she raised her head and let out a small cry as she recognised her saviour. 'François!'

'Ah, I see you are coming round.'

He gently lowered her to her feet. Laure looked around and saw they were within view of the convent. He steered her away but she held on to him and covered his face with kisses.

'Don't go. Take me with you.'

'You don't want me, darling,' he said softly. 'I am no good for you. Find yourself a good husband.'

'But I don't want to get married,' she cried. 'I want to be with you.'

Tears rolled down her face as she peered into his eyes.

He took her in his arms and kissed her passionately. 'Do you really? Then I shall be back.'

'No,' she pleaded. 'Take me with you tonight.'

'No, not tonight. I must go, I can't explain. I will come back for you.'

He pushed her towards the path leading to the building and disappeared back into the woods. Laure stared at the spot where he had vanished, hoping he would reappear. But then she heard the sound of a crowing rooster and she knew she couldn't wait any longer.

Chapter Thirteen

'What did you expect?' Marguerite asked sarcastically. 'You can't have it your way every time.'

Laure walked along, sighing dejectedly. Her second visit to the soldiers' barracks had been far less enjoyable than her first. Word had spread through the garrison and the men were ready for her this time.

Unable to get her hands on a crop – or anything else she could have used – she threatened in vain. The soldiers wouldn't give in and just took what they wanted from her. Of course, there had been plenty of hungry mouths, eager hands and hard pricks to pleasure her. But she hadn't been in control of everything. It just wasn't like the last time.

They hurried back in complete darkness. There was no moon tonight. Laure trailed behind again. Not because she felt sick – she had stayed away from the whisky this time – but because she secretly hoped to see François. After all, he only seemed to appear under cover of darkness, and tonight was as good a night as any.

By the time she arrived at the convent, the others had already gone in. Laure made her way up the winding staircase, but it wasn't until she reached the top that she sensed somebody walking behind her. As she crossed the hall leading to the dormitory, an arm fell on her shoulder and forced her to turn around.

Surprised, she let out a small cry. The early-morning light came in through the window and she easily recognised Louise, that older, plain girl who was rumoured to have come to the colony because she couldn't find a husband back in France. Even though she had arrived quite a few months ago, she still hadn't received a single proposal. Meanwhile, Marguerite, Antoinette and Marie had refused more than half a dozen suitors each. They were too busy having fun and Louise resented them all the more for it.

'Well,' the woman croaked. 'At least I caught one of the lot. I'm sure Mother Superior will be very interested to know her girls leave their beds at night to go to the soldiers' barracks.'

Before Laure could say or do anything, Louise had taken off. Laure turned around and saw Marguerite coming towards her.

'Did she see you?' she asked as she caught her breath. 'You were too far behind. We couldn't warn you. I don't know exactly how she found out, but she knows where we've been. She is bound to tell someone.'

Laure shrugged. 'Let her talk all she likes. She has no proof. It's her word against ours.'

It was a hot day. Too hot to be making candles. Laure could hardly believe the tales she had heard about this land; how long and harsh the winters were, and how poor the crops.

So far she had seen nature at its most magnificent. The orchards bore luscious fruits, and the crops were plentiful. And the heat: from sunrise until late evening, there was hardly a refreshing moment. And working in the kitchen didn't make things any easier.

The king's girls were, on the whole, from good families and had to be taught to cook, sew and clean a house.

Laure was one of only a few who had worked as a maid, and she wondered what kind of wives her companions would make.

This afternoon, the nuns were teaching them how to make clothing out of all sorts of discarded pieces of cloth. Laure knew more than their teacher, so she had been relegated to the kitchen and asked to make tallow candles.

Had she known, she would have kept her mouth shut. Over a fire, a large pan full of suet was slowly melting. Now and again Laure would ladle out the liquid and pour it into the moulds where wicks had already been inserted.

She stopped for a while to undo the top of her bodice and wipe her brow. Sweat trickled down her back and between her breasts. Usually she didn't mind, but today her dress felt tight and she was most uncomfortable.

The moulds were neatly lined up on the large table. It would take forever for the suet to set. She had almost finished filling them when Mother Superior appeared in the kitchen. Mother Henriette was nothing like Mother Eloise at the convent where Laure had stayed after the fire at the château. This nun was short and stout, completely unattractive, and lacking the restrained lust Mother Eloise had displayed.

At first, Laure didn't make much of this visit. But then she remembered only two nights ago Louise had threatened to tell what she knew. And judging from the look on Mother Superior's face, it hadn't been an idle threat.

'I had been warned about you,' the woman started. 'But I was willing to give you the benefit of the doubt.'

Laure stopped what she was doing and listened carefully. What exactly had Louise said? And how much of it had Mother Superior believed?

'When the convent at La Rochelle advised me of the life you had led before you went to live there, I understood perhaps fate had crossed your path with that of bad people and you had been a victim of strong influences. I was quite ready to help if I found you needed guidance. But now . . .' She stopped and paced in front Laure. 'I was very, very upset when Louise came to tell me where you go at night. That was most disturbing. I would have been able to turn a blind eye, providing you repented, but then I talked to Sister Mélanie about you and . . .'

Her voice broke, and Laure understood her chaperone on the boat had been unable to keep their secret.

'You are a vile creature, Laure Lapierre. You have no place in this house of God. But it is my duty to find you a husband and I shall keep the promise I have made to my superiors. However, it would be in everyone's best interest if we found somebody for you as soon as possible. Unlike your companions here, you shall not have the luxury of choosing. You will marry the first man we find for you.'

'What if I refuse to marry him?' Laure said defiantly.

Mother Superior smiled smugly. 'I had a feeling you would say something like that. If you refuse to marry, I will arrange for you to be sent to Ville-Marie de Mont-réal, another settlement further up the river. Life is quite rough there, so I think you would rather agree to marry of your own free will. There will be no comfortable dormi-tory to shelter you. We don't have a convent there, only a farmhouse. You will be living quite far from the town itself, and all visits from potential suitors will be chap-eroned. There will be no young man within walking distance with whom to sin. And certainly no soldiers' barracks.'

She stepped back and slipped her arms under her apron. Her face had remained serene under her coronet. 'You will either be married tomorrow,' she said. 'Or you will leave for Ville-Marie the next morning. The choice is yours.'

Laure looked at her, seething with rage. She didn't particularly like either of those options. Get married by tomorrow? To a man she didn't even know? And what about this town of Ville-Marie? What kind of life would she have there?

Somehow she felt going away would be the better choice. That way, she could buy some time, choose her own mate, perhaps even find a way out of getting married at all. If only François had taken her with him. Why hadn't he come? Now it was too late.

'It would be best if I left,' she said as a sob rose in her throat.

'As you wish,' Mother Superior breathed. 'I'll make arrangements for you to leave on the coach, the day after tomorrow.'

Left alone in the kitchen, Laure sobbed uncontrollably. Once again, just as she thought things were going her way, fate had decided otherwise. Would she ever be able to find peace again? She was tired of not knowing what would happen next, of things constantly changing just as she got accustomed to them.

It seemed not so long ago that life was sweet. Then her father had decided to make her work. Later on, just as she had found her way into her mistress's bed, fire had destroyed everything. After that, she could have been happy with Father Olivier, but he had betrayed her.

Recently, she truly believed François would come for her, but he hadn't. And now, she was on her own again, on her way to yet another place. Her cheeks burnt with rage, and the tears rolling down her face didn't soothe them. She tried not to think about her situation, but concentrate on her task. Not that it mattered anymore. She was leaving, so why should she have to do anything the nuns asked of her?

Yet Mother Superior's words kept echoing around in her mind and she couldn't think of anything else. She would have to leave for Ville-Marie. From what she had heard, this was several leagues away. Would François ever find her there? If he returned and couldn't find her at the convent, he might think she was married and give up on her.

Why, oh why had she believed Father Olivier's lies? Why had she embarked on the boat at La Rochelle? All she had done was exchange one prison for another. When would life finally reward her, instead of constantly making her miserable?

She took the pan full of melted suet off the fire and put it on the table. There were no empty candle moulds left, and the suet she had poured into the first batch probably hadn't yet set. It would take all day; it was so hot in the kitchen.

As she walked around the table to check her work, she could feel sweat trickle along the inside of her legs. She wanted to get out of this place, kitchen, convent and all. She wanted out of her agreement to marry. And she wanted François, of all people, to be the one to take her away from all this.

As she turned around the corner of the table, her skirt caught the handle of the pan and toppled it over onto the floor. The melted suet splashed everywhere as the copper pan bounced on the pale marble with a deafening crash.

Laure watched, incredulous, as the suet formed an enormous puddle all over the kitchen floor. It thickened on the cooler surface and soon stopped spreading. What a mess, she raged inwardly. Naturally, she would have to clean it before anybody walked in.

She looked around hopelessly. There was only one way to go about it. Tucking the hem of her dress into the apron strings tied around her waist, she retrieved the copper pan, grabbed a large metal spoon and got down on all fours to scoop up as much as she could.

The floor felt slippery under her knees and shins. No doubt her legs would soon be covered in half-melted suet, but it was better than getting stains on her dress, and exposing her legs and cooling off was a welcome relief.

At one point her knee slipped sideways and her legs parted. Her behind touched the floor and she squealed like a little girl. This was actually quite enjoyable. The suet felt soft on the inside of her thighs and she wriggled about in it.

Some of the suet was still quite warm and smooth on her naked vulva. Putting down the pan and the spoon she spread her legs in front of her, and rubbed her flesh against the slippery marble floor.

Her clitoris reared readily and she moaned. Bracing herself on her hands, she ground her pubis hard and fast, enjoying the contrast of warm suet and cold marble.

'Laure? What are you doing?'

Laure quickly grabbed the pan and the spoon and rose to her knees. Over the top of the table, she saw Sister Mélanie peering from the entrance to the kitchen. From her position, Laure could barely see her, so she concluded the nun could see she was on the floor, but couldn't guess what she had been up to.

They held each other's gaze for a moment. Since her arrival, Laure hadn't seen much of her chaperone from the boat, but she fondly remembered their last night together. Pity Mélanie had confessed to what they had done together, Laure thought. In a way, it was her fault if she now had to leave.

A wicked idea sprang to mind. 'I spilled the suet,' she confessed in a child-like tone. 'Mother Superior will be so angry with me now . . .'

Mélanie walked around the table to see for herself. 'Oh dear,' she said in a sweet voice. 'What a mess. Let me help you.'

Laure stopped her just as she was about to kneel. 'Be careful. You don't want to get any on your habit.'

Mélanie paused for a moment and silently stared at Laure's bare legs. She blushed and bowed her head silently. Laure's heart pounded fast. If only she could get Mélanie to join her on the floor, she would give the nun something else to confess.

Sister Mélanie took the rosary hanging around her neck and quickly brought it to her lips before crossing herself. Then, taking a deep breath, she grabbed the hem of her habit to tuck it into her belt.

Laure waited and watched as Mélanie pulled up her bloomers to uncover her thighs. The sight of them brought back more memories of the time they had spent together on the boat, especially the last night, when Laure had been daring enough to caress that chaste body.

Together they tried to scoop up as much of the suet as possible. Mélanie concentrated meticulously on the task at hand, whilst Laure only pretended to work. In fact, she was trying to come up with a way to get the nun to shed her bloomers and sit on the floor.

At one point, Mélanie stood up and rubbed her sore knees. Instead of kneeling again, she simply squatted, her feet flat on the floor but her balance precarious. This was the moment Laure had been waiting for.

She pretended to move about, gathering yet more suet. As she neared the nun, she bumped her with her hips. Just as she had hoped, the nun fell back with a small cry and ended up sitting squarely on the floor.

Laure apologised and watched as the nun struggled to get up. Mélanie only succeeded in increasing the amount of greasy stains on her bloomers. When she got to her feet, she shot Laure a glance – half amused, half despairing and briefly surveyed the damage.

Large patches of tallow stuck to the seat of her bloomers, as well as the whole of the back, weighing down the fabric and making them sag, not to mention rather transparent.

'I have to go and change,' Sister Mélanie said in a small voice.

Laure tried to look distressed and pretended to cry. 'You can't leave me,' she sobbed. 'I can't clean all this by myself.'

Sister Mélanie sighed and got down on the floor again. This time she sat squarely, with her legs apart. As she slid about, her bloomers began to slip and she had to hold them up with one hand to make sure the old, worn laces didn't give.

Laure let herself slide from one part of the floor to the next. Although they had gathered most of the suet, a thin film remained on the marble floor and made it amusingly slippery.

'How will we finish cleaning this?' she asked.

'I honestly don't know,' Sister Mélanie admitted.

'Maybe we could wipe it up,' Laure suggested. 'But we don't have any rags. Unless ...' She paused and looked intently at the nun's ruined bloomers. Sister Mélanie followed her gaze and blushed when she understood what Laure was thinking.

'Well,' she conceded. 'They are ruined, that's for certain. I suppose we might as well use them to wipe the floor.'

Laure lent a helping hand as Mélanie wriggled out of her bloomers. Quite innocently, she slid her hand along the nun's thigh as she pulled down the garment. Her skin was hot and soft and the nun shivered under Laure's touch.

Sister Mélanie tried to tear the bloomers into two pieces, winding the pant-legs around her wrists and pulling as hard as she could.

'Let me help,' Laure said as she took the bloomers from the nun's hands. She grabbed one leg and instructed the nun to pull on the other. As hard as they pulled, they were unsuccessful. Sitting on their naked behinds on the slippery floor, they only managed to pull one another closer. What started out as a clean-up session soon turned into a children's game.

They pushed and pulled each other back and forth, their bare skin sliding along the marble floor, and laughed like children. Sister Mélanie lost her cornet in the process, triggering another burst of giggles.

Laure kept the game going for as long as possible, wanting her friend to relax before she put the rest of her plan into action. After a while she pulled herself closer

198

to the nun and innocently tangled the Vs of their legs. Mélanie didn't seem to find anything wrong with that, so Laure slipped her arms around the nun's tiny waist and held her close for a moment.

Mélanie looked at her with wistful eyes, but already Laure's mouth was approaching hers and she couldn't refuse the girl's kiss. Laure kissed her gently at first whilst her thigh casually pressed against the nun's crotch.

When Laure felt quite sure the nun wouldn't pull away, she let her hand stray and brush against the woman's chest. At first, Mélanie remained unmoved and completely still. But her breathing grew shallow and heavier with each of Laure's kisses.

When Laure's hand then moved down to caress Mélanie's flesh, she still didn't move. Laure was pleased to find her folds were already moist. Without breaking her kisses, she showed her chaperone how to rub her flesh along the cold surface.

Mélanie obeyed silently, but when Laure brought her hand towards her own flesh, the nun suddenly pulled away.

'We must not,' she urged, coming to her senses. 'It is so sinful.' She tried to wriggle out of the girl's embrace and get back on her feet, but she slipped again and ended exactly where she had started.

'Please stay,' Laure whispered huskily as she pulled the nun closer. 'I will be leaving in two days. I might never see you again.'

Sister Mélanie was startled. 'You are leaving? Where are you going?'

'Mother Superior is sending me to Ville-Marie, the day after tomorrow. I don't expect I'll be coming back.'

'But why?'

'I don't know,' Laure lied. 'She gave me no choice.'

With a sigh, Mélanie gave in and relaxed in the girl's embrace. Laure resumed her kisses. Her greasy hand wandered up one pale leg and gently brushed the nun's slit. She felt her tremble and increased her ministrations, setting her thumb on the swollen bud and rubbing it lightly.

Mélanie moaned loudly but didn't returned the caress. Once again Laure directed the nun's hand to her own flesh. This time, Mélanie made no protest. Shyly, she returned Laure's kisses, hesitant at first but slowly more eager as Laure's thumb circled her clitoris.

She mirrored the caresses of the girl's hand. Soon Laure moaned in unison with her chaperone and her hips swayed of their own accord against her tiny hand. Their mouths still bonded, they writhed against each other as pleasure swept over them. Laure brought Mélanie to climax again and again. It didn't matter if the nun later confessed to having sinned again. Laure would make sure Mélanie never forgot her, and that no penance would ever erase the guilty memories of this day.

As the nun grew weak in her arms, Laure settled back and continued rubbing her flesh on the floor to bring herself to climax. Now she could let go of the body shaken by the last subsiding waves of pleasure. She was satisfied that, in her own mind, Mélanie would believe she had sinned horribly.

Laure abandoned herself to her own climax, sliding and writhing as she freed her breasts from her bodice to caress them. She lost her mind for a long while, numb with pleasure and oblivious to everything else. When she opened her eyes, she saw Mélanie kneeling piously and clasping her rosary in her trembling hands.

The nun stopped her prayers for a moment and turned her tear-stained face towards Laure.

'You are a sinful child,' she sobbed. 'But I will save you. The devil is in you, and I will rid you of it, even if I have to lose my own soul.'

Laure smiled and stood up slowly. The devil? That was one way of looking at it. But, of course, Laure didn't have to share that opinion.

Chapter Fourteen

She didn't want to say goodbye to anybody. Before sunrise, she had risen, dressed and left the dormitory before anyone else had woken up. Everyone knew she was leaving but no-one had said a word about it. Marguerite and her partners in crime had been very quiet. No doubt they had figured out Louise had told Mother Superior about the nocturnal escapades, and they didn't want to be found out as well.

Alone in the dark stables, Laure paced aimlessly for a while. The smell of the hay reminded her of home, of her childhood. She stumbled around in the dark, sat on a large stack of hay and reclined, closing her eyes. For a moment, she could almost pretend the last few months hadn't really happened. She was back in France, in the stables at the Château de Reyval, impatiently waiting for René to come and join her.

He would enter silently, see her lying down with her eyes closed, basking in the warm hay, and slowly lift up her skirt. The image was so vivid in Laure's her head she could almost feel it happening. In fact . . .

She opened her eyes and crawled back in surprise. At first, she didn't recognise the man standing between her parted legs and cunningly slipping his hands under her skirt. But as his mouth broadened into a bright smile, Laure's heart warmed and she held her hands out to him. 'François!'

He knelt as he continued lifting her skirts then came to lie on top of her.

'You're here,' she cried incredulously. 'You came for me.'

His mouth on hers silenced her and they exchanged passionate kisses. His lips were full and soft and just as hot as hers. Tasting him in her mouth, she relaxed and sighed with relief.

His hands stroked her neck briefly before gliding under the collar of her bodice. He stood and pulled her to her feet. Laure squirmed lasciviously as she pressed herself against him. The warmth of his kisses radiated through her entire body. Her nipples puckered with arousal and her flesh seeped its excitement. Now that he was finally here, she would never let him go.

She held him tight and pressed her hips against his. His penis grew hard against her tummy and she was satisfied he wouldn't leave her again. As she ran her hands along his back, his body felt new, almost foreign. Laure realised at that moment she had never even touched him. She had fantasised about him often, but he wasn't what she had imagined.

At times she hadn't been entirely convinced he ever existed outside the confines of her imagination. And now he was here with her. She fed on his mouth hungrily. At last she could have him and abandon herself as she hadn't done in a long time.

He was just as eager as she and his breathing betrayed his excitement. With astonishing dexterity, his hands quickly undid the buttons of her dress and the laces of her bodice without ever fumbling. Her bonnet disappeared and her hair cascaded around her shoulders. Then he pulled her dress over her head and helped her out of her chemise in a matter of seconds.

In contrast, Laure had to desperately tug at his shirt to

get it off. She almost ripped it. He laughed as his hands joined hers and pulled his shirt over his head, then he braced himself on an upright beam to take off his boots.

Laure was impatient to see him, to feel his naked skin on hers. She had more luck with his breeches. The buttons gave easily and they glided down to his ankles with no effort. Finally, they held each other tightly.

But it still wasn't enough. She wanted more. Pushing him against the beam, she practically threw herself upon him. Her body yearned to discover his, to feel his blood pulsing at the surface of his skin, to have him caress her.

And then there were his hands. Until now, that was all she had known of him, really. Yet the one time he had touched her was still embedded in her memory. If this man could, with only one finger, bring her to such ecstasy, what else was he capable of triggering within her using his entire body?

He pushed her back and she landed, half sitting, half reclining, in the haystack. Their clothes were scattered around them. The air was cool but Laure was so hot for her man she hardly noticed. Under her behind and her legs, the hay felt prickly and even rough, but that was also beyond her concern. All that mattered was that François, her François, was here with her. And he was all hers.

In the early morning light, Laure could barely make out the contours of his body. Instead, she had to rely on her hands to get to know him. Her mouth closely followed her fingers and she caressed him from head to toe, letting her hands trail from his cheeks, down his neck and over his chest. She liked the way his nipples contracted under her fingertips and she toyed with them for a while before continuing her exploration.

His hard stomach was ridged with sinewy muscles and Laure's fingers slowly bobbed up and down as they traced down to his hips before going back up along his flanks and across his back. She massaged him as he

203

rolled her onto her back and came down on top of her, writhing lasciviously.

His manhood briefly brushed her legs as he lowered himself. His mouth explored her neck and shoulders whilst she clasped his back. The rough hay made her bare skin even more sensitive, especially as she grew hot and sweaty with excitement. But Laure wouldn't have it any other way. This morning she was at one with nature, wild and unbridled.

Her feet settled on the back of his legs and she brought them up and down. She could feel the muscles of his thighs play against her soles, powerful and eager. The haystack underneath them slowly gave and soon Laure found herself sitting up again, with her lover sprawled in front of her.

His mouth was still on her neck, slowly making its way down. After a while François pulled away and stood up. His silhouette was neatly cut by the incoming morning light. Laure turned around and crawled back up the haystack.

He swiftly followed behind, knelt in front of her and sat back on his heels. Laure straddled his leg and pressed her flesh against his bare thigh, then brought his head to her breasts. He suckled her hungrily, massaging her back and her buttocks as she writhed against him. His member twitched against the front of her thighs, making Laure want him more.

Little by little, his hands found their way to her legs and she shifted her weight to straddle his thigh. He teased her expertly and she gasped as his thumb located her clitoris and rubbed it frantically. He slipped two fingers into her tunnel and held her in a vice-like grip, now working her bud with the base of his palm.

She climaxed immediately, letting out a loud cry that escaped from deep within her soul. Pleasure flowed through her and transported her outside her own body. When she came back, he was still teasing her. His hand had let go briefly but returned to pleasure her again. She panted endlessly as he skilfully handled her breasts and her vulva.

By then she didn't want to play an active role in their lovemaking anymore. She just wanted to let him have his way. She had been waiting for him for so long, she wanted to take all the pleasure she could get. Now.

His member reared against her thigh and again she was hungry for it. He continued stroking her whilst she let her hand trail down his hip and take hold of him. He was hard yet so soft to the touch; like a rod of iron enveloped in silk. At first she touched him with her fingertips only, then gradually increased the intensity of her caresses until she heard him moan.

He let go of her flesh, settled his hands on her hips and pulled her down with him as he lay back. She writhed on top of him, unable to prop herself up because their bodies were sinking in the hay. Like a sinuous snake, she spread herself over his chest and let her mouth do the work. She sucked on his nipples just as greedily as he had suckled hers. He arched his back and pushed her up, his arms gently coaxing her into turning around.

Her knees straddled his face and her flesh descended towards his face. She readily seized his member with her mouth and she covered it in hundreds of kisses all along its length before engulfing him.

His hips jerked and he thrust in her mouth, but she held him back with her hands. His tongue flickered furiously over her bud and she was close to climax again, but she didn't want it just yet and she forced her breathing to slow down. Instead, she concentrated on pleasuring him, on discovering this new marvel and on finding out how to trigger its sensitivity.

Holding his prick delicately between her lips, she gently sucked it. He throbbed in her grasp and she encircled the base of his shaft with her thumb and forefinger, holding him tight to calm him down.

He moaned between her legs, and his shallow breath

brushed her hot flesh. His member shrank somewhat so Laure lightly rubbed its length until it grew hard again. The plum swelled and seeped.

Suddenly, she wanted to feel him inside her. He bent his knees and dug his heels deep in the hay. Laure saw the opportunity his position afforded her and decided to make the most of it. Setting her hands on his knees, she pulled herself up and slowly eased her behind down across his chest and belly. She kept on moving, rubbing her chest against his bare thighs, until her flesh met his engorged dick. For a while, she teased him by letting the motion of her hips rub along the length of his prick, grinding down on the hard rod.

It twitched a few times, as if looking to insert itself within her. But Laure delayed penetration for as long as she could. She liked the way his hardness caressed her slick folds and she growled wantonly. Her hips rotated over his, his shaft pressing against her bud. After a while his hands grasped her buttocks and he lifted her. He entered her with a slow, delving thrust.

Laure gasped. It was so good to feel him move deep inside her, to let his hips push up slowly, triggering an exquisite tingle as he glided in and out. Her nipples ground into the rough skin of his thighs. Laure was overwhelmed by the medley of sensations which now linked her groin and her breasts, as if there was a connection, a string stretched inside her and vibrating under the power of her arousal.

She moved to counter his thrust, coming down to meet him as he pushed up, rising as he pulled away. Their synchronised tempo increased without missing a beat. Laure felt him come alive within her, endlessly pulsating as he approached his climax.

Parting his legs with her hands, she bent down until her chest touched the hay. He brought his legs back under him and, without letting go of her, managed to get up onto his knees.

Together they crawled across the top of the haystack,

his thrusts pushing her forward. Laure stopped when she reached the beam supporting the roof and propped herself against it as she straightened up. Behind her, François thrust harder, squeezing her between his chest and the beam. His hand glided around her hips and he rubbed her mound roughly.

Then, just like he had done that morning on the boat, he set a single finger on her swollen bud, and tortured it skilfully. His hips slowed for a while, as if he wanted to make her climax first. Holding her impaled upon his shaft, he never stopped caressing her body. His free hand took hold of her breasts and lightly brushed the warm skin. Laure panted and almost choked as his caresses brought her to another peak. She yelled her pleasure, feeling her flesh contract around his and jerking her hips back in an attempt to escape his hand.

But he wouldn't let go. He kept tickling her clitoris, endlessly worrying it, faster, harder, sending her into a wild explosion of successive orgasms and still keeping her at the edge of excitement, where pleasure is triggered and doesn't subside.

Pleasure rampaged through her in an everlasting wave. Her lungs burnt, her throat was raw from all her cries of joy; she felt exhausted. He let go of her vulva and her breasts, set his hands on her hips, and resumed thrusting.

Laure climaxed again. And again. Just to feel his powerful thrusts was enough to bring her even more exquisite torment. Only now he shared it. He moved at a dizzying speed, holding her fast and pushing her back and forth as his groin slapped her behind.

Her breasts quivered in reaction to his momentum. Breathing hard, he let out loud cries with every drive of his body, then spaced them out as his tempo decreased but his thrusts grew more intense.

With a final stroke, he penetrated her to the core, and held her tight against him. She felt his seed gush within her, and she heard him sigh just before he fell, lifeless, on top of her.

She let go of the beam and together they dropped into the hay, on their sides. His arms encircled her waist and he held her for a few minutes. Laure closed her eyes for a moment. The hay slowly gave under their weight and they slid down with the stack, but neither of them let go of the other.

Laure ended up face down in the hay. She breathed in deeply. The scent reminded her of her childhood, of those carefree days, back in France.

'When I was little,' she said in a hoarse, strained voice, 'I used to play in the stables for hours. I would dig tunnels through the haystacks and hide there. Sometimes I would fall asleep and my father would have to come and fetch me.'

François stirred behind her and kissed her neck. 'What else did you do as a child?' he asked.

'I remember we spent a lot of time in the woods. My father knew a lake, deep in the forest, and he would take me fishing. We had to go up the river in a row boat, and he taught me how to steer.'

François sat up. 'So, you can find your way around in a forest?'

His question took her aback and she waited before replying. 'That was a long time ago,' she said as she pulled him back towards her. 'It wouldn't be the same now.'

She turned onto her side and pulled his arm over her. He kissed her gently and lazily let his hand trace the contours of her body. Laure closed her eyes again and drifted away, watching hazy images of trees and streams dance behind her closed eyelids. She dozed off for a moment.

He stirred and stood up rapidly, but she didn't react right away. When she turned around he was almost completely dressed. He was fretful, as if in a hurry. The sun was now up and cast a faint light through the window. Every few seconds François would glance out and look around with a worried expression on his face.

Laure stood up and gathered her clothes. She had to hurry; she didn't want to make him wait. And she had to be gone before anybody came for her.

François grabbed his bag and came to kiss her. 'Until we meet again,' he said with a smile.

Laure looked at him incredulously. 'What? You are taking me with you, aren't you?'

François gave her a puzzled look then laughed softly. 'No, of course not,' he said as he made his way to the stable doors. 'Whatever made you think that?'

Laure ran after him, half naked and thoroughly horrified. 'But you must,' she screeched. 'You must take me away from this place. I want to go with you.'

'I can't take you with me,' he said as he gently pushed her away. 'I must leave this town for a while. But I'll be back.'

'But I won't be here. I'm leaving today.'

François stopped to look at her. 'Where are you going?'

'They are sending me to Ville-Marie to find a husband. But I don't want to go! I want to go with you!'

He looked at her silently for a moment. 'I will meet you there,' he said after a while. 'I really must go now, it is late. But I will come for you in a few weeks, as soon as I find my way there.'

'Come with me on the coach,' Laure said, suddenly excited. She cuddled up to him and put her arms around his neck. 'We can pretend to meet and you can ask to marry me and then take me with you.'

'No.' He prised her arms away from his neck and held her back. 'No-one can see me. You must never tell anyone that you know me, or where I am. But I will come for you.'

Before she could say anything else he turned around and left. She was alone again.

Chapter Fifteen

Sister Mélanie was the last person to board the coach, and she was the last person Laure expected to be her chaperone. From the time she took her seat, the nun never once looked at Laure. Instead, she kept her eyes closed, her lips moving in silent prayer as her hands clasped her rosary.

Only when they stopped to rest the horses did Laure speak to the nun. After the other passengers had disembarked, the two women were alone. Sister Mélanie was about to step out when Laure grabbed her arm and stopped her.

'Why are you coming with me?' she asked.

'I have sinned because of you,' the nun replied in a cold voice. 'As a penance I shall endeavour to help find you a suitable husband. That is how I will redeem myself in God's eyes.'

She struggled out of Laure's grasp and stepped out. It was the only thing she said all day. At night they stopped at an inn. When Laure entered the room and saw there was only one bed, she bit her lip and fought to wipe the smile off her face. Sister Mélanie could try to resist, but Laure knew the nun's flesh was weak.

She undressed and hopped into bed. The nun kneeled

at the foot of the bed and said her prayers. Laure was impatient for her to join her. She would seduce her in her sleep, as she had done on the boat.

But Sister Mélanie stayed exactly where she was. After a while Laure dozed off, and when she awoke, Mélanie was still kneeling at the foot of the bed.

By the time the inn-keeper knocked on their door to tell them the coach would be leaving soon, the nun hadn't moved. Laure sat up in bed, only then noticing it was dawn. Mélanie had spent the whole night in prayer, never once joining Laure in the bed.

The town of Ville-Marie de Montréal was nothing like Québec. It was a tiny settlement, surrounded by fortifications, on a very large island. There weren't as many houses, and their construction was shabbier. The only thing the two towns had in common was that there were very few women around.

As they boarded a smaller coach to reach their final destination, Laure figured that it would be easy to find her way around this town. Her spirits dampened, however, when she realised the coach turned off on a side road and was heading further and further from the centre of town. Then she remembered what Mother Superior had told her: she would be housed at a farm outside of town. Far enough away to discourage any ideas of nocturnal escapades.

The coach turned onto a road cutting across fields. Laure immediately concluded, with some relief, that, if there were fields, there must be men to mind them, but she quickly realised her mistake when she saw a group of nuns working the fields themselves.

The Maison St-Gabriel was a large stone farmhouse where Laure would share an attic room with three other girls. One of them, Aline, had the bed next to Laure's.

'I understand you are quite eager to find a husband,' she said to Laure as they were getting ready for bed that first night. 'I'm afraid it might take longer than you would have hoped. This is harvest season and the men are too busy to come and visit right now.'

'Am I to understand they are not that eager to take a wife?' Laure asked.

'Oh, no. They are. Only most of them work quite far away from here, and they simply can't make the time to call on us.'

'But what about the men from the town?'

The other girls looked at one other and then at Laure. 'They are not looking for wives,' Aline explained. 'Noblemen and clergymen, or else they're old or already married. The only transient visitors in town are fur trappers, and they are not looking to marry.'

'Aren't there any soldiers?'

'Yes, but they don't come here. They are busy, you understand. The British are not all that far south, and there have been problems with native tribes.'

Laure stopped listening. Aline had just confirmed what Mother Superior had said: there would be no distractions for her here.

Although the days were getting shorter, the weather was still hot. The leaves on the trees had turned from green to yellow to red, and the wild animals had shed their dark summer coat in exchange for a paler, thicker one.

Laure had been at Maison St Gabriel for almost four weeks. Nothing had happened since her arrival. Absolutely nothing. There was plenty of work to be done, from sunrise to sunset, but life was as flat as the floorboards in the day room.

As days went by and harvest drew to a close, the other girls grew excited. The young men would soon have more time on their hands than they knew what to do with. Suitors would soon start filing in.

At first, Laure was intrigued. A visit from a man – any man – would be a welcome change. But after the first night she saw there was nothing to get excited about.

After the evening meal, the girls gathered in the day

room and the nuns brought in an unusually large amount of candles and oil lamps. Then, about half a dozen young – and, at times, not so young – men arrived. The group sat and chatted under the nuns' watchful eyes, playing games and singing songs. A good time was had by all, then the men left. The following morning, the girls were cunningly questioned by their chaperones to see which of the young men they had preferred.

Aline accepted a marriage proposal after a third visit from a lad called Philippe. He was rather short, strapping and robust, but he knew how to make her laugh and he owned the largest farm for leagues around.

By the end of the second week, Laure herself had received no less than five proposals. She had refused all of them, even the one coming from a man called François. She was waiting for *her* François.

Two days before Aline was due to leave, three other girls arrived. Laure saw this as a blessing. Her companions were now engaged and their departures only days away. She didn't want to sleep alone in the large room.

The men continued to come, but at times she didn't even want to come down and meet anybody. Life had become more boring than she ever could have imagined. Until that morning when, for the first time, she thought perhaps the wait was drawing to an end.

Her water bucket somehow got caught in the well and she couldn't pull it out. She cursed and yelled, pulled on the handle as hard as she could and tried to rattle the chain, but to no avail.

Everyone else was busy in the fields. Only Sister Mignonne was around, but her frail and old body could never accomplish what Laure herself wasn't able to.

Her hands clasped around the chain and her knuckles quickly turned white as she tried to pull it one last time. Tilting her head back, she let out a loud scream and several words that would assuredly send her straight to hell, and pulled with every ounce of strength she could muster. This was definitely quite unladylike, but that was the least of Laure's concerns. A moment later she realised what a bad idea this was when her fingers suddenly lost their grip on the slippery chain and she fell backwards.

She cursed again as she flew through the air, bracing herself for the bump as she hit the gound. Yet instead of the hard, rocky surface, she landed on something much more comfortable: a man.

At first, all she could see were his legs sticking out between her own. Surprised, she slowly turned her head and saw she was sitting on a stranger's lap, a stranger who now lay flat on the ground beneath her, his eyes wide open and staring at the sky.

He slowly sat up, rubbed the back of his head with the palm of his hand, and winced in pain. Only then did he realise there was a young lady sitting on top of him.

Laure sprang to her feet, helped him up and apologised profusely. 'The bucket ... The bucket was caught,' she stammered as she brushed the dust from his clothes.

'I know,' the stranger said. 'I saw you from afar. And I certainly heard you. I was just about to ask if you needed help.'

Laure was about to reply when she looked up and saw his smile. Suddenly, the sight of him dumbfounded her. He was just a bit taller than her, and by far the most attractive man she had seen since arriving at the farmhouse. His hair was the colour of copper, neatly tied at the back. His beard was curly, a little paler than his hair but just as soft-looking. His teeth were white as milk, and shone brightly. She let her gaze wander and, under the pretence of dusting him off, quickly felt his body under his clothes.

The heat of his skin radiated through the cotton of his shirt. She could feel strong and youthful muscles; his shoulders were large and squared, his waist unusually narrow. His shirt was open and revealed the tan skin of his neck and upper chest. Laure came closer, mesmerised. Her lips were inexorably attracted to this skin; she longed to kiss it, then let her tongue gently brush his earlobes.

Her eyes met his and Laure could see that he had been looking at her with just as much interest. She frantically searched for something to say. What she really wanted to do was to slip her arms around his neck and press her body against his. Her nipples puckered under her dress as his eyes travelled over them and he blushed slightly.

He opened his mouth and was about to say something else when Sister Mignonne trotted out of the house as fast as her old legs could carry her. When he saw her, his face lit up and he ran to greet her.

'Jérome,' the nun said, beaming. 'We haven't seen you in a while. It is so nice to see you.'

Laure remained by the side of the well, suddenly feeling jealous. What business did Sister Mignonne have, coming out to interrupt them like this? Now, Jérome had completely forgotten about her, and she wasn't the least bit pleased.

Jérome put his arms around the nun's waist, held her tight and lifted her off the ground as if she were no more than a child. His hands on her back were large and powerful, yet handled her frail body delicately. Laure discreetly continued her examination from where she stood. His ample breeches revealed nothing of what she would find inside. It didn't matter. She wanted to feel his hands on her, not playfully touching her as they touched the nun, but slowly and intensely caressing her bare skin.

She couldn't hear what he and the nun were saying, but it seemed quite funny, judging from the laughter and broad smiles. After a while, he bid Sister Mignonne goodbye, turned to leave, and noticed Laure was still waiting by the side of the well. He walked up to her and bent over the edge to peer inside.

'There's an enormous root piercing the side,' he stated.

215

'That's where the bucket is caught.' His voice echoed inside the well. 'You should have someone remove it otherwise you'll never be able to haul water from there.'

He yanked the chain forcefully a couple of times and the bucket was freed. Without a word, Laure followed him to the house as he carried the water.

'Thank you,' she said faintly as he set the bucket at her feet. She desperately tried to think of something witty to say, but couldn't. He tipped his hat and went on his way. He never once glanced back at Laure, whose eyes remained fixed on his buttocks as he walked off.

'Is he gone already?' said Sister Mignonne. She stepped from the house, out of breath, brandishing a large canvas bag. 'I thought I would give him some food to take with him.'

She followed Laure's gaze in time to see Jérome disappear at the end of the road. She clutched the bag to her flat chest. 'Such a nice young man,' she said in a soft voice.

'Who is he?' Laure asked.

'He's from the parish of St Agnes,' the nun replied. 'His father owns a farm there. We don't see enough of him. Last winter he went away to the lumber camps. Many men do that around here. There is so little work for them after harvest time. Jérome is very hard working, you know. Now that he's back, he wanted to know if he could call on us to meet our girls. Who knows, maybe this year he'll find one he likes.'

Laure had hoped to make conversations stop when she appeared in the day room. She had taken her time before coming down. If Jérome was there, he would undoubtedly be looking for her and she wanted to make him wait a little. This way, he would think she wasn't coming down and her arrival would be a nice surprise.

The surprise was on her, however, when she entered the room and saw he was doing all the talking. Everybody else was listening in awe as he told them about his adventures at lumber camp.

Laure dragged a chair from across the room, trying to make as much noise as possible. But Jérome took no notice of her. The only reaction she got was a reproachful glance from the young men who didn't want to miss any of the fascinating story.

To make matters worse, the only source of light came from an oil lamp next to where Jérome was sitting. He wouldn't even see her unless she cut her way through the audience to get closer to him.

'The water was ice cold,' he continued. 'In the spring, the river also carries large chunks of ice that can knock a man dead in just one strike.'

The girls sitting at his feet huddled together as if they were feeling the cold for real. The tale involved a man who had fallen in the river as the lumber was sent down with the force of the current. Jérome had had to jump from one log to the next to reach him, navigating through the current and risking his own life in the process.

Sister Mélanie clutched her rosary, trembling with fright as if she could see the scene Jérome was describing. Even Sister Mignonne, who usually dozed off in her rocking chair, listened intently, wide-eyed.

Naturally, the story had a happy ending. Jérome had saved his companion's life and modestly admitted he hadn't really thought about the risk to his own life. For the rest of the evening, he remained the centre of attention. Nuns, girls and even the young men visiting that night were totally captivated by him. He had charmed them all.

Only at the end of the evening, when everyone was about to leave, did he finally noticed Laure's presence.

'Good evening,' he said with a curt bow. 'I cut that root from the well when I arrived earlier. It shouldn't bother you now.'

'Thank you,' Laure said. All the words she had so carefully rehearsed, the witty repartee, the clever comments, had vanished from her mind and once again she could find nothing to say.

He gave her a puzzled look and turned away to bid everybody else good night. Laure thought he had probably mistaken her silence for a lack of interest and she silently cursed herself. The other girls walked him to the door and seemed genuinely sorry he had to leave. He promised to return and left, escorted by the other young men, who perhaps already knew they didn't stand a chance next to such good-looking and interesting competition.

'You are being impossible, Laure,' Sister Mélanie said. 'Of all the young men I have introduced you to, not a single one was to your liking. They are about to leave for the lumber camps. If you don't agree to marry now, you will have to wait until the spring, or perhaps even later.'

Laure didn't reply and continued churning the butter. Sister Mélanie was right, of course. So far almost a dozen proposals had been thrown her way. The other girls had gone or were about to leave. Only Laure would remain. But how could she tell the nun she still hoped François would come for her? How could she confess that was the reason she had kept to herself and had quickly given up even on Jérome?

Moreover, how could she admit her hopes had now waned and she felt herself a fool for having believed him? She had been stupid to wait. She should have made more of an effort to trap Jérome. He was the only one she would settle for. But Jérome had paid very little attention to her, no doubt discouraged by her distant manner. And now he was to marry Agathe.

Agathe had been the last girl left apart from Laure. She wasn't especially pretty, but she was available. There were whispers amongst the nuns that Jérome had proposed mainly because he wanted his own farm. He was the youngest of several brothers, and he would find himself with no possessions upon his father's death. In marrying, the government would give him a piece of land.

From what Laure had seen, however, Jérome had been rather picky. She suspected he had failed to propose to the girls because he was waiting for a rare pearl. But now Agathe and Laure were the only ones left.

Laure cursed herself. If only she hadn't been so aloof, if she had shown more interest, he wouldn't have been afraid of rejection and he would have proposed to her, not Agathe. For it was clear, in Laure's mind, that Jérome's proposal was motivated by desperation at this point.

'Be honest with me, Laure,' Sister Mélanie continued. 'Wasn't there at least one young man you would have liked? I would have done anything to see you married, you know that.'

Laure didn't reply. Naturally, the answer was clear in her mind: Jérome was the only one she would have settled for. But he was engaged. Unless . . .

She looked at the nun as a diabolical idea formed in her mind. She knew it was cruel, but well worth a try.

'Actually,' she said in a broken voice. 'My heart has been taken and horribly broken.' She burst into fake tears and hid her face in her apron. Sister Mélanie came to her and put her arm around her shoulders.

'What is the matter? Tell me everything.'

'God help me,' Laure sobbed loudly. 'I love Jérome with all my heart, but he has chosen another one . . .'

Sister Mélanie sat her down on the long bench and hugged her tight. 'My poor child,' she said tenderly. 'I had no idea. Had I known, perhaps I could have done something about it, but I'm afraid it is too late.'

'I know,' Laure said. 'I never should have come here. Now I will never marry. I might as well go back to Québec and leave the convent for good. I think I may be paying the price for all my sins. My soul is doomed.'

She felt the nun tremble as she spoke the words. She

219

still remembered Mélanie telling her that she would strive to find Laure a husband as a penance for her own sins. Reminding her of that couldn't hurt.

'And you, my dear Sister Mélanie. You have vowed to find a husband for me. But what are you to do if the only man I love loves another?'

Sister Mélanie swallowed hard and Laure knew she had hit her target. 'Actually,' the nun said. 'My companions and I have reason to believe Jérome proposed to Agathe only because he thought you wouldn't want him.'

Laure broke free from the nun's embrace and looked up at her hopefully. 'Really?' she said in a shaky voice. 'Then, there is still hope for me. Perhaps if you were to talk to him, see what his intentions really are.'

Sister Mélanie stiffened and turned pale. 'I don't know,' she said carefully. 'That would mean perhaps breaking up his engagement to Agathe.'

'But she doesn't love him,' Laure lied. 'She told me in confidence she had agreed to marry him because she doesn't want to spend the winter here.'

Sister Mélanie hesitated for a moment.

'You have to do it,' Laure insisted. 'You vowed to find me a husband. You have to keep your promise.'

'I'll see what I can do,' the nun replied as she rose to her feet. 'I think Jérome will be coming this afternoon. Sister Mignonne has asked him to repair something in the barn. I'll have a word with him.'

Agathe's wailing persisted throughout the night and there was nothing anyone could say or do to comfort her. Naturally, Laure had been moved to another room to avoid any confrontation between them.

The poor girl's reaction had taken everybody by surprise, except Laure. The truth was Agathe had accepted Jérome's proposal because he was the only one ever to have ever asked for her hand. Before then, she was desperately afraid that she would never marry. And now that he had broken their engagement, her last hopes had vanished.

Yet Jérome had remained a true gentleman. He had told his fiancée himself that he had changed his mind and now wanted to marry Laure. He never admitted Sister Mélanie had been the one to provoke that decision, nor would he tell anyone what she had told him. But the result was the same: he had proposed to Laure and she had accepted.

And now she was patiently waiting by the door for him to come and pick her up. She was to meet his family and attend Mass with them. She didn't feel any remorse when Mélanie pointed out Agathe was the one who was supposed to have met his parents that day. In Laure's mind, if Agathe had been more of a woman, she would have found a way to stop him from breaking up the engagement.

And today, Laure was going to make sure he would never do the same to her.

As usual, Mass was utterly boring. Even more boring was the meal that followed. The Thibodeau family all lived in the same large house. Jérome had four brothers who were already married, and they had about a dozen children between them. As soon as she stepped into the house, Laure was immediately required to help serve the food, feed the babies, make sure the men always had plenty to eat and then wash up the plates.

Before she had time to finish her own meal, she was already exhausted. The older brother, Fernand, was quick to point out she would have to toughen up once she married.

'Look at my wife,' he said proudly. 'She is up before dawn, takes care of our five children, helps out in the fields and is the last one to go to sleep. But she's never tired.'

Laure glanced in Lorraine's direction. The poor woman had large blue patches under her eyes, which made her look about ten years older than she was. She carried her youngest son around wherever she went, although she was obviously close to giving birth to another one.

The other wives didn't look much better. They would never dare complain of being tired, but Laure could see it for herself that they were plainly exhausted.

'That's enough talk,' Maman Thibodeau said as she playfully slapped her son behind the head. 'You'll be scaring the poor girl.' She turned to Laure and ushered her towards the door. 'Go and see if you can find Jérome,' she advised. 'It will be time to head back soon.'

Laure was more than happy to get out of there. At soon as she stepped outside she took in a deep breath. Now she had serious doubts as to whether she really should trade in her life at Maison St Gabriel for this.

As it was, there was always work to be done. But at least the nuns shared out the chores fairly and there was nobody to wait on, no children to feed, clean and dress. And no husband to order her about. On the other hand, however, there was no husband to share her bed either.

She looked at Jérome as he came out of the barn and walked towards her. He had a good body, and judging from the way he moved, she could guess he would most probably hold his own in bed. But it was a gamble. She would have to get accustomed to having only one man, at least for the time being.

He smiled, leant towards her and gave her a playful peck on the cheek. Jérome was indeed affectionate, but would that be sufficient?

'I think we ought to head back,' he commented. 'I promised Sister Mélanie I would get you there in time for the evening meal.'

As she climbed into the trap, Laure realised it was unusual for the nuns to have let Jérome take her without a chaperone. Either they trusted him unconditionally, or they wanted to give them time to get to know each other better. They might have known they could trust Jérome, but as for Laure . . .

As soon as the farm was out of sight, she cuddled up against him. Jérome didn't seem to mind, yet he made no effort to return her affectionate gesture. She tilted her head on his shoulder and slipped her arm under his. There again, her fiancé showed no reaction.

More than ever, she was determined not to marry without first making sure Jérome would be a good lover. She wouldn't settle for a man who couldn't satisfy her. But how could she trick him into revealing the nature of his sexuality?

As the road wound around a small lake, Laure let out a cry. 'Can't we stop for a moment?' she wheedled. Jérome didn't reply, but simply pulled on the reins to stop the horses.

Laure jumped off and gestured for him to step down as well. Without waiting for him, she went for a stroll around the lake. She watched him from the corner of her eye, waiting for the opportunity to get close again. Instead of following her, Jérome sat by the water and silently watched her picking flowers.

Every now and again she would stop and glance towards him demurely through the reeds, as if playing some silly game. What she really wanted was for him to come after her, but right now he was content to just watch and smile at her.

She walked around the lake a couple of times and came back towards him. At the last moment, she pretended to slip in the mud and conveniently landed beside him. He held out his arms to catch her and she immediately slipped her arms around his waist.

'I'm very sorry,' she cooed as she nestled her head against his chest. 'I'm so clumsy sometimes. And you're always there to catch me . . .'

Looking up at him, she gently stroked his cheek with his fingertips. He blushed and returned her smile. For a moment all was silence. She pressed herself against him.

'Kiss me,' she said in a husky voice.

His smile vanished and he hesitated before gently brushing her mouth with his. A second later, he was pulling away. Laure grabbed hold of his neck to stop him. He didn't try to break free, but neither did he attempt another kiss.

Laure took control. She gently nibbled on his lips for a while, then inserted her tongue in his mouth. Jérome was docile, but soon he returned her kisses. Yet his reaction was still too tame for her taste.

Tightening her embrace, she writhed and rubbed her body against him. He tightened his own embrace and she heard him breathing harder. A few seconds later, she felt his member growing against her ribs. It twitched a couple of times, to her delight, before Jérome suddenly pushed her away.

'We should leave,' he said as he tried to break away from her. Laure held on tighter.

'Why?' she asked in a childish tone. 'It is still very early.'

He stopped struggling and held her gaze. Her hand trailed down his chest and gently brushed over his crotch. He blushed further and trembled violently.

'We shouldn't stay here,' he continued. But the tone of his voice betrayed a lack of conviction.

Sensing she was winning, Laure slowly undid the buttons at the front of her dress and then pulled on the laces of her bodice. He watched silently, mesmerised, as she gradually revealed the pale skin of her breasts.

When she felt him stiffen further, she rose to her feet. She walked around him, her legs brushing against his back and his shoulders, as she continued to undress. Jérome never took his eyes off her, yet seemed unable to move.

Her dress fell to the ground. Her petticoats followed. Soon she stood in front of him, clad only in her chemise, which flowed around her in the soft breeze. She raised it inch by inch, then used her bare knee to brush his mouth.

Jérome shyly took hold of her calf and gently caressed it with trembling fingers. His beard tickled her and his lips hovered over her skin. She pulled away a moment later, setting her foot between his parted legs. She continued raising her chemise, gradually exposing more of her thighs.

He sobbed and closed his eyes as she finished undressing. Laure couldn't believe how shy he was. She was just inches from him, almost naked now, and he couldn't even stand to look at her. Yet the bulge in his breeches made it obvious he wasn't insensitive to her charms.

Her chemise was carelessly thrown into the bushes, just a few steps away. Laure took off her bonnet, pulled out the pins holding up her hair and dropped them in Jérome's lap.

Throwing her head back, she quickly ran her hands over her neck, chest, belly and thighs, moaning in satisfaction. The sun warmed her and she felt alive again, at one with nature; as it should be.

Her blood pulsed right underneath the surface of her skin. The touch of her own hands triggered delicious shivers. This was what she wanted her whole life to be. All she needed was a man who could make her feel this good.

She looked down at Jérome and saw his eyes vacantly fixed on something on the other side of the lake. His face had turned crimson and a large vein palpitated at his temple. Grabbing his face in her hands, Laure forced him to look up at her. He averted his eyes and stared at the sky instead.

This was the most disappointing man she had ever encountered. Here she was, gloriously naked, offering herself to his contemplation, yet he wouldn't even look at her. Not to worry, she thought. She would have him. Even if she had to force him.

She sat down, setting her naked bottom in the dust and leaning back against his chest. She had to prise his hands off his knees to put them on her body. His fingers

225

were cold and trembling on her belly, and she couldn't help but be amused.

Jérome didn't know what to do, she thought. Obviously, he had never been with a woman. Stroking his face, she resumed her kisses. Desire boiled within her. She hadn't touched a man for months. Her passion awoke furiously and she knew there was only one way to quell it.

'Take me,' she whispered between two kisses. 'I want you.'

Jérome's hands clenched around her shoulders and he pushed her away from him.

'I can't,' he said in a trembling voice. 'We are not married.'

'What does it matter?' she continued. 'We will be married soon.'

'Yes, but right now it would be a sin.'

'No-one would know.'

'Even so. We have to wait.'

'And what will you do when we are married?'

He hesitated before replying. Laure squirmed free of his hold and pressed her naked body against him. Her nipples grew stiff and poked his through his shirt. She let her hands wander, feeling his chest and his flanks before slowly making her way towards the buttons on his breeches.

'Touch me,' she coaxed softly. 'I need to feel your hands on me.'

She seized his hands and put them directly on her breasts. She made him caress her, directing his fingertips over her nipples to gently tweak them.

Jérome was hot and sweating profusely. Against her hip, Laure could feel his member hard as a rock and ready for her. She quickly undid the buttons of his breeches. His phallus sprang out on its own. She felt it stir but didn't have time to touch it. In just a fraction of a second, he had pinned her to the ground.

All at once he was inside her. Laure didn't even have

time to react. He entered her forcefully and began thrusting immediately. She squealed with delight as his girth stretched her, wanting this to last. He glided in and out a few times, then gave three or four powerful pushes. She heard him gasp as he came. Before she could say or do anything, it was all over.

Jérome swiftly rolled onto his back, buttoned up his breeches and jumped to his feet.

'I'll wait in the trap,' he said in a trembling voice.

Laure rolled over on the ground and laughed out loud. How ridiculous! How utterly, desperately ridiculous! She lay on her stomach on the warm, fragrant earth. The blades of grass tickled and warmed her, and she felt elated.

She was glad she had decided to check him out first. Now she knew that if she married him, she would have to teach him everything. His big hands would learn to caress her voluptuous body, his beard to tickle every inch of her warm skin.

This would be hard work, but fun. She could train him, teach him obedience, get him to perform exactly as she pleased. She could taunt him, test him as she had herself been tested when she lived at the château. He would be at her mercy.

Yet it would take a while to achieve the results she wanted. Would it be worth the effort? And she wondered why he didn't know anything about pleasing a woman. He lived on a farm, so he knew about mere copulation. But what else? Hadn't any of his brothers told him anything?

Or perhaps he wasn't all that innocent, Laure suspected. A vague idea formed in her mind and she sat up, her heart pounding with something not unlike fear. She tried to make some sense of the ideas now flashing through her head and she feared she might have discovered the key to Jérome's behaviour.

If Jérome had learnt from watching the animals mate, and figured this was what married life was about, he wouldn't know about giving pleasure. With him, it would always be a matter of seconds, mere copulation.

What could he have learnt from his brothers? Absolutely nothing, probably. Laure couldn't chase from her mind the dismal image of the Thibodeau wives. Sad, unhappy women who served little purpose besides keeping the house and having babies. Perhaps the fact that they rarely smiled was simply the result of their husbands' ineptitude.

Laure stood up, brushed the dirt from her skin and quickly got dressed. She had to talk to Jérome, find out what he knew about women.

As she climbed back into the trap, she kept her distance. She would give him the cold treatment, make him yearn for her, and reject him for as long as she could. Then, she would have him on her terms. The training had already begun.

'Have you been with a woman before?' she asked point blank.

Jérome turned red again.

'Answer me.'

'Yes,' he said painfully. 'I have.'

'When? Where?'

'During the winter. In the lumber camps. Sometimes we had visits from ladies who came just for that.'

'What did they teach you?'

Jérome looked at her quizzically. 'Teach?' he asked cautiously.

'Yes. Didn't they tell you what they wanted you to do? Didn't they show you how to please a woman?'

'Women are not supposed to have pleasure,' he said in a grave tone. 'It's a sin. Those women were whores.'

Laure put her hand on his leg and drew it back immediately when she felt him shudder. 'Is that what you think of me?' she asked softly.

'No,' he protested. 'You are my fiancée. You will be having my children.'

228

'And once we're married, is it always going to be like it was just now?'

Jérome took a deep breath. 'Yes,' he said in a strong voice. 'This is the way it's supposed to be. Anything else is sinful.'

Laure didn't reply. She had heard enough; enough to know it would take a long time to turn him into a decent lover. Now she wasn't so sure he was worth the effort. For there would be a price to pay for her as well: children to raise, meals to cook, a house to clean.

Not another word was exchanged during the rest of the trip back to the farmhouse. Jérome was more relaxed by the time they arrived. In fact, he looked rather pleased with himself. But there was no reason for him to gloat. Laure despised him now.

His farewell was just as dry as his former lovemaking. Laure received a light peck on the cheek. He then hopped back into the trap, whipped the horse into a frenzy and disappeared in a cloud of dust.

Laure was confused. What kind of life would they have together once they became man and wife? Yet staying here meant being without a man, probably at least until next year. She could still change her mind. Or she could marry him and find herself a lover if her husband couldn't satisfy her. The thought made her smile.

She grabbed a bucket and walked to the well. She remembered that morning, not very long ago, when she had first met the man who was to become her husband. He had indeed made a good impression on her that day. Of course, that was easy for Jérome, as long as he kept his breeches on.

As she hoisted the bucket out of the well, she suddenly heard someone call out her name in a whisper. At first she wasn't quite sure whether her imagination was playing tricks on her, but she put the bucket on the ground and listened intently.

'Over here. In the barn.' It was a voice she knew, but couldn't quite place.

The door of the barn was ajar. Beyond it she could just make out a silhouette, a man waving at her. She looked around and, not seeing anybody else, made her way over.

As she approached, the man stuck his head out to look around, and Laure finally recognised him.

'François!' She threw herself at him and yelped with delight. He put one arm around her waist and set his hand flat on her mouth.

'Shhh. Nobody must know that I am here.'

'You came. You came for me.'

'I can't stay very long,' he said before he kissed her.

She lost herself in his embrace, already feeling the heat of his body through his clothes. She wanted him so much. Being with him, albeit for a brief moment, would make up for everything she had put up with since her arrival here. She rubbed herself against him, whimpering as she fondled him through his breeches.

He laughed softly and pushed her away. 'Don't be so impatient. I told you I couldn't stay.'

'Just a few minutes,' she whined as she threw her arms around his neck. 'I need you so much.'

'That's always nice to hear,' he said as he broke free from her embrace. 'But I really must leave.'

'Take me with you,' Laure insisted. 'I can't stand living here any longer.'

He cupped her chin and brought her mouth to his lips. 'I have to go far, far away,' he said as his eyes pooled into hers. 'Do you really want to come with me?'

'I would go anywhere, as long as it's with you.'

'I know, I know. But it will be a long and hard journey, and we will be away from any town or village. Are you sure you want to come?'

'Yes. Anything is better as long as I'm with you!'

'Then meet me here after everyone has gone to sleep.

We will be going through the woods, so bring warm clothes and good shoes, and nothing else.'

He put his finger on her mouth, opened the door of the barn and looked out. 'Tell no-one,' he whispered as he grabbed his bag. 'Don't even leave a note. If anyone ever finds us, you will lose me forever.'

He slipped out silently, looked around one more time, and disappeared without making a single sound.

Chapter Sixteen

*L*aure was too excited to ask François where he was taking her. She didn't even want to know what was in the large bag he was carrying, or why he had three rifles with him.

They had been walking for several hours now, and she was tired. Yet she knew better than to complain. He had said they would be spending the night in the woods. She didn't care where she spent it, as long as she was with him.

They moved quickly. Laure couldn't see anything, for there was no moon tonight, but she trusted him to find his way. She held her breath as they stopped suddenly and he held his finger to her lips. He listened expectantly for a moment, then resumed his trek.

Laure's eyes grew accustomed to the dark but she still couldn't tell where they were. Soon she recognised the sound of flowing water. She knew they were walking alongside a stream, but she couldn't tell exactly where it was or which way they were going.

The night was damp and cold and she couldn't stop shivering. She had to make a tremendous effort to stop her teeth chattering. The cold penetrated her to the bone and her feet were frozen and painful. Yet they kept on walking steadily, hardly ever stopping to rest, until the sky turned pale.

Laure still couldn't see much. Above her head, the trees formed a ceiling that held dawn at bay. After a while, François stopped and bent down to pick something up. She watched silently, too tired to even display amazement when he lifted a large branch from a pine tree which hid the entrance to some sort of cavern. He ushered her in and followed closely.

The cavern was pitch-dark. Crouching on all fours, Laure felt her way through rocks and dead leaves and slowly progressed until her hand touched something furry, warm and soft. She let out a cry of surprise. Behind her, François laughed and lit a candle.

In the flickering light, the whole cavern became visible and Laure looked around in awe. Pile upon pile of skins were laid out in front of her: bear, racoon, beaver, and others she didn't recognise.

François egged her on and she crawled further in then lay down on a large bearskin and covered herself with another. He set the candle in a holder and immediately came to join her under the improvised blanket.

'We'll stay here today,' he said as he began undressing her. 'We need to rest, and it's not safe to be about during the day.'

Laure didn't reply. She was more than willing to go along with whatever he said. She writhed as he undressed her, rolling around on the soft fur. She was in his arms again, and she wouldn't do anything to risk losing him now.

She tried to undress him but he stopped her. He pushed the bearskin away, exposing her naked body which looked like velvet in the candlelight. He wet his forefinger and toyed with her left nipple, rubbing it until it grew stiff and pointed.

Laure shivered with delight. She wasn't cold anymore, only tremendously excited. He stuck out his tongue and playfully flickered over her other nipple. Laure's back

233

arched violently, pushing her chest towards his mouth. François lay back and laughed.

'You are such a little wanton,' he said aloud. His voice sounded muffled now. Sounds penetrated the stone face of the cavern and didn't echo. Laure closed her eyes and ran her hands along her ribcage. How right he was. It felt good to be naked again, and to know that for once there was no risk of getting caught. She had no convent to go back to, no-one waiting for her. She wanted to make the most of it.

What would the nuns at Maison St Gabriel say once they realised she had left? She didn't really care. It didn't matter anymore. Sister Mélanie would surely be worried, but soon enough she would understand Laure's disappearance was indeed a blessing.

Laure opened her eyes and looked at François. He seemed content to simply watch as she caressed herself. She remembered how little effect it had on Jérome.

She closed her eyes again and pressed her body against her lover's. She didn't want to think about her fiancé. Jérome would soon realise she wasn't coming back and would marry Agathe. And now Laure had all she had ever hoped for: François.

His hands followed hers over her body and he cupped both her breasts. He could take his time to caress and re-discover her body, which had been consumed with desire for him from the very first time he had touched her. He would slowly build her passion until she overflowed with utter pleasure.

Leaning back, she parted her legs and brought her knees up. His hand immediately glided between her thighs but simply rested on her flesh for a while. Under his touch, she could feel the flow of her dew increase and her clitoris stiffened as she rubbed it against the palm of his hand.

Her hips swayed but his hand remained still. Laure used it to arouse herself. She also fondled her own breasts and slowly brought herself to climax as he watched and enjoyed the sight of her.

But as pleasure sweetly swept through her, his groans and shallow breathing told her he was also growing excited. She didn't wait for her orgasm to subside before she turned to him and eagerly began to undress him.

He grunted but let her have her way. She tore off his shirt, uncovering his hard chest which she immediately covered in wet kisses. It felt good to be near him again. This was familiar territory.

As she lay on top of him, he brought the bearskin up to cover her. He grabbed handfuls of the pelt and used it to caress her skin. The softness was exhilarating and arousal fired up within her again.

She moved her hips until she felt his hardness nudging her flesh. He pushed deep inside her, and she let him thrust slowly, rocked by the gentle motion of his pelvis. They held each other tight as bolts of pleasure pierced them each in turn.

Laure needed this to be slow and gentle. There would be plenty of time for hot, unbridled passion later. Quickly vanquished by the long walk and the strength of her feeling for her lover, she fell asleep in his embrace.

They came out of the cave silently. François instructed Laure not to move or talk, then looked around and listened. All that could be heard was the rumbling of a large river nearby, punctuated by the occasional call of a bird.

Laure dreaded having to walk through the night again. But if that was what François wanted, then she would obey him unconditionally. He still hadn't told her where they were going, or why. And she wasn't going to ask. Yet she was eager to know what exactly he was always listening for.

When they had arrived at the cave, she had concluded he was always on the look out for some small animal whose fur could fetch a fair price. But now she wasn't so sure.

After a rather short walk they came to a junction of two rivers. François headed straight for the bushes and, after pushing a few branches aside, pulled out a bark canoe. He dropped his bags into it, took out two paddles and handed one to Laure.

'I hope you know how to use this,' he mocked.

Laure took the paddle and clenched her hands around it. Of course she knew. She remembered telling him about the times her father took her fishing when she was a little girl. Now she understood why he had been interested in her story.

He helped her into the canoe, pushed it into the water and hopped in. Silently, they glided along the river. At times the current grew strong and all they had to do was steer. But now and again, the water was as flat as the sky above them and they had to paddle if they were to make any progress.

As dawn approached, François grew worried. He instructed Laure to paddle harder, faster. But after hours on the river she was tired. Once again, it had been a long night and she was feeling cold. Her shoulders ached and she could barely go on.

Suddenly, François let out a cry of triumph and they stopped. The river flowed past a small inlet that was practically impossible to see if one didn't already know it was there.

He helped her out and she fell to the ground. François hid the canoe under a large pile of branches, and then pulled some on top of himself and Laure. By the time he slipped his arms around her, she was already asleep.

She was awakened by his hand on her shoulder, shaking her vigorously.

'Wake up,' François whispered. 'We have to go. Now.' His voice was low and urgent.

By the time she was completely awake, Laure was already in the canoe, paddling furiously as instructed by

François. The sun was still quite high in the sky and his behaviour told her this hadn't been in his plans.

He looked behind him every minute or so. Laure got worried and also turned around to see what he was looking for. By now, she knew he wasn't looking for furry animals; she concluded he was being chased.

That would explain why she only ever saw him under cover of darkness, why he was always in a hurry to leave, never showed himself in town, and had urged her not to tell anyone when she had seen him. The mystery increased her excitement. Of course, she was still worried about the rifles he carried, but she was confident they would escape whoever was chasing them.

The sun beat down on her head and her back as she kept paddling. At first, she had been thankful for its warming rays. For the past couple of nights the humidity and the cold had been most unpleasant and both the light and the heat of the sun were a welcome change. But soon she grew too hot and uncomfortable. Her arms were tired and they hadn't stopped at all for hours.

François turned around. 'We'll be going down the rapids soon. We don't have any choice. We can't stop and continuing on foot is too risky right now. I need you to brace yourself and do exactly what I tell you.'

Laure nodded weakly. She didn't know how long the rapids would be, or if the canoe would hold together if it hit the rocks repeatedly. Already she could hear the sound of rushing water, growing louder as they approached.

The river had been rather narrow and calm, but suddenly the current picked up and carried them around a bend. Another river merged with the one they were on and together they formed a junction as large as a field, where the water turned white and foamy.

François stood up in the canoe, balancing precariously, and surveyed the hellish scene.

'We'll have to steer to the right,' he yelled above the

237

roar and pointed in that direction. 'Whatever you do, try to keep us to the right.'

Laure nodded and he sat back. A moment later, the canoe jerked violently and water splashed her from all sides. The first upsurge hit her directly in the face and blinded her. In a matter of seconds she was drenched.

The water made a deafening noise, but she could still hear François's screams as he urged her not to stop paddling. Her hands were frozen stiff around the handle but adrenaline coursed through her veins giving rise to a burst of warm energy and she found the strength to keep going.

Only instinct dictated what she had to do. Her feet firmly planted on the bottom of the canoe, she parted her legs until her knees touched the sides to keep her balance. She kept her eyes shut tight to protect them from the stinging spray. Already the sun had started its descent behind the trees and she couldn't see much anyway. She would let François's voice guide her.

Water splashed her face, entering both her mouth and her nose. She spat out most of it, but sometimes had no choice but to swallow large gulps. She choked when it took her by surprise, invading her nostrils and falling down the back of her throat.

She felt the sleeves of her dress rip under the strain, but it didn't matter anymore. Only one thing remained in her mind: right, always keep right.

At one point the water was deeper and, although the current was strong, they didn't have to dodge any rocks hiding below the surface. For a while they sat back, letting the current transport them. Laure shook her head and brushed her hair from her face.

'I think the worst is over,' she yelled.

'Afraid not,' François yelled back. 'Brace yourself.'

She slipped the paddle under her knees and held on to the sides of the canoe. Through this part of the rapids all they could do was go with the flow. François steered occasionally. Yet although the rocks weren't visible, they still diverted the flow quite violently and the canoe was mercilessly tossed from side to side.

Suddenly, more rocks. François cursed, instructed Laure to paddle and together they grunted with exertion as they propelled themselves further along. Now, it wasn't just a matter of fighting the rapids. They had entered a steep and treacherous gulley which looked more like a series of small waterfalls.

The canoe jolted and hit the water at an angle. Laure had to lean back to prevent herself from being thrown forward, but as her end of the canoe fell back into the water, the impact was almost impossible to counteract.

The second step was even worse. Laure lost her balance and almost fell out of the boat. She caught the side at the last moment, but dropped the paddle. She ended up scrabbling on the bottom, tossed about violently and unable to sit up again.

As the canoe flew over the next bump, François was almost thrown out. One hand clenched around a handle on the side of the canoe, Laure managed to grab his belt and pull him back. Now they both lay in the boat, having lost their paddles and completely powerless to steer themselves as the current grew stronger and pulled them on inexorably.

At some point they got caught in a whirlpool. They veered aimlessly to and fro. Then, nothing. For a few seconds they seemed to be flying, propelled forward as the river suddenly dropped below them.

The canoe gave a loud cracking sound as it hit the water and Laure felt herself pulled through a black, wet hole. She barely had time to take a deep breath as she vainly tried to find something to hold on to.

She glided into the cold water, then felt the bottom of the canoe brush the top of her head. She flailed and kicked, trying to swim through the current. Under water she couldn't see anything, even with her eyes open. Her lungs burnt and she was sure she would soon drown.

At the last moment, her foot touched something hard

and flat. She kicked as hard as she could, and a moment later broke through the surface.

She continued kicking and brushed her hair away from her face. A wall of water thundered down in front of her and she realised with horror the height they had just dropped. The current pulled her on, then gradually subsided until she was able to swim to shore.

Collapsing on the rocky ground, she breathed as hard as she could, still coughing up water occasionally. She was alive.

She half expected François to show up behind her. Yet as she lay shivering in the cold night air, she had little notion of time. Only when the sky turned pale did she realise she was still alone.

She sat up and looked around. There was no sign of him. On the other side of the river, the front half of the canoe lay on its side, bobbing in the faint waves. A piece of fabric floated in the water and she recognised her own bonnet. But François?

Trembling with fright, she stood up and called out to him. Her voice echoed in the forest and a large flock of birds took off. She went into the water, as far as she could, and tried to search up and down the river for any sight of him. Looking down she could see her own two feet and the river bed. Nothing else.

Still shivering with fright and cold, she waded back to the shore and curled up in a ball in the bushes. She couldn't believe he had drowned. He had to be alive. He would come back and find her, she thought, as she slowly dozed off.

Chapter Seventeen

Voices woke her. Laure jumped to her feet excitedly.
François! But who could he be talking to?

She looked around, suddenly feeling warm and wide
awake. She couldn't see anyone, but the voices were
getting closer. Then, from behind her came the sound of
rustling leaves. She turned around and jumped forward.
'François, François.'

Branches parted and a tall, blond man came out of the
woods. Laure froze in surprise. The man wore a soldier's
uniform, but he looked nothing like any of the soldiers
she had met before.

Other men followed, all dressed like him. They spoke
to one another and Laure realised they were British.
The man in front of her looked like the leader of the
pack.

'Where is the man?' he demanded angrily. '*Où est
l'homme?*'

Laure trembled but didn't reply.

'*Où est l'homme?*' he repeated. '*Où est François Dupuis?*'

Laure was baffled. What did the British want with
François, she wondered? Were they the reason he had
fled both Québec and Ville-Marie? But why? Were they
his friends or his enemies?

'You were with him when he left Ville-Marie,' the officer said. 'Where is he now?'

'We fell through the rapids,' Laure replied cautiously. 'The canoe broke on the rocks; I think he drowned. I almost did.'

The officer looked at Laure for a moment without really seeing her. She felt his eyes boring through her, as if she were just an obstacle in the path of his pensive gaze. Suddenly, he turned around and barked a few orders. The soldiers dispersed, wading into the river or searching the banks, looking for clues as to François's whereabouts.

Laure was filled with dread. The last thing she wanted was to find his lifeless body. Slowly, the soldiers came back, one of them holding something that looked like a dripping rag, but which Laure recognised as François's torn shirt.

She hid her face in her hands and burst into tears. Was this all that was left of him?

The officer took a few steps away, then stopped and came back towards Laure. He took his tunic off and threw it over her shoulders.

'You come with us,' he said in broken French.

After a few days on the road, Laure was becoming impatient and testy. She didn't like the British, and she still didn't know where they were taking her or why. But at least she didn't have to walk with the soldiers. Lieutenant Lyndsay had taken her up on his horse with him. At times he would even let her ride alone as he walked alongside.

On the whole, he had been very kind and civilised, but the place they were headed was so far away she quickly lost hope of ever being able to find her way back.

Dead or alive, François was far behind her now. As sad as she was, she was pleased to have a whole detachment of young men waiting on her hand and foot. As they silently walked through woods and fields, Laure could feel their gaze on her and was rather flattered. When they stopped every evening, soldiers rushed to give up their tent for her benefit and sleep outside. Others would make all kinds of padded cushions for her to sit on, and always made sure she had plenty to eat.

They all vied for her attention: they brought her flowers, handed her their handkerchief to cover her head if the sun shone too brightly. But in their eyes she could read their real motives, their lustful desire. And although so far they had treated her with the utmost respect, she knew a single gesture on her part would change that.

But the man she fancied most, curiously enough, was the lieutenant himself. He reminder her of René, the lover she had now almost forgotten. They had the same build, and the same sun-bleached hair. The most striking difference was that the lieutenant seemed totally disinterested in her as a woman. Laure had been quiet, disregarding all the questions she burnt to ask for fear of making him angry. She still didn't know where he was taking her, or how François had figured in his plans.

The nights got colder and after four days it started to rain. In just a matter of hours, it was as if summer had died. Laure was constantly wet, cold and utterly miserable. She would have given anything to be back at Maison St Gabriel. She would even have settled for the convent in Québec.

Yet as they progressed further into the British-held territories, Laure was pleased to be back in civilisation. The towns they passed were as densely populated as Québec, and it was good to see people again.

The English dressed differently, and their demeanour was a bit more orderly. But for Laure, it was like finally coming home. When they arrived in the town of Albany, the lieutenant traded his horse for a trap. The final leg of their trip was the shortest. They rode out and around town, until they arrived at a military camp. The trap stopped in front of a large stone house and Laure stepped out.

A smiling, blonde woman appeared in the doorway and embraced the lieutenant. Without even being introduced, Laure knew she was his wife. The woman reminded her of Madame Lampron, albeit a bit younger. She had the same slender, frail body; the same flaxen and wispy hair; the same small, delicate features.

Laure looked at them and decided they made the perfect tableau. Memories of her days back at the château flashed through her mind and her heart raced: she was home, indeed. She would stay with this couple and they would take care of her. Her life would be as it should have been at the château: pampered and careless.

Mrs Lyndsay looked at her and smiled as her husband talked to her. Laure couldn't understand what they were saying, and it was obvious the woman didn't speak any French. But together they smiled at Laure, then silently ushered her indoors. It was their way of welcoming her.

The big stone house was furnished quite frugally, but seemed comfortable nonetheless. A fire roared in the large fireplace and cast its warmth all around. As they entered the kitchen, Mrs Lyndsay said a few words to their servant, an old lady who seemed on the verge of collapsing. The woman fetched a large pot of water and set it to heat over the flame.

'You stay with us,' the lieutenant told Laure. 'I will come back in two days.'

He kissed his wife and left. Mrs Lyndsay made Laure sit at the kitchen table and the servant brought her some food. Laure devoured everything ravenously, never once stopping to look at her surroundings. Mrs Lyndsay watched and laughed at this little ogre.

As soon as the last morsel disappeared into Laure's mouth, the woman took her to a small room at the back of the kitchen, where the servant was busy preparing a bath. At this point, Laure didn't need to be told what to do. By the time the servant had left the room, Laure was already naked and stepping into the large wooden tub filled to the brim with warm, fragrant water.

She lowered herself into the tub and shivered deliciously. The water tickled as it crept up along her ribcage and lapped at the underswell of her breasts. Her nipples puckered under the warming effect of the water and the sight of them made her giggle. Warmth radiated through her and erased all the cold and the aches of her long journey.

Looking up, she saw Mrs Lyndsay was watching her from the corner where she stood. The woman was busy filling another, smaller wooden tub with warm water and a bit of soap. As she gathered the clothes Laure had discarded, she couldn't take her eyes from the bathing beauty. Her expression betrayed both curiosity and lust.

Naturally, Laure liked the idea of having this lovely lady watching her. Grabbing the heavy bar of soap waiting on the stool by the tub, she rubbed it slowly down the length of her arms before letting herself sink deeper. She sighed loudly. This was so good, so yearned for.

She hadn't been allowed the luxury of a warm bath in many years. Even when she lived at the château, she had to bathe in the river during the summer months, and in winter, water was too precious to waste filling a whole tub. Then, at the convent, there was no warm water to speak of. Now, she felt spoilt.

Sensing that Mrs Lyndsay was still watching from the corner of her eye, Laure lifted her right leg, set her foot on the edge of the tub and ran her soap-covered fingers up and down her calf and thigh.

Mrs Lyndsay was indeed still watching. She only pretended to wash Laure's clothes, for they both knew her dress had been ripped so badly from her descent down the river it would have been better to shred it for rags. Yet, it gave the woman an excuse to stay in the room and contemplate the sensual brunette her husband had just brought into their household.

By now, Laure had realised there was another way in which this woman was different from her mistress at the château: by now Madame would have gladly joined her in the large tub. Mrs Lyndsay was no doubt enthralled by the sight of Laure's naked body, but she would need more encouragement.

Laure sat up, toyed with the bar of soap until her hands grew thick with foam, and then started washing her neck and chest. She washed herself thoroughly, letting her fingernails gently scrape across the delicate skin of her neck. But once her fingers began their descent over her breasts, Laure purposely slowed her movements and proceeded to subtly caress herself.

Soft moans of delight rose from her throat and she closed her eyes as she traced the contour of her smooth globes, letting her fingertips lightly, slowly brush her erect nipples.

Demurely glancing towards Mrs Lyndsay, she saw the woman blush, then leave the clothes to soak in the bucket and walk out. Laure was disappointed. How could anyone refuse to watch such a lovely display of sensuality? Or did Mrs Lyndsay have such a sense of propriety that even lustful curiosity couldn't get the better of her?

Laure let herself sink back into the water. At last, she was enjoying life again.

It wasn't until the following morning Laure realised why the lieutenant and his wife had taken her in. As she left the breakfast table, the servant handed her a bucket and gestured for her to go fetch water. Puzzled, Laure looked towards Mrs Lyndsay who leisurely sat by the fire doing embroidery.

She didn't think much of it at first, but when she came back and the bucket was traded for a broom, she understood everything. They wanted her to stay with them so she could become their servant. Laure breathed deeply, trying to quell the tears of rage that rose to her eyes. How dare they! How could they assume she would agree to stay with them and be their maid just because the lieutenant had rescued her from the woods?

She went about her chores without complaining or protesting, but her mind worked frantically. She knew very well she couldn't leave. There was no way she could find her way back now, and she didn't even speak their language. The only solution was to wait for the lieutenant's return and ask him to take her back to the French settlement. If François was dead, she would have to rely on her own resources. Her determination was her only weapon, but once out of the house, what could she do if no-one understood what she said?

Then she thought of what awaited her if she went back. In a word: nothing. As she silently churned butter in the wooden vat, she looked at Mrs Lyndsay sitting comfortably by the fire. She remembered the way the Lamprons had treated her. They had been quite happy to invite her to take part in their games, but when it came to making her life better . . .

An idea slowly took shape in her mind. Her situation right now was not all that different. There was a way out from a life of labour, along the same path which had taken her to Madame's bed. Only this time she would make sure to get there quickly, on her own terms.

She would seduce the young Mrs Lyndsay. Judging from the way the women had watched Laure as she bathed, the attraction was already there. Now, it was up to Laure to make her realise that her husband had brought more than a servant back from the woods.

The snoring sounds coming from the other bed told Laure that old Sarah was fast asleep. During the day, the housekeeper was grumpy and quite keen on bossing Laure around, but as soon as her head touched the pillow, she turned as stiff as a log and nothing seemed to disturb her slumber.

Laure rose silently and made her way to Mrs Lyndsay's bedroom. Under her bare feet, each step gave a slight squeak but she kept going nonetheless. At the top of the stairs, the door to the woman's bedroom was open already.

On the bedside table, the candle was now a small stump protruding from a large puddle of wax. The woman had fallen asleep without taking the precaution of blowing out the flame.

As she approached, Laure could see the silhouette sprawled in the bed, the blanket pulled up only to her waist. But what really caught her attention was the round breast left uncovered by the unfastened, gaping chemise.

On the pillow, the woman's hair was spread around her face. It was thicker, much curlier than that of Madame, but it was enough to bring back delicious memories of those times at the château.

Also different was the nipple that lay dormant, large and dark. Madame had small, pink nipples, always erect. Laure lightly sat on the edge of the bed, and used her index finger to slowly trace round the inviting breast.

She watched with glee as the peak gradually contracted under her touch, puckering into a stiff, long point. The woman let out a sleepy sigh, but didn't stir. Laure's hand strayed, gliding under the open chemise to offer the same treatment to the other breast.

Under the blanket, Mrs Lyndsay's hips moved suggestively. Laure increased the pressure of her hand, now gently cupping the full breast. Mrs Lyndsay's face twitched a few times, then she opened her eyes.

Laure didn't move away. For a while, the women silently held each other's gaze. Laure slowly pulled her hand out, opened the chemise to completely expose her mistress's chest, then dipped her thumb in the puddle of wax.

Wickedly, she covered the woman's nipples with the liquid wax, letting it cool, then gently peeling it off. The shape of the nipple remained in the solid piece that Laure brought to her lips.

The woman still didn't stir, not even when Laure pulled the blanket down and lifted the chemise to reveal her legs. In the candlelight, her skin appeared rosy and smooth. Laure bent down and lovingly caressed the exposed thighs, letting her fingers wander to the inside but never coming close to the place where they met. That would have to wait.

Mrs Lyndsay writhed slightly and sighed, obviously aroused. Laure was just as excited. She hadn't touched a woman since that time with Sister Mélanie in the kitchen. The prospect of once again losing herself in a long, smooth embrace made her flesh seep with desire, but she forced herself to hold back. She had planned to go slowly, no matter how inviting the scent of the woman's dew.

For she could smell its fragrance, sweet and enticing. Under her hand, the woman's thighs trembled and Laure knew she had been right to come. Her mistress moaned as Laure increased the intensity of her caresses, bringing her hands closer to the wet slit still hidden under the edge of the chemise.

Only once did she touch it – a brief stroke with the tip of her middle finger. The woman gasped and opened her thighs, but Laure didn't accept the invitation. Instead, she stood up, blew out the candle and went back to bed.

Mrs Lyndsay couldn't look at Laure the next morning. Yet she was always close, following the maid around for no reason. Whenever Laure looked at her, the woman would blush and avert her gaze. But still she wouldn't go away. Laure knew she had enthralled her prey. Although the woman wouldn't come to her, she wouldn't refuse her advances either.

That night, when Laure entered the room again, Mrs Lyndsay was sitting up in bed, naked. She reached out as Laure approached her, grabbing the maid's hand and hastily putting it to her breasts.

Laure bit her lip to hold back the laugh that rose to

her lips. This had been so easy. It had taken just two days to make this woman want her. What else could she do now to make the most of this situation? The possibilities were endless. But she didn't want to think about that now.

Laure quickly removed her chemise and slipped under the warm blanket. Mrs Lyndsay reached out hesitantly, set her hand on Laure's hips, and waited for her to make the next move. Laure didn't waste any time. Squeezing the woman in a tight embrace, she fondled the rosy skin it had been so difficult to resist the previous evening. This time it was all hers for the taking.

Her mouth followed right behind her hands. She was hungry for the woman. Her mistress seemed happy just to be caressed, lying idly and letting her maid take care of her. Laure was excited. It seemed like years since she had been with a woman. The softness of the skin rubbing against hers was incomparable. She wanted more of it, endlessly stroking the whole length of the lovely body, writhing on top of her, its touch tiring delicious sensations deep within her.

She finally set her mouth on the nipples she had tortured the previous night and suckled them gently. Under her mouth, they puckered further and Mrs Lyndsay let out a loud moan as Laure drew them deeper in her mouth.

Laure moved aside and brought her hand down to caress the woman's swollen flesh. She was amazed at how juicy it already was, as if Mrs Lyndsay was still aroused from the previous night.

Under her fingers, the wet folds were slippery and engorged, the clitoris swollen and hard as a pebble. The moment Laure touched it, she triggered the woman's first orgasm. Her mouth still fastened on the woman's nipple, she sucked hard as the woman arched her back and cried with joy. Yet Laure didn't let go. Instead, she kept on caressing the moist flesh, feeling all the dew now covering and warming her hand.

Her hand moved back and forth along the wet slit, and Mrs Lyndsay flew into a series of spasms as successive waves of pleasure rocked through her. Laure let go to allow her mistress to recover, and straddled the woman's thigh. With wanton movements of her hips, she ground her flesh on the rosy skin, feeling her own dew flow and ease the friction of her clitoris on the clenched thigh.

She climaxed soon after, her mouth once again glued to her mistress's skin. The woman became more daring, her hands stroking Laure at first hesitantly then gradually growing more eager.

Laure moved onto her back, grabbed her mistress's hand and placed it on her moist flesh to show her how she liked to be stroked. The woman was a keen and obedient pupil. Her fingers flickered all over her folds, tickling her deliciously. Then her own hand came to join that of her mistress and together they rubbed her slit until she climaxed again.

Without taking time to recover, Laure snaked around on the bed and quickly fastened her mouth on the woman's vulva. She licked it briefly, letting the taste of fragrant dew fill her mouth before returning for more. The woman followed her lead and gently pressed the tip of her tongue against the girl's stiff bud before darting deeper into her tunnel.

Laure wasn't as gentle. She pinched the clitoris between her lips and sucked it as she would a tiny prick, tweaking its head with the tip of her tongue.

Mrs Lyndsay screamed as she climaxed then increased her ministrations on Laure's flesh. Together they reached their peak and pulled away to catch their breath.

Laure returned to lie next to her mistress. She tried to think of something to say, but she knew it was pointless. Instead, she let her hands and her mouth do the talking.

Lasciviously, Mrs Lyndsay threw one leg over the maid's hip. Together they rocked, each woman using the other's leg to kindle her arousal whilst waves of pleasure slowly subsided. Laure was overjoyed. Now that she had worked her way into Mrs Lyndsay's arms, she would likely stay there, at least on the nights the lieutenant was away.

She awoke late the next morning, unwilling to pull herself away from the smooth embrace that had enveloped her through the night. Against her bosom, Mrs Lyndsay's delicate face was calm and child-like.

Laure stirred and her mistress tightened her grip around her waist. She blinked several times, surprised to see the sun so high in the sky already. As her eyes surveyed the room, they stopped suddenly when they encountered the lieutenant.

His bewildered look slowly vanished to be replaced by anger. His face was rough and unshaven, and the amount of dirt and mud on his boots and uniform indicated the ride home had perhaps not been very pleasant. Finding his wife in bed with Laure, the two naked bodies voluptuously entwined after a blissful night of passion, was not what he had expected upon his return.

Laure stirred herself from her slumber and forced herself to think fast. Heaven only knew what he would do to her now. She had come too far to let him kick her out of their house. The floor shook as he stormed over to the bed. His riding crop whipped through the air with a whistle and landed on top of the blanket, right in the middle of the bed.

Mrs Lyndsay awoke abruptly. Surprise turned to terror and she pulled the blanket to cover her bare chest. The lieutenant barked a few words, which Laure couldn't understand. Immediately, Mrs Lyndsay pushed Laure away and hid her face in her hands, crying.

The lieutenant kept shouting and his wife became more upset. In his hand, the riding crop trembled and Laure could see he was making a tremendous effort not to strike again. As the shouting match continued, Laure silently rose, walked to him and subserviently knelt on the floor, facing the bed and offering her bare bottom to his gaze.

He paced around her a few times, clearly pondering what he should do with her. As he came within her reach, Laure grabbed his boot and kissed it.

She was excited by his anger. She was offering herself to him. How could he refuse? She crossed her arms on the bed, bowed her head and braced herself for the first blow.

It came, but not as hard as she would have expected. Her bottom contracted and her skin turned hot, but Laure moaned with pleasure. It brought back so many memories.

Lifting her head, she looked at Mrs Lyndsay who was still lying in the bed. The woman's eyes betrayed both terror and fascination. After the third blow, the lieutenant dropped to his knees next to Laure and proceeded to spank her with his bare hand.

At first the blows were short slaps. Little by little, however, his hand slowed and lingered on Laure's buttocks a trifle longer each time. After a while she felt his long fingers grab at her flesh and she moaned louder.

The lieutenant held back. Laure turned to look at him and saw his eyes fixed on her displayed flesh. Crawling behind her, he parted her legs, lifted her bottom towards his face and suddenly went down.

Laure squealed as his mouth hungrily licked her slick folds as he drew them into his mouth. She heard him grunt like a bear as he relished her, his breathing fast and hard, his fingers probing deep inside her and caressing her frantically.

Laure gestured for Mrs Lyndsay to come near, making her sit on the edge of the bed and part her legs. Pulling the woman's thighs over her shoulders, Laure set her mouth to the flesh she had so often enjoyed the previous night.

Squeezed between the lieutenant and his wife, she

253

was offering herself for their pleasure, silently but obediently available to them. Behind her, the lieutenant rose to his knees and kept stroking Laure's wet slit whilst he undid the buttons of his breeches. He penetrated her fully and abruptly, his powerful thrusts propelling Laure forward and forcing her face into his wife's exposed flesh.

Laure did her best to bring her mistress to her peak. The moist folds were soon covered in a mix of the woman's dew and her own saliva. It tasted musky and at times bitter, but Laure diligently licked and sucked as if it were the only beverage.

Using the tip of her tongue expertly, she flicked the swollen clitoris. Then she took it between her lips and gently sucked, sending a wave of bliss rampaging through the woman's body.

Behind her, the lieutenant thrust harder but not as quickly. Each stroke brought him closer to his own climax and soon Laure felt his member twitch inside her. He slapped her bottom a couple of times as he climaxed, then fell across her back.

His hands slipped under her and he seized her breasts forcefully. Laure screamed and panted as he toyed with her bud, rubbing it with his rough fingers until the sensation became so intense she had to struggle away from him.

She crawled away and climbed into bed with her mistress. The lieutenant followed closely behind. The two women helped him undress and all three of them then cuddled up together, stroking each other as they dozed off.

Chapter Eighteen

*L*aure lost all hope when she learned that Sarah had gathered her few possessions and left. No doubt she had been waiting for someone to replace her before retiring. Now that Laure had arrived, she could finally go.

For the past week, Laure had been spending her nights in bed with the lieutenant and his wife. During the day the old servant always had some small chore for Laure to do, but little by little, Laure had hoped the Lyndsays would realise she was too precious to them to be put to work.

Yet on the day the lieutenant told her she would now be expected to cook, clean and do all the work around the house, Laure protested violently.

'How can you do this?' she yelled. 'I am not a servant. I refuse to do this. I . . .'

The lieutenant slapped her face and seized her wrists.

'We are providing for you,' he said in broken French. 'If you are not happy, you can always leave.'

He gave her a disdainful look and left the kitchen. Fuming with rage, Laure decided to sit in the corner and refused to lift a finger. She would show him. Everything remained untouched until the lieutenant came to see what she was up to at the end of the day.

When he realised she had done absolutely nothing all day, he flew into a rage, knocking the pots and pans off the shelves and throwing handfuls of food at her. He took hold of her by the arm and tried to slap her again. Laure covered her face with her free arm and he ended up hitting her on the back. He then violently threw her into the corner and left, slamming the door and locking it behind him.

Alone by the dying fire, Laure hid her face in her apron and cried. What had she done to deserve this? Why was it that whenever she managed to make a good, comfortable life for herself, she was then always forced to give it up?

It seemed every time she managed to make the most of her situation, everything changed. The short time she had spent with François had been heavenly, but then he had drowned. And now, if only the lieutenant would help her back to the French side, she knew she'd find a way to cope. At least she would choose her own fate.

She stood up and walked to the window. The sunny days were gone. The weather had turned cold and the ground was now frozen. In the distance, she could see people walking hurriedly, warmly wrapped in clothing so heavy she couldn't tell the men from the women.

As Laure looked out of the window, the steam from her breath clouded the pane of glass. Around the edges, a thin layer of frost had already built up. Soon, it would be winter: that long, dreadful season she had heard so much about. It was too late to think of leaving. She had nowhere to go, and nobody could help her.

She would have to bide her time, spend the winter here with the Lyndsays. By spring she would perhaps know a few words of English; she would gather all her energy and find the courage and the strength to make her way north. Would she go to Ville-Marie or Québec? It didn't matter. She would go back to the nuns, and beg for their forgiveness.

She never should have left in the first place. Even being married to a farmer like Jérome would be better than life as a servant. At least she would have been in charge of her own destiny.

The lieutenant was on leave. During the day, he would tell Laure what was to be done around the house, and supervise her work.

Mrs Lyndsay watched from afar, with a disdainful look on her face. The lieutenant had been rather abrupt with his wife since he had come back, and the woman seemed to think it was Laure's fault. At night when they retired, they locked their door.

Alone in her tiny bed, Laure would often cry as she shivered in the cold, wondering how much longer she could take this.

Things seemed to improve one evening when, as she was getting ready for bed, the lieutenant called her to their room. In the previous days, the tension between him and his wife had subsided. That night, Laure felt quite sure he would ask her to join them in bed. But as she entered the room, she suddenly realised it was not to be.

In the corner by the side of the bed, chains and shackles lay on the floor. The moment Laure walked in, she knew they were meant for her. The lieutenant made her take off her chemise and kneel on the floor.

He bound her as if she were a prisoner, tying her wrists and her ankles to the wall so that she knelt with her arms and legs apart. This position excited her nonetheless. The mere notion that the lieutenant had asked her to join them gave her hope.

The heat from the fire at the other end of the room was barely enough to keep Laure warm. Behind her, the wall was cold. The shackles around her wrists and ankles didn't warm up and bit cruelly into her skin.

Yet Laure was so excited she didn't let that bother her. On the bed, the lieutenant and his wife were both naked and looking at her. She was reminded what a good body the lieutenant had. His broad chest was covered with fine, golden hair, as were his arms and legs. His member appeared to her in all its glory, long, stiff and ready for the taking. He knelt on the bed, and his wife obediently took him in her mouth. From the corner where she knelt, Laure instinctively licked her dry lips, hoping she would also get a taste of him tonight.

But as husband and wife slowly grew excited and eager for each other's body, they paid less and less attention to Laure. She was condemned to the role of a lone spectator, watching them as they caressed and kissed each other, cruelly taunted by their lustful display.

The sight of them both frustrated and excited Laure. Even when she closed her eyes, their sighs and moans reached her ears and she couldn't do anything to shut them out. Her nipples pointed towards them in a silent plea. Her dew oozed from within her and now trickled down her bare legs.

She would have given anything to be freed and invited into their bed, even if it meant spending the rest of her life working as their servant. But as she watched them climax, one after the other, her hopes soon vanished. She was mesmerised by their expressions of joy as they were transported by pleasure. Her ears resonated with their cries of ecstasy long after they had died down. It only lasted a few hours, yet for Laure it seemed like an eternity.

So, this was hell. A perpetual taunt that never fulfilled its promise. She would be required to watch, but never be allowed to touch. Not for one night, not for moments, but for ever.

The lieutenant rose lazily, took a shawl that had been left on a chair, and threw it over Laure's shoulders. He then went back to the bed, blew out the candle, and went to sleep.

* * *

As Laure had feared, the same scenario repeated itself every night the lieutenant was home. She remained obedient, never once refusing to come to the bedroom, always hoping that one of those nights they would ask her to join them.

But it never happened. When the lieutenant was away, Mrs Lyndsay locked her door and made sure to stay away from Laure. This went on for weeks, and Laure gradually lost all hope of the situation ever changing.

Some nights she would watch, but the sight of their naked bodies no longer aroused her. She looked at the lieutenant and his wife, yet saw right through them.

They had broken her lustful will. There was to be no more pleasure for her, with or without them. By the middle of the winter, Laure had completely lost any desire to get away from them. All she wanted was food, clothes, and shelter. The Lyndsays were good providers, and she didn't care how they treated her.

The lieutenant took her out a few times, showing her how to get to the market, how to ask for what she wanted and how to pay for her purchases. On those rare occasions, Laure wasn't even excited. Being outdoors was dreadful, even clad in her heavy coat. He seemed to choose the coldest, windiest days to make her go out. If he sent her out on her own, he kept track of when she left and when she returned, as if he didn't want her to mingle with anybody else.

Yet Laure didn't even seem to attract anybody's eye. She was nothing but a servant, not to mention French. She kept her head low and hurried on, no longer wishing to meet anybody.

The news that the lieutenant was to be posted further up north triggered tears from both his wife and Laure. Neither of them wanted to leave, at least not now. It would be a long journey, on horseback, and they didn't know what kind of accommodation they would find once they arrived.

But there was no choice. The British army had decided

a whole detachment would be posted closer to the French settlements, and the lieutenant had to go with them. It also seemed this house was too big for just the three of them, and soon a major and his young family would be taking their place.

They packed the bare necessities, all they needed for the three-day trip. When the time came to leave, it was decided Mrs Lyndsay would ride in the sleigh, along with the wives of other officers, but Laure would walk with the soldiers. She was given sturdy boots and an extra coat. It didn't bother her. The soldiers were polite and she now knew a few words of English. Besides, it was better than having to share the sleigh with Mrs Lyndsay.

A few hours into the trip, it started to snow and Laure was chilled to the bone. The first night they pitched camp around a road-side inn. Laure slept indoors, on the floor at the foot of the Lyndsays' bed. Before retiring, the lieutenant locked the door and tucked the key under his pillow. Laure couldn't decide whether it was to stop her from wandering out or to make sure none of the soldiers would come and pay her an impromptu visit.

Either way, she didn't care. The floor was hard but the room was warm. But she knew one night's rest wouldn't be long enough to recover from the long day, and be strong enough to face the next.

The next morning she came down behind her master and mistress. Most of the soldiers were already assembled in the dining room, not wanting to leave the warmth and comfort until the last minute.

As Laure let her eyes wander around the room, she noticed a man intently looking at her. He looked familiar, although his dishevelled hair, dark beard and shabby clothes made him most unattractive. Laure looked away, but for the rest of the day his image remained embedded in her mind. She thought she knew him, but from where?

She tried to search her memory, from the earliest years at the château. There she had seen so many men coming to help for the summer and then leaving, never to be seen again. He could have been one of those workers. Yet her recollections dated back several years, and the stranger from the inn seemed quite young.

Unable to figure out of whom he reminded her, Laure chased him from her mind. By the middle of the afternoon, the snow was coming down quite heavily and the horses were exhausted from ploughing their way through the drifts.

As they pulled into yet another inn, Laure silently watched as the soldiers unloaded the horses. Then the news came: the trip would take longer than planned, at least an extra day, perhaps two.

Laure grabbed her bag and dragged herself inside. Before going in, she looked around for the Lyndsays. Amongst the soldiers, she thought she saw the man, the stranger from that morning. But as she looked again and tried to find him in the crowd, there was no trace of him. She wiped her brow, turned around and went indoors. She must have imagined him. Why would he have followed the detachment?

The third day wouldn't get them much closer to their destination. The men were exhausted and the wind blew so hard at times they could scarcely move.

The blizzard caught them quite suddenly. At the time, they were far from any settlement, and they couldn't stop. At first, Laure had walked amongst the soldiers. But as the weather turned for the worse, the men gradually broke ranks, blindly putting one foot ahead of the other, disregarding orders to stay regrouped for the sake of making progress along the road, their only guide the sound of the sleigh bells ahead of them.

They waded in loose snow that reached above their knees. Laure's coat was covered in ice and frozen stiff. She walked painfully, her feet freezing cold.

She couldn't walk as fast as the soldiers, and as a result soon found herself lagging behind everybody else.

Ahead of her, the others were barely visible in the blizzard, but she followed them obstinately, not wanting to be left behind.

Yet the wind blew hard and she couldn't keep her head up for very long. Whenever she did, she would notice, to her horror, they were gradually disappearing in front of her. Even the bells sounded faint.

She turned around a few times, sensing somebody was still behind her. She thought she heard him breathe loudly, but whenever she paused in search of him, he was nowhere to be seen. She couldn't afford to wait for a man who probably didn't even exist. The others were too far ahead already. Mustering whatever strength she had left, she bowed her head and kept on walking.

Things improved when the road took them into the forest. The trees provided some shelter from the wind, but the snow was coming down just as heavily. Laure was straggling far behind, but at least the detachment was still in view.

She stopped to catch her breath and wipe away the tears rolling down her face, threatening to turn into ice. Her scarf had blown off in the wind sometime earlier, and she hadn't taken time to retrieve it. Her lips were cracked and sore, her cheeks rough and stinging.

All she wanted was to fall into the snow and go to sleep. She didn't care if she died. She watched, completely disinterested, as the soldiers slowly disappeared ahead of her.

The wind picked up and whipped her face. Laure didn't move. She remembered the time she had struggled to get out of the fire at the château. Her will to live had helped her find the strength. Then when she fell into the river, she had made her way back to the surface through sheer desperation.

But, in this blizzard, she was too numb to fight. She unclenched her fist, tilted her head back, and let out what she thought would be her last breath. She couldn't go on; didn't want to take another step. She didn't want to fight; didn't want to live.

The wind pushed her backwards and she knew she would fall if her coat wasn't so stiff. She didn't even have the strength to react. But when something wet and rough assaulted her mouth, Laure faintly kicked and tried to scream.

'Shhhh.'

The voice in her ear sounded familiar, but she couldn't tell if it came from a man or a woman. It could have been the wind. Maybe her frozen mind was imagining it all. Yet the arms picking her up and carrying her into the woods were real. Opening her eyes, Laure saw him: the bearded stranger from the inn.

His face was half covered in a thick shawl, but she knew it was him. He was taking her away. She didn't know where, and she didn't care.

He huffed and puffed as he leapt over snowy knolls. She knew she was probably very heavy in his arms, but he was strong. He didn't say a word as he made his way through the forest, away from the road and the detachment. At times he would stop and look behind. Laure looked over his shoulder and could see his foot steps were erased as soon as he made them.

The soldiers wouldn't be able to follow and find her, once they realised she had disappeared. She didn't know whether she was glad or angry about that. The stranger now made his way laboriously onwards, and Laure dozed off in his arms. It was dark when he finally dropped her to her feet.

They were at the foot of a small mountain. The stranger climbed up, using snow-covered rocks like steps, and gestured for Laure to follow him. She caught his extended hand and he helped her up until they arrived about halfway up the mountain.

There, to her amazement, the stranger bent down, rummaged through the thick snow with his bare hands, and lifted a large bundle of pine branches. This time,

Laure was not surprised when the entrance of a cavern appeared in front of her.

The stranger went in ahead of her. Laure followed, dragging herself painfully along in the dark as the branches fell and closed the entrance behind them. Her heart pounded fast. Under her gloved hands, she felt the hard ground suddenly become soft and smooth.

Hesitantly, she took off her gloves and touched it with her bare hands. Fur! It couldn't be . . .

But as the stranger lit a lamp and held it up in front of her, Laure felt tears spring to her eyes and a sob rise in her throat. She couldn't bear to look at the hand holding the lamp, afraid of what she would see. Or, rather, terrified she wouldn't see what her mind was telling her to expect. But in the darkness, she could see the stranger's eyes watching her intently. She let out a small cry, convinced she knew those eyes, the two black pearls she had seen before.

But the only way to appease her pounding heart was to look at the hand. Immediately, warmth filled her and she wept as she threw herself into his arms. How could she not have recognised him?

It was his hand; the same hand she had seen holding a lamp that morning on the boat, and then again as the nuns' coach was stranded by the side of the road, so many months ago. The long, pale fingers, crooked around the handle of the lamp, the first two twisted in a way she would never forget. The distinct bump on the side of his wrist.

She looked at his face again. He looked older, thinner, and his beard had grown so long it hid the sunken cheeks she had found so attractive. Yet the smile was definitely the same. But how could it be? François had drowned.

'I thought . . . I thought you had drowned,' she said as she began to shake uncontrollably.

'And I thought *you* had drowned,' he replied before kissing her.

He held her and rocked her like a baby for a while, then helped her get out of her wet clothes. The cavern where he had taken her was bigger than the first one, but it seemed much warmer.

She stood limply as he undressed her. Her nipples, already erect from the cold, now reacted to his touch. Little by little, she felt herself warming up. His fingers felt boiling hot and slowly caressed her cool skin. By the time she slipped under the bearskin, the blood was flowing in her veins again.

François undressed quickly and joined her. The moment she felt his body against hers, it was as if the time she had spent with the Lyndsays was just a dream. She was back in her man's arms, although she couldn't quite get used to the beard which tickled her wherever he kissed her.

She liked the feel of it as it trailed along the inside of her legs, then brushed along her own bush. François's mouth was rough and chapped from the cold, but that only made his kisses on her flesh more intense. She liked the scratchy caresses as he relished her, his lips quickly homing in on her clitoris and rubbing it so hard her squeals echoed through the cave.

She came almost immediately, holding his head between her legs. He toyed with her endlessly, triggering pleasure so intense she soon felt lifeless. He moved back up and kissed her, his mouth and his beard wet with her juices.

Nestling into his arms, Laure laughed as she dozed off. She longed to fondle and deliciously torture him, but she didn't have the strength. Besides, there would be plenty of time for that later. Right now, all she wanted to do was sleep, happy and secure in his arms.

Chapter Nineteen

Winter came early. Through the window, Laure smiled as she watched a family of racoons hurriedly heading for shelter. They had not completely shed their coats and the first snow had surprised them. The fur trade would be good this year.

She turned away and crouched down by the crib where baby Roland slept peacefully. Papa would be home soon. Good thing, too: she needed François's help to chop more wood.

Pulling her shawl tightly around her shoulders, she threw another log on the fire and sat in the rocking chair. He had said this time he would stay for the winter. She couldn't wait for him to return.

He wouldn't bring back as much money, but it wasn't important. Now that he had stopped spying for both the British and the French, they wouldn't be as rich but at least they would be safe. Playing double agent was too dangerous. They both still vividly remembered how they had almost drowned when attempting to ride the rapids. Everyone had been after him back then, but that was all far behind them now.

In the distance, Laure could see a boat slowly sailing upstream towards Québec. It would probably be the last boat this year. She couldn't help smiling again as she remembered her own arrival, so many months ago. Never would she have expected just over a year later she would be a wife and mother.

Yet this was better than anything she could have ever hoped for. Their house on the road to the village was tiny but comfortable, and overlooked the most magnificent part of the St Lawrence river. So what if they didn't have any land of their own? She had François, and he knew how to take good care of her.

She didn't miss Québec, nor Ville-Marie for that matter. She was so far away now. Indeed, this house was near to where she had wanted to get off when she had first arrived in the colony. But if she had insisted on getting off, she probably never would have met François.

Every now and again she thought of Sister Mélanie, and what she would say if she knew Laure was finally settled. Maybe she wouldn't approve of her choice. Laure knew François wasn't the most honest of men, but at least he had always kept his promises. He had come back for her every time. And only he knew how to treat her right.

WESTERN STAR – Roxanne Carr
ISBN 0 352 32969 6

A PRIVATE COLLECTION – Sarah Fisher
ISBN 0 352 32970 X

NICOLE'S REVENGE – Lisette Allen
ISBN 0 352 32984 X

UNFINISHED BUSINESS – Sarah Hope-Walker
ISBN 0 352 32983 1

CRIMSON BUCCANEER – Cleo Cordell
ISBN 0 352 32987 4

LA BASQUAISE – Angel Strand
ISBN 0 352 329888 2

THE LURE OF SATYRIA – Cheryl Mildenhall
ISBN 0 352 32994 7

THE DEVIL INSIDE – Portia Da Costa
ISBN 0 352 32993 9

HEALING PASSION – Sylvie Ouellette
ISBN 0 352 32998 X

THE SEDUCTRESS – Vivienne LaFay
ISBN 0 352 32997 1

THE STALLION – Georgina Brown
ISBN 0 352 33005 8

CRASH COURSE – Juliet Hastings
ISBN 0 352 33018 X

THE INTIMATE EYE – Georgia Angelis
ISBN 0 352 33004 X

THE AMULET – Lisette Allen
ISBN 0 352 33019 8

GOTHIC BLUE – Portia Da Costa
ISBN 0 352 33075 9

THE HOUSE OF GABRIEL – Rafaella
ISBN 0 352 33063 5

PANDORA'S BOX – ed. Kerri Sharp
ISBN 0 352 33074 0

THE NINETY DAYS OF GENEVIEVE – Lucinda
Carrington
ISBN 0 352 33070 8

THE BIG CLASS – Angel Strand
ISBN 0 352 33076 7

THE BLACK ORCHID HOTEL – Roxanne Carr
ISBN 0 352 33060 0

Published in July

LORD WRAXALL'S FANCY
Anna Lieff Saxby

1720, the Caribbean. Lady Celine Fortescue has fallen in love with Liam, a young ship's officer, unaware that her father has another man in mind for her – the handsome but cruel Lord Odo Wraxall. When Liam's life is threatened, Wraxall takes advantage of the situation to dupe Celine into marrying him. He does not, however, take into account her determination to see justice done, nor Liam's unlikely new alliance with some of the lustiest pirates – male and female – to sail the Spanish Main.

ISBN 0 352 33080 5

FORBIDDEN CRUSADE
Juliet Hastings

1186, the Holy Land. Forbidden to marry beneath her rank, Melisende, a beautiful young noblewoman, uses her cunning – and natural sensuality – to seduce Robert, the chivalrous, honourable but poor young castellan she loves. Capture, exposure, shame and betrayal follow, however, and, in her brother's castle and the harem of the Emir, she has to exert her resourcefulness and appetite for pleasure to secure the prize of her forbidden crusade.

ISBN 0 352 33079 1

Published in August

THE HOUSESHARE
Pat O'Brien

When Rupe reveals his most intimate desires over the Internet, he does not know that his electronic confidante is Tine, his landlady. With anonymity guaranteed, steamy encounters in cyberspace are limited only by the bounds of the imagination, but what will happen when Tine attemps to make the virtual real?

ISBN 0 352 33094 5

THE KING'S GIRL
Sylvie Ouellette

The early 1600s. Under the care of the decadent Monsieur and Madame Lampron, Laure, a spirited and sensual young Frenchwoman, is taught much about the darker pleasures of the flesh. Sent to the newly established colony in North America, she tries in vain to behave as a young Catholic girl should, and is soon embarking on a mission of seduction and adventure.

ISBN 0 352 33095 3

To be published in September

TO TAKE A QUEEN
Jan Smith

Winter 1314. Lady Blanche McNaghten, the young widow of a High-
land chieftain, is rediscovering her taste for sexual pleasures with a
variety of new and exciting lovers, when she encounters the Black
MacGregor. Proud and dominant, the MacGregror is also a sworn
enemy of Blanche's clan. Their lust is instantaneous and mutual, but
does nothing to diminish their natural antagonism. In the ensuing
struggle for power, neither hesitates to use sex as their primary
strategic weapon. Can the conflict ever be resolved?

ISBN 0 352 33098 8

DANCE OF OBSESSION
Olivia Christie

Paris, 1935. Grief-stricken by the sudden death of her husband, Georgia
d'Essange wants to be left alone. However, Georgia's stepson, Dominic,
has inherited Fleur's – an exclusive club where women of means can
indulge their sexual fantasies – and demands her help in running it.
Dominic is also eager to take his father's place in Georgia's bed, and
further complications arise when Georgia's first lover – now a rich and
successful artist – appears on the scene. In an atmosphere of increasing
sexual tensions, can everyone's desires be satisfied?

ISBN 0 352 33101 1

If you would like a complete list of plot summaries of Black Lace titles,
please fill out the questionnaire overleaf or send a stamped addressed
envelope to:-

Black Lace
332 Ladbroke Grove
London W10 5AH

WE NEED YOUR HELP . . .
to plan the future of women's erotic fiction –

– and no stamp required!

Yours are the only opinions that matter.

Black Lace is the first series of books devoted to erotic fiction by women for women.

We intend to keep providing the best-written, sexiest books you can buy. And we'd appreciate your help and valued opinion of the books so far. Tell us what you want to read.

THE BLACK LACE QUESTIONNAIRE

SECTION ONE: ABOUT YOU

1.1 Sex (*we presume you are female, but so as not to discriminate*)
Are you?
| | |
Male ☐
Female ☐

1.2 Age
| | | | |
under 21 ☐ 21–30 ☐
31–40 ☐ 41–50 ☐
51–60 ☐ over 60 ☐

1.3 At what age did you leave full-time education?
still in education ☐ 16 or younger ☐
17–19 ☐ 20 or older ☐

1.4 Occupation _____

1.5 Annual household income
     under £10,000 ☐   £10–£20,000 ☐
     £20–£30,000 ☐   £30–£40,000 ☐
     over £40,000 ☐

1.6 We are perfectly happy for you to remain anonymous;
but if you would like to receive information on other
publications available, please insert your name and
address

_____

_____

_____

_____

SECTION TWO: ABOUT BUYING BLACK LACE BOOKS

2.1 How did you acquire this copy of *The King's Girl*?
     I bought it myself ☐   My partner bought it ☐
     I borrowed/found it ☐

2.2 How did you find out about Black Lace books?
     I saw them in a shop ☐
     I saw them advertised in a magazine ☐
     I saw the London Underground posters ☐
     I read about them in _____
     Other _____

2.3 Please tick the following statements you agree with:
     I would be less embarrassed about buying Black
     Lace books if the cover pictures were less explicit ☐
     I think that in general the pictures on Black
     Lace books are about right ☐
     I think Black Lace cover pictures should be as
     explicit as possible ☐

2.4 Would you read a Black Lace book in a public place – on
a train for instance?
     Yes ☐   No ☐

SECTION THREE: ABOUT THIS BLACK LACE BOOK

3.1 Do you think the sex content in this book is:
      Too much   ☐   About right   ☐
      Not enough   ☐

3.2 Do you think the writing style in this book is:
      Too unreal/escapist ☐   About right   ☐
      Too down to earth   ☐

3.3 Do you think the story in this book is:
      Too complicated   ☐   About right   ☐
      Too boring/simple   ☐

3.4 Do you think the cover of this book is:
      Too explicit   ☐   About right   ☐
      Not explicit enough ☐

Here's a space for any other comments:

SECTION FOUR: ABOUT OTHER BLACK LACE BOOKS

4.1 How many Black Lace books have you read?   ☐

4.2 If more than one, which one did you prefer?

4.3 Why?

SECTION FIVE: ABOUT YOUR IDEAL EROTIC NOVEL

We want to publish the books you want to read – so this is your chance to tell us exactly what your ideal erotic novel would be like.

5.1 Using a scale of 1 to 5 (1 = no interest at all, 5 = your ideal), please rate the following possible settings for an erotic novel:

Medieval/barbarian/sword 'n' sorcery ☐
Renaissance/Elizabethan/Restoration ☐
Victorian/Edwardian ☐
1920s & 1930s – the Jazz Age ☐
Present day ☐
Future/Science Fiction ☐

5.2 Using the same scale of 1 to 5, please rate the following themes you may find in an erotic novel:

Submissive male/dominant female ☐
Submissive female/dominant male ☐
Lesbianism ☐
Bondage/fetishism ☐
Romantic love ☐
Experimental sex e.g. anal/watersports/sex toys ☐
Gay male sex ☐
Group sex ☐

Using the same scale of 1 to 5, please rate the following styles in which an erotic novel could be written:

Realistic, down to earth, set in real life ☐
Escapist fantasy, but just about believable ☐
Completely unreal, impressionistic, dreamlike ☐

5.3 Would you prefer your ideal erotic novel to be written from the viewpoint of the main male characters or the main female characters?

Male ☐   Female ☐
Both ☐

5.4 What would your ideal Black Lace heroine be like? Tick as many as you like:

Dominant	☐	Glamorous	☐
Extroverted	☐	Contemporary	☐
Independent	☐	Bisexual	☐
Adventurous	☐	Naive	☐
Intellectual	☐	Introverted	☐
Professional	☐	Kinky	☐
Submissive	☐	Anything else?	☐
Ordinary	☐	_____	

5.5 What would your ideal male lead character be like? Again, tick as many as you like:

Rugged	☐		
Athletic	☐	Caring	☐
Sophisticated	☐	Cruel	☐
Retiring	☐	Debonair	☐
Outdoor-type	☐	Naive	☐
Executive-type	☐	Intellectual	☐
Ordinary	☐	Professional	☐
Kinky	☐	Romantic	☐
Hunky	☐		
Sexually dominant	☐	Anything else?	☐
Sexually submissive	☐	_____	

5.6 Is there one particular setting or subject matter that your ideal erotic novel would contain?

_____

SECTION SIX: LAST WORDS

6.1 What do you like best about Black Lace books?

_____

6.2 What do you most dislike about Black Lace books?

_____

6.3 In what way, if any, would you like to change Black Lace covers?

_____

6.4 Here's a space for any other comments:

_____

_____

_____

_____

_____

Thank you for completing this questionnaire. Now tear it out of the book – carefully! – put it in an envelope and send it to:

> **Black Lace**
> **FREEPOST**
> **London**
> **W10 5BR**

No stamp is required if you are resident in the U.K.